*HEAR YE! HEAR YE!
HIS MAJESTY, THE KING,
WISHES TO ANNOUNCE
THE NUPTIALS OF
PRINCESS KATHERINE,
HIS SECOND-YOUNGEST
DAUGHTER, TO
TREY SUTHERLAND*

LET IT BE KNOWN that **Katherine** (once regarded as the shyest of the royal siblings—now considered quite the accomplished spy!) will become not only a wife, but also a ready-made mom to a teenage daughter and six-year-old son.

LET IT BE KNOWN that **Trey Sutherland** (whose killer business instincts and likewise good looks once had the rumor mill spinning upon his first wife's tragic death) has made the former Plain-Jane princess his beautiful bride.

All of Wynborough congratulates the newlyweds—and wonders which of the remaining princesses will be next to have a royal wedding....

Dear Reader,

Happy holidays! In honor of the season, we've got six very special gifts for you. Who can resist *The Outlaw Bride,* the newest from Maggie Shayne's bestselling miniseries THE TEXAS BRAND? Forget everything you think you know about time and how we move through it, because you're about to get a look at the power of the human heart to alter even the hardest realities. And you'll get an interesting look at the origins of the Texas Brands, too.

ROYALLY WED, our exciting cross-line continuity miniseries, continues with Suzanne Brockmann's *Undercover Princess.* In her search to find her long-lost brother, the crown prince, Princess Katherine Wyndham has to try life as a commoner. Funny thing is, she quite likes being a nanny to two adorable kids—not to mention the time she spends in their handsome father's arms. In her FAMILIES ARE FOREVER title, *Code Name: Santa,* Kayla Daniels finds the perfect way to bring a secret agent in from the cold—just in time for the holidays. *It Had To Be You* is the newest from Beverly Bird, a suspenseful tale of a meant-to-be love. Sara Orwig takes us WAY OUT WEST to meet a *Galahad in Blue Jeans.* Now there's a title that says it all! Finally, look for Barbara Ankrum's *I'll Remember You,* our TRY TO REMEMBER title.

Enjoy them all—and don't forget to come back again next month, because we plan to start off a very happy new year right here in Silhouette Intimate Moments, where the best and most exciting romances are always to be found.

Enjoy!

Leslie J. Wainger
Executive Senior Editor

Please address questions and book requests to:
Silhouette Reader Service
U.S.: 3010 Walden Ave., P.O. Box 1325, Buffalo, NY 14269
Canadian: P.O. Box 609, Fort Erie, Ont. L2A 5X3

UNDERCOVER
PRINCESS

SUZANNE
BROCKMANN

Published by Silhouette Books

America's Publisher of Contemporary Romance

For Jason, who has a thing for princesses!

Special thanks and acknowledgment are given
to Suzanne Brockmann for her contribution
to the Royally Wed series.

 SILHOUETTE BOOKS

ISBN 0-373-07968-0

UNDERCOVER PRINCESS

Visit us at www.romance.net

Printed in U.S.A.

Books by Suzanne Brockmann

Silhouette Intimate Moments

Hero Under Cover #575
Not Without Risk #647
A Man To Die For #681
Prince Joe #720
Forever Blue #742
Frisco's Kid #759
Love with the Proper Stranger #831
Everyday, Average Jones #872
Harvard's Education #884
It Came Upon a Midnight Clear #896
The Admiral's Bride #962
†*Undercover Princess* #968

*Tall, Dark & Dangerous
†Royally Wed

SUZANNE BROCKMANN

lives just west of Boston in a house always filled with her friends—actors and musicians and storytellers and artists and teachers. When not writing award-winning romances about U.S. Navy SEALs and other heroes, she sings in an a cappella group called SERIOUS FUN, manages the professional acting careers of her two children, volunteers at the Appalachian Benefit Coffeehouse and always answers letters from readers. You can send a SASE to P.O. Box 5092, Wayland, MA 01778.

THE WYNDHAMS

Prince Phillip Wyndham (King of Wynborough)
m.
Gabriella Clark (Queen of Wynborough)

James
(presumed dead)
*MAN...
MERCENARY...
MONARCH*
Special Edition
on sale February 2000

Alexandra
m.
Mitch Colton
*A ROYAL BABY ON THE
WAY*
Special Edition #1281
on sale October 1999

Elizabeth
*THE PREGNANT
PRINCESS*
Desire #1268
on sale January 2000

Katherine
m.
Trey Sutherland
*UNDERCOVER
PRINCESS*
Intimate Moments
#968
on sale November 1999

Serena
*THE PRINCESS'S
WHITE KNIGHT*
Silhouette Romance
#1415
on sale
December 1999

Chapter 1

"Have you been with the agency for long?"

Princess Katherine of Wynborough gazed at the neatly dressed woman who was pacing nervously in the entrance hall of the Sutherland estate. "Excuse me?"

"You *are* here for the job interview, too, aren't you?" the woman asked. "I've worked as the Hendrickson's nanny for years, but they're moving overseas. I wanted to stay in the Albuquerque area, but now I'm not sure which would be worse—living in Hong Kong or working for Trey Sutherland."

And right then, for Katherine, suddenly everything was crystal clear.

Job interview. *That's* why it had suddenly become so easy to get onto the Sutherland estate. His secretary had thought she had called for a job interview.

Trey Sutherland was, without a doubt, the most difficult man in the entire state of New Mexico to meet face-to-face. For nearly a week, she'd been given a complete runaround every time she'd called. No, Mr. Sutherland was unable to

take the princess's call. No, Mr. Sutherland was unavailable
to meet with anyone until after the New Year at the earliest.
I'm sorry, Mr. Sutherland sends his regrets.

She suspected Trey Sutherland hadn't even received her
messages. It wouldn't have surprised her one bit to find out
the man had given his assistant authority to screen his calls.
And if it wasn't pure business, it wasn't getting through.

But then, this morning, just like that—jackpot. Katherine
had called, and without identifying herself, had asked to speak
to Mr. Sutherland. His secretary had put her on hold, and then
had come back on the line to ask if she wanted to set up an
appointment. Katherine had barely had time to say yes, of
course, before the woman had told her, ''Three o'clock.
Sharp.'' She'd rattled off the address of the Sutherland estate
on the outskirts of Albuquerque, and hung up, leaving Katherine somewhat taken aback by the rapid-fire, no-nonsense
American pace.

It hadn't occurred to her at the time that the secretary hadn't
taken down Katherine's name. The implications weren't
clear—until now.

And now, after a harried flight from Colorado, it was obvious that the only reason she'd been waved in through those
heavy cast-iron gates out front was because she'd been mistaken, first from her well-schooled British accent, and now
again from her less than regal demeanor, as a candidate for
the position of nanny.

Oh, dear.

''You've heard the rumors.'' The other woman in the waiting area simply couldn't sit still. ''You know, about Trey
Sutherland?''

''Actually,'' Katherine said evenly, ''I haven't.''

The woman moved closer to Katherine's chair as she lowered her voice. ''His wife died a few years ago. Definitely
under mysterious circumstances. I've heard *he* was a suspect,
but the police never found enough evidence to convict him.''
She shivered. ''It's so gloomy in here.''

''It's raining,'' Katherine pointed out. The thunderstorm

had started, the clouds opening up, as she'd pulled into the driveway of the estate. "It's gloomy everywhere right now."

There was a mirror on the wall opposite her, and she looked critically at her reflection. Neat white blouse buttoned nearly to her chin. Dark-gray wool skirt, dark-gray jacket. Sensible low heels. Her hair was neither red nor auburn like her sisters'. Although it gleamed slightly in the dim light that came through the windows, it was completely, unremarkably brown, her bangs framing a face that wasn't exotically beautiful like Elizabeth, or elegantly regal like Alexandra, or charmingly pretty like Serena.

No, while her three sisters truly looked like princesses, Katherine looked like…someone's nanny. Her face was a little too round, her mouth a little too soft, and her eyes were a very, very sensible shade of gray.

"How would you sleep at night?" the woman asked. "Wondering if he really did kill her?" She gathered up her purse and raincoat. "I think I'd rather go to Hong Kong."

"But that's silly," Katherine said as the door closed behind the woman. "You don't know any of the facts. It's only a rumor."

Another door opened, and a diminutive Mexican-American woman peeked out. "Are you the only one?" she said in a lilting Spanish accent as she entered the room for a closer look, as if more nanny candidates might be hiding beneath the long bench that lined one wall, or under the other straight-backed chair that sat on the earth-colored tile.

"I appear to be," Katherine said apologetically. "However—" She closed her mouth abruptly. She would apologize for the mistake only *after* she met the elusive Trey Sutherland.

"I'm Anita," the little gray-haired woman said. "I'm Trey's housekeeper."

Anita and Trey. It was charmingly informal. Anita wore jeans and a big bulky sweater, Katherine realized. And sneakers on her feet.

"He's not quite ready for you," Anita said, "but why don't you follow me anyway?"

As the housekeeper led the way down a long corridor, Katherine had to jog a bit to keep up. The estate was beautiful, a sprawling hacienda with Mexican-tile floors and windows set into arches, overlooking a lush center courtyard. The last of the fall flowers bloomed, bringing color to the garden, even in the cool autumn rain.

Katherine followed Anita up a flight of stairs, and then up yet another. The hallway here was wide enough to hold several chairs and a soft leather couch, positioned together in a sort of sitting area.

"Trey's suite is in the tower," Anita explained. She stopped outside a thick wooden door. "His office is here, his bedroom the floor above. The children and the nanny—you—sleep in the east wing, on the second floor." She gestured toward the sofa. "Why don't you have a seat? Trey will be with you in a minute."

As Katherine slowly sat down, Anita descended the stairs, swiftly and silently.

Katherine drew in a deep breath. Well. Here she was. Moments from meeting the man who could well help answer all her questions.

But how thrilled would he be to help her after he found out she'd used trickery and deceit to worm her way into his home? Of course, she'd been as tricked as he, but he couldn't know that. She'd better figure out what she was going to say, and she'd better do it quickly.

Katherine drew in another deep breath and practiced her most winsomely royal smile. "Mr. Sutherland. What a pleasure it is to finally meet you. But I do believe there's been something of a mix-up, sir. Your staff has mistaken me for the hired help, while in fact I am a princess. And that, sir, is why I've come to see you today. My elder brother, Prince James Wyndham, was abducted as an infant. He's been presumed dead these past nearly thirty years, but my three sisters and I have recently found reason to believe he may *not* have perished all those years ago. Mr. Sutherland, we believe that your equally elusive business partner, one Mr. William Lewis, could in fact be our missing brother, and the true heir to the Wynborough throne.''

Ah, yes.

That would go over quite excellently.

Katherine closed her eyes, imagining her sister Elizabeth and their social secretary, Laura Bishop, having to fly from Colorado to New Mexico to bail Katherine out of the lunatics' wing of the city jail.

This was a mistake—coming to Albuquerque this way, assuming that she could find Bill Lewis, assuming she could get through Trey Sutherland's tightly closed gates. She wasn't cut out to play James Bond. That was much more Elizabeth's or Serena's speed.

Katherine was the one who should have gone to search through old records at The Sunshine Home for Children in Arizona, where James was now believed to have been brought after his abduction all those years ago.

But something crazy had possessed Katherine. She'd agreed to come to Albuquerque, and now here she was.

Mistaken for a nanny.

Her fault completely.

She looked from the tightly closed door of Trey Sutherland's home office to the stairs that led back down to the front entrance.

Oh, dear.

As much as she wanted to, now that she was here, she simply couldn't walk away. If she were going to fail, it wasn't going to be from lack of trying.

She took a deep breath. ''Mr. Sutherland. What I have to say to you is going to sound *completely* insane, but I must ask you, sir, to—''

The door opened.

And there was Trey Sutherland.

Katherine had seen his picture. She had known that he was outrageously handsome, but his photograph hadn't prepared her for the reality of the man.

He was taller than she'd expected—well over six feet. His

shoulders took up nearly the entire doorway—shoulders clad in a dark-gray business suit that looked as if it had been tailored to his exact measurements. His shirt was a lighter shade of that same gray, his collar unbuttoned, his tie rumpled and loose.

His hair was jet-black and messy, as if he'd been running his fingers through it in frustration. His face was harshly handsome, his mouth set in an expression of grimness. His eyes, although tired, redefined the color *blue*.

"Sorry to keep you waiting." His voice was a smooth baritone, without even a trace of a Southwestern American twang. "Come on in."

She had to move past him to enter his office. She went swiftly, aware of the subtle fragrance of his cologne, aware once again of his sheer size.

The phone on his desk rang, and Katherine froze, uncertain whether to go any farther or to retreat and wait, once again, out in the hall.

But Trey Sutherland closed his office door. "I'm sorry, I've got to take this. Why don't you sit down? I'll be right with you."

She gestured toward the door. "If you want, I don't mind…"

"No, this won't take long. Please. Sit."

As Katherine slowly perched on the edge of one of the leather armchairs positioned in front of Trey's rather lovely wooden desk, he picked up the telephone. He took the call standing behind his desk, his back to her as he gazed out the big picture window, his hand on his neck as if he were trying to loosen the tightly knotted muscles there.

"Sutherland."

Katherine tried not to listen, gazing down at her hands tightly clasped in her lap.

"No." Trey's voice left no room for doubt. "Absolutely not." He laughed, but it was an expulsion of disbelief rather than humor. "No, I'm not hiding him. Believe me, if I knew where Bill Lewis was, I'd be leading the charge to knock down his door.''

Bill Lewis. The man she and her sisters believed might be their brother. Katherine stopped trying not to listen.

''Yeah, he could call or even drop in at any time. That's his usual MO,'' Trey continued, sitting on the edge of his desk in that casual way of an American male, completely comfortable within his well-developed body. His strong back seemed better suited to a T-shirt and a pair of dusty blue jeans, although she *did* have to admit that his suit fit him exceedingly well. Exceptionally well. ''But I can't make any promises. And, no, I won't hold him down until you get here.'' He laughed again—it was a rich sound that made her own lips move up into a smile. ''God, I don't know. He could be anywhere. Last time he went to Nepal. *Nepal.* I love him like a brother, but *Nepal?*''

He stood and turned to face her, and Katherine hurriedly erased her smile and shifted her gaze to one of the framed watercolors that hung on the wall, pretending to be completely absorbed in the shades of blue used in the ocean scene.

Trey Sutherland didn't know where Bill Lewis was. But he believed it likely that Mr. Lewis could ''drop in'' at any time. If Katherine truly wanted to find Mr. Lewis, and she *did,* then—

He was looking at her. He was making noises of agreement into the telephone and, while he thought she wasn't paying him any mind, he was sneaking a look at…her *legs?*

That was absurd. If anyone was going to dare to look at a princess's legs, he would look at Alexandra's or Elizabeth's legs, not Katherine's. While her legs weren't precisely unattractive, she simply didn't dress in a manner to draw a man's eyes in that direction. That is, assuming the man was bold enough to check out a princess in the first place. Most men weren't.

But, of course, Trey Sutherland had no idea that Katherine was a princess. Trey Sutherland thought that Katherine was in his office to apply for a job as a nanny.

He hung up the phone. "Sorry."

"It's all right."

In the brighter light of his office, she saw that there was a trace of silver at his temples. And his eyes really were a quite disarming shade of blue. His gaze swept over her again in a most disconcerting way. This time, it wasn't so much checking her out as assessing. Taking stock. Studying. There was nothing disrespectful about it—he was simply doing it in an extremely male way.

"You're younger than I'd hoped you'd be," he said bluntly, coming around to sit in the other leather armchair in front of his desk.

Katherine blinked at him. "Younger...?"

"This is a live-in position," he explained. "If you've got a husband and family—"

"I don't. Have a husband, I mean."

"A boyfriend?"

She felt herself blush. "No."

"How old *are* you?"

"Twenty-five." This was absurd. This man's questions were so direct as to be rude. And she wasn't even here to be hired on as a nanny. "How old are *you?*" Oh dear, where had *that* come from?

But he answered her. "Thirty-five. At least until the beginning of January, and then I'll be thirty-six."

"I'm sorry, I—"

"No, that's fair. You've got every right to ask as many questions as you want. This interview is a two-way street. Do you like kids?"

She was blinking at him again. "Do I...?"

"Yeah, I know. It seems like a stupid question considering the job you're applying for, but I've run across more than my share of people claiming to be nannies who don't particularly like the children they've been hired to care for. They don't particularly like children at all." His eyes were hot with intensity as he leaned toward her. "My kids need to be respected and liked at the *very* least. And you better believe if I could pay you to love them, I would.''

He stood up suddenly, as if he'd given too much away, or if there was a limit to how long he could contain his sheer energy and stay seated in a chair.

''My turn to apologize,'' he said, as he moved behind his desk. ''Our last nanny left without even saying goodbye to Stacy and Doug. It's important to me that I find someone who fully understands the extent of the burden I'm placing upon them. These are kids who know too damn well what it means to be deserted, and— I'm getting way ahead of myself. I haven't even asked you your name.''

''I do like kids,'' Katherine said softly. She liked kids, Trey Sutherland seemed in rather desperate need of a nanny, and, if she kept up this insane subterfuge and moved into the Sutherland estate, she'd be here when and if William Lewis turned up.

She'd also be here to watch Trey Sutherland's amazingly beautiful eyes blaze with intensity and passion. She imagined his eyes lit up that way at least several dozen times a day.

He smiled only very slightly, yet it was enough to soften the somewhat harsh lines of his face. ''That's good to know, Miss…?''

She tucked her hand behind her back, crossed her fingers, and for the first time in her life, acted on complete impulse.

''Wind,'' Princess Katherine of Wynborough said in her very best Sean Connery. ''Kathy Wind.''

It was funny, but as Trey reached to shake Kathy Wind's hand, it was almost—at first—as if she were extending her knuckles to be kissed, as if she were the Royal Queen of England.

But although her hand was soft, her nails were short, some of them bitten. Whoever heard of a queen who bit her fingernails?

She had a solid, warm handshake, and although it was absurd to base such things on gut reactions, he liked her even more for it.

"Where are you from?" he asked, releasing her hand.

She had to crane her neck to look up at him, and he sat down on the edge of his desk to put them slightly more on the same level.

She had a very direct way of looking steadily into his eyes, and he liked *that* about her, too.

"I'm from the country of Wynborough," she told him in her Mary Poppins accent. "It's a small island not far from England."

"So what brings you all the way out here to the American Southwest?"

"I have…family…in Aspen. Colorado," she added in that earnest way she had, as if he might not know where Aspen was.

Yeah, Trey liked her. And that was a damn good thing, because, as Anita had let him know, Kathy Wind was the only surviving candidate for the position of nanny. The others had either been scared off by the size of the estate, or by the dark rumors that surrounded both this place and its master.

He gazed into Kathy's wide gray eyes, wondering what she'd heard about him, and wondering, if she *had* heard something, why it didn't matter to her. Of course, this interview was only just starting. She still had time to bring the subject up.

"Ever been arrested?" he asked. It was amazing the variety of answers he'd received to *that* question when interviewing potential child care providers for his two kids.

Kathy laughed, a sudden burst of startled surprise. "I should hope *not!*"

"I should, too," Trey said dryly. "But *have* you?"

She flushed slightly. That was the second time she'd done that. The effect was completely sweet and totally charming. "No!"

"Good. Neither have I," he told her.

Something nearly imperceptible shifted in her eyes, and he

knew that she *had* heard something about him. But she didn't take the opportunity to question him about it. She was either too nervous or too polite.

Too polite, he decided. Despite the chewed-on fingernails and an undercurrent of some kind of emotional energy, Kathy Wind wasn't afraid of him. God, he would sure love it if some of those quiet manners rubbed off on Stacy. His daughter had become completely wild since Helena's death. And as for Dougie—the kid had completely stopped talking. All Trey wanted was to hear his son's voice again. At this point, he wouldn't even care if the boy used it to tell him to go to hell.

"How long have you worked as a nanny?" he asked her, moving behind his desk to shuffle through the meager pile of résumés the agency had sent him. "The agency hasn't sent me your references."

"No?" Kathy blinked at him. "Well, I'm...new. But I'll...have them faxed to you." She shifted in her seat. "Actually, Mr. Sutherland, I've got to be honest. I'm not from the agency. I heard about this position through an, um—" she cleared her throat "—an acquaintance. But I'll see that you receive a full list of references later today. However..."

Trey watched her closely, aware that something still wasn't quite kosher—as his college friends at NYU would have said—despite her honest admission.

She drew in a deep breath and steadily met his gaze. "I'm afraid you might find me slightly underqualified for this position. I've never actually been a nanny before." She gave him the sweetest, most crookedly hopeful smile. "But everyone's got to start somewhere, right?"

She was adorable. She warmed him in a way he couldn't quite remember being warmed before. It wasn't that he found her attractive. Not sexually attractive, that is. Sure, she had a great pair of legs, and her figure—at least what he could see beneath that incredibly non-feminine wool suit—was slender and rather well-proportioned and... Okay, so she *was* attractive. She was outrageously attractive, but in a fresh-faced, sweet little sister sort of way. Not that he'd ever had a little sister. But if he had, this warmth might be what he would feel toward her.

She was quietly pretty with a slightly round face, innocently free of makeup, that made her look closer to fifteen than twenty-five. Her features were even, almost delicate—small, straight nose, slightly pointed chin. Her mouth was full and friendly, but her eyes were what he liked the best—gray and wide with thick dark lashes. She played at being cool and remote, but she couldn't hide the very appealing mix of intelligence, interest and innocence that lingered there.

And while Trey would have preferred hiring an experienced nanny, everyone *did* have to start somewhere.

"You'll need a driver's license," he said. "Do you have one?"

"Of course." Blink, blink. "Why?"

"You'll be in charge of getting the kids to and from school," he said. "They both attend a private school about four miles from here. And then there'll be parties and things they'll need rides for." At least, he hoped there would be. Even though Stacy was in eighth grade this year, her social calendar remained rather empty. "And Stace has clarinet lessons several times a week."

"So basically, you'd be hiring me as a chauffeur," Kathy noted, one eyebrow elegantly lifted.

"No, believe me, there's supervision involved," Trey told her. "A lot of it, actually. You'd put in long days. You'd have the hours off that the kids are in school, but I'd need you available in the evenings. And during school vacations, I'd need you twenty-four/seven."

She blinked at him again. "Twenty-four…?"

"Twenty-four hours a day, seven days a week," he explained. What rock had she been hiding under, that she hadn't heard that expression before? "You'd be compensated for the overtime, of course."

"Of course, but…" Her eyes were innocently wide. "When do *you* see them?"

"My time's going to be really tight between now and the

New Year," he said as if that answered her question. He stood up abruptly. "Before we go any further, you need to meet them. Anastacia's thirteen and Douglas is six. Neither of them are easy to get along with." He forced a tight smile. "But that shouldn't be surprising considering who their father is."

She studied him seriously. "You seem all right to me."

Yeah, well he wasn't. "Their mother died three years ago and neither of them have adjusted very well."

"That doesn't seem like something *any* child would adjust to—at least not well."

That was a good point, but Stacy and Doug's lack of adjustment sometimes seemed off the map. Of course, Trey was a fine one to talk. He hadn't adjusted particularly well to Helena's death, either.

"Stacy's pretty hostile," he told Kathy. Understatement of the year. "Her grades are abysmal, she's actually left home a few times—sometimes in the middle of the night. She hasn't gotten far, not enough to call it running away, but still it's…"

"Frightening," she supplied the word. "I can imagine. You must have been terrified."

"She needs…something that I don't seem to be able to give her," Trey said honestly. "And as for Doug…" He shook his head. His son had chosen a different way to escape the realities of life after his mother's death. Trey gestured toward the door. "Now would probably be a good time for you to meet them—that is, if you're still interested in the job."

Kathy didn't stand up. Not a good sign. She sighed. "Mr. Sutherland."

"Trey," he said. "Please. We don't stand on ceremony in this house."

"Trey." She looked up at him. "Please would you mind sitting down for just a moment? You're quite relentlessly tall and I'm afraid that what I have to say to you is an eye to eye sort of thing."

Trey smiled. This woman was a riot. Only she hadn't intended any of what she'd said to be funny. But since she was probably going to tell him she didn't want the job, it no longer seemed very funny to him, either. He sat obediently in the chair next to hers, resigned to what she was about to say.

She turned slightly to face him. "As much as I'd love this position—and I *truly* would—I'm not sure I'm the right woman for the job," she told him earnestly, her eyes so serious. "You see, I'm not looking for long-term employment, and it seems to me, sir, that you and Stacy and Doug would be best served by hiring a nanny who would be prepared to stay until the children are grown. It seems to me that they—and you—have had enough upheaval in your lives."

This was too much. She wanted the job, but here she was, trying to talk him out of hiring her—for the sake of his children.

"I suppose it's too much to hope I could change your mind," he wondered aloud. "Talk you into staying on for, say, ten years?"

She smiled at that. She had the cutest dimples when she smiled. "Ten years of twenty-four/seven?" She shook her head. "No, thank you."

"Are you sure this isn't negotiable?" he asked. "We could rethink the twenty-four/seven thing or—"

"I'm flattered that you think so highly of me after only one brief meeting," Kathy told him. "But, no, sir. It's not negotiable. I'd like to hope that someday I'll have a family of my own and…well…"

"Of course," Trey said, backing down. "I understand. It's just…I'm kind of in a bind. This isn't exactly the time of year where people want to change jobs. The agency said I'd have a better selection of candidates in January, but I can't wait that long. I can barely wait until tomorrow. I need someone starting *now*."

She gazed at him thoughtfully. "I *could* stay until January, provided I'd have a week off for Christmas," she told him. "It wouldn't be the best scenario, but… Maybe if the children knew from the start that I'd only be here temporarily…?"

"Maybe what you better do is meet them first," Trey countered, "before you start making such generous offers."

Kathy stood up. "Then lead on," she commanded in that royal manner she had.

"Right this way, Your Majesty," he said, leading the way to the door.

She faltered. "Excuse me?"

"Bad joke," he said. "I think it's probably your accent. Very...regal."

"Really?" She looked completely taken aback. "I'm so sorry, I didn't realize—"

"Relax," Trey told her. "It suits you. It's very cute."

Chapter 2

Cute.

Of all the things Princess Katherine of Wynborough had been called in her relatively uneventful life, *cute* had not been one of them.

Until now.

She followed Trey Sutherland down the stairs, down another endless hallway. If she were going to live here, she'd need to take a few hours and go exploring with a map. As far as she could figure, the house was shaped like a square U, with two long wings stretching back from the main building, forming the shelter for the center courtyard. The tower was on one front corner of the building—at the beginning of the opposite wing than the one they were heading down now.

In fact, if she looked out the window, across the courtyard and up, she could see the windows of Trey's office, lights still blazing through the late-afternoon dreariness.

Trey slowed his pace and glanced at her. "I meant what I said," he told her. "Instead of coming to a definite decision after you meet the kids, you go home and think it over. Fax me your references, and tomorrow, if we still both think this will work—temporarily, of course—we'll talk again.''

He was giving her an out.

''This is the playroom,'' he said, taking a deep breath before he opened the door.

Katherine wasn't sure exactly what horror she'd expected to find, but the cheerful, brightly lit room, filled with books and games and toys, furnished with two big, overstuffed sofas and a small handful of rocking chairs wasn't it. There was a huge fireplace. It was cold and dark now, but when lit it would be capable of warming nearly the entire large room. Windows and skylights let in what little light remained of the darkening afternoon. A cabinet was open, revealing a TV and VCR. A Disney tape was playing to the otherwise empty room.

Trey strode to the VCR and turned both it and the TV off. He then went to an intercom system that was built into the wall. He leaned on one of the buttons, bent close to the microphone. ''Stace. I thought I asked you to stay with Doug in the playroom this afternoon.''

A young girl's voice came through the speaker, tinny and thin and clearly annoyed. ''I was. But then he chewed through his leash....''

Chewed? Through his *leash?*

Trey didn't look too happy about that, either. ''How many times have I told you that if we treat him like a boy, he'll act like a boy and...'' He shook his head, clearly exasperated. ''Just come down here,'' he ordered. ''There's someone here I want you to meet.''

''Leash?'' Katherine echoed weakly.

''Imaginary leash,'' Trey said quickly. ''I may not be father of the year, but I don't tie my kids up.''

''Doggie—Dougie—thinks he's a dog.''

The girl's room must have been right next door, because Stacy arrived in no time at all.

She stood in the doorway, arms across her chest. She was dressed entirely in black. Black leggings, black oversize turtleneck that hung down to her thighs, black lace-up boots with big clunky heels. Her short hair was black, too, although Katherine would have wagered she hadn't been born with it that extreme color. She wore thick black eyeliner, an extremely pale shade of pancake base, an almost blackish red shade of lipstick, and black nail polish.

The effect was…striking, but perhaps a little much for a thirteen-year-old.

"A *dog*," Katherine echoed.

"Yeah." Stacy gazed at her, unsmiling, sullen to the point of near rudeness. "You know, arf, arf." She turned to her father. "If you whistle for him, Trey, he'll come."

Trey looked decidedly displeased, the muscles in the sides of his jaw jumping. "I'm not going to whistle for him because he's *not* a dog."

Stacy turned to Katherine. "You must be nanny number 4,515." The girl looked at her critically. "The suit's cool, the knee-length skirt's kind of retro, but you should lose the dorky blouse and just go with the jacket with nothing underneath— except maybe one of those black Miracle Bras from the Victoria's Secret catalog. Trade in the nerd shoes for something with a three and a half inch heel and—"

"And I don't think so," Trey interrupted.

"Yeah, you wouldn't," Stacy said with an exaggerated sigh. "You're the one who hasn't gone out with anyone but the awful Ice Queen in years—unless you've been getting busy on the sly with someone I don't know about."

Oh, dear.

For one awful moment, Trey Sutherland looked as if he were going to throttle his daughter. And then for one truly dreadful moment, Katherine was afraid the man might cry. Then everything he was feeling, anger and hurt and embarrassment, was tucked neatly away. And when he spoke, his voice was devoid of all emotion.

"What did I do to deserve that?" he quietly asked his daughter.

Stacy knew perfectly well that she had completely overstepped the boundaries of propriety by saying such a thing in front of a stranger. She could apologize, or she could take the defensive route. As Katherine watched, the girl unwisely chose defensive. "It was just a joke. Lighten up, Trey."

Oh, dear. He clearly hated that she called him by his first name, and Stacy knew it. Katherine could see that the girl certainly had learned how to push her father's buttons.

"If I'm nanny number 4,500 and something," Katherine said, stepping boldly into the fray, "I can understand how this all might be a little overwhelming for the pair of you—and for Doug, too, poor thing. So why don't we start again?" She looked at Trey. "Why don't you give your son a break and whistle for him—obviously that's what he wants you to do. And as for *you*—" she turned to Stacy "—let's do this nicely, without embarrassing your father any further, shall we?" She held out her hand as Trey sighed and let out a piercing whistle. "I'm Kathy Wind. How do you do? Shake my hand and say 'Fine, thanks.'"

Stacy's fingers were cold and she had a grip about as firm as a fish. But her mouth twisted into what could almost be called a smile. "Fine, thanks."

"Excellent." Katherine smiled, and squeezed the girl's hand before letting go. "I think it's important you're in the information loop, so you need to know that your father's only considering hiring me temporarily—until you and he and Doug can find someone that you'd like to hire for the long-term. I'll be faxing my references and resume as soon as possible. I imagine you'll want to look them over, too. If you have any questions you'd like to ask me then—or now, for that matter—please go right ahead."

"Do you ride horses?"

A flash of movement near the farthest of the two sofas caught Katherine's eye. Two very large brown eyes blinked at her and then quickly disappeared. Douglas had appeared. So to speak. Katherine looked back at Stacy. "Not well, I'm afraid. Do you?"

"I hate horses. Is that hokey accent for real?"

Trey closed his eyes. "Stacy—"

"More real than your hair color," Katherine pointed out.

Doug was back, peering around the back of the sofa, and this time, Katherine didn't look directly at him. She simply let him look at her.

Stacy leaned against the wall, feigning disinterest, but there was a definite spark in her brown eyes. "Don't you like my hair this way?"

Katherine didn't hesitate. "The style? Yes. The color, sorry, no. However, it *is* your hair and you have the right to dye it whatever color you like."

It was the right answer, Katherine noted, because Stacy had to work to prevent her approval from leaking past her facade of boredom. "Do you have any tattoos?"

Good heavens. "No, I'm tattoo free—and completely unpierced as well."

"Not even your ears?" The girl was actually remarkably pretty, with a heart-shaped face that—even through the last layers of baby fat—boasted a pair of dramatic cheekbones that were quite a bit like her handsome father's.

And from what Katherine could see of Doug in her peripheral vision, he looked quite a bit like his sister. Same delicately shaped face. Significantly lighter shade of brown hair, though.

"Not even my ears," she told Stacy cheerfully.

"You're kidding. Are you a virgin, too?"

"Anastacia." Trey bristled, his beautiful mouth set in a grim line. "The idea was that you could ask Kathy questions pertaining to her employment here. If you'd rather go to your room, just keep it up." He strode tensely toward the hallway. "*Where* is Douglas?"

"I imagine he'll come out when he's ready." Katherine looked at the little boy and smiled.

He didn't smile back, but this time at least he didn't retreat.

"I understand you play the clarinet." Katherine moved to the couch and sat, and, as if Doug really were a dog, she casually draped her hand over the arm rest, down close to him, as if for him to sniff. "I used to play the oboe."

"The oboe? Man, double reeds are *really* hard to—" Stacy cleared her throat, uncomfortable, it seemed, that she'd actually almost been enthusiastic.

Out of all her sisters, Katherine was the only one who had glided almost quietly through her early teens. And although she'd mostly kept her mood swings to herself, preferring to hide away in her room with a good book, she'd lived through all three of her sisters' significantly noisier bouts of thirteen-year-old angst.

"How about you, sir?" Katherine asked Stacy's father. "Are you at all musical?"

"You've really got to stop calling me that." He turned to look at her, his blue eyes just as shuttered as Stacy's brown ones. This was *quite* a family. Of course, she should talk. The Wyndhams weren't known for their lack of repression, and out of all the princesses, Katherine was perhaps most guilty of keeping her true feelings under wraps.

"Trey used to play the piano, but these days he only plays the stock market," Stacy said.

"Sir," Trey said, sidestepping Stacy's last remark. "It makes me feel like some medieval lord of the manor."

He spotted his son, who had gotten close enough to breathe on Katherine's hand, but not close enough to touch. "There you are." Several long strides brought him next to the sofa, and he leaned over, scooping Doug up and into his arms. "Doug, this is Kathy Wind. Kathy, this is…"

The boy was dreadfully, painfully shy, and he clung to Trey, burying his face in the man's shoulder. "Douglas," Trey finished somewhat apologetically. "Well, it's the back of Doug's head, anyway."

He embraced the boy tightly, resting his cheek against the small tousled head for a long moment. "Come on, Dougie. Don't you want to meet Kathy?" he asked quietly.

Doug shook his head no.

"It's all right," Katherine said. "We both got a chance to look each other over. He looks all right to me, and as long as I look all right to him, and to Stacy, as well—" she turned to the girl ''—I think we'll get along all right. What do *you* think?''

Stacy shrugged. ''I guess.'' She looked at her father. ''Can I, like, go now?''

Trey glanced at Katherine, and nodded. ''Yeah,'' he said. ''Sure.'' He let Doug slide down to the floor as well, and the two children were gone from the room in a flash.

Katherine would have risen to her feet, but Trey sat down on the other end of the sofa as if he were exhausted, as if every bone in his body had turned to liquid. He stretched his long legs out in front of him, his head against the back cushions, as he stared up at the slightly vaulted ceiling.

''So,'' he said with a laugh that didn't have much to do with humor. ''There we are. In all our dysfunctional glory.''

He turned his head to look at her, and was unable to hide a glint of despair in his eyes. ''I'm not very good at this parenting thing,'' he admitted. His smile was self-deprecating. ''I guess that was pretty obvious.''

Katherine chewed thoughtfully on her lower lip. ''What was obvious was that you love them. They certainly are—'' she couldn't keep from smiling ''—unique.''

His smile became much more genuine. ''Understatement.'' He stood up and she, too, rose to her feet. ''I appreciate your spending all this time here this afternoon, Kathy. I won't keep you any longer.''

Kathy. Her sisters had sometimes called her Kathy, but no one else ever had. She'd always, *always* been Princess Katherine. It was funny, actually, hearing her childhood nickname on a man's lips.

On this man's very attractive lips.

His very maleness seemed to linger about him, never far from the surface. Even now, as he gazed at her, there was something in his eyes that wouldn't let her forget that he was a man, and she was a woman.

Katherine wanted him to hire her as a temporary nanny because she wanted to locate one Mr. William Lewis. She also wanted to help Trey Sutherland out of this bind he was

in. And, yes, she had to be completely honest here. She liked
being looked at and spoken to as if she were a normal woman.
Not a princess to bow and scrape and be obsequiously polite
to at all times.

"I'll get those references to you as quickly as I can," she
told him. "By tonight, if possible."

"Tomorrow will be fine." He started toward the door. "If
and when you decide that—"

"Oh, I've decided."

"I meant what I said about you taking the time to think it
over."

"I don't need time," she told him. "I'll fax them to you
tonight. I want this job, and if, as you've led me to believe,
you're desperate, well, then... If my references meet your
approval—and I believe they will—I see no reason why I
shouldn't start tomorrow."

"It's perfect, Laura," Katherine said into her cellular phone
as she drove back into Albuquerque. "If William Lewis
shows up, I'll be there. Already inside the gates of the Sutherland estate."

"As the *nanny*." Laura Bishop was both Royal Social Secretary and friend. Currently she was an extremely skeptical
friend.

"I'd really just be a glorified baby-sitter," Katherine explained. "And *that's* perfect, too. After I drive the children
to school in the morning, I'll have nearly the entire day to try
to find out where Bill Lewis has gone. *Someone* in Albuquerque knows where he is, I know it."

"And you want me to, what? Make some fake references
for you?"

"Not fake references." Katherine pulled into the parking
lot of a shopping mall to consult her street map. She had the
most dreadful sense of direction of anyone in the world. She
searched for the avenue she had just been on, craning her neck
to check the name of the cross street. "Real references. Let
Alexandra be one. A princess of Wynborough as a refer-

ence—that ought to make something of an impact. And I
know you could talk Dr. McMahon into vouching for Kathy
Wind's character, too.''

Laura sighed. ''Katherine, this could be a complete wild-
goose chase. We don't even know if Bill Lewis is our man.''

''We don't know that he's not.'' Katherine found the avenue, found the cross street and...yes, she'd been heading
away from the hotel. Drat.

''You know, this place has been in something of an uproar
since you left this morning,'' Laura told her, referring to the
royal vacation home back in Aspen. ''Gabriel Morgan's been
positively grim about the fact that you just flew off to New
Mexico without arranging any kind of a game plan with him.''

''Oh, shoot.'' Katherine cringed. Gabe Morgan was in
charge of the royal bodyguards. ''It's just...I called Trey
Sutherland's office this morning and was told I could see him
at three. I just grabbed the first plane reservation I could get.
I didn't have time to do more than leave a note on your desk.''

''Which I found only about an hour ago.''

''Oh dear, I'm so sorry!''

''I was just glad it was you. If it were Serena who'd gone
missing that way, I think Gabe might've had an aneurism on
the spot.''

''Laura, it's going to look extremely peculiar if the new
nanny shows up with a bodyguard, so—''

Laura sighed again. ''I'll take care of that, too.
Just...promise me you'll be careful.''

''Of course, I'll be careful. And, oh, as far as the references
go, I've been completely honest with Trey—except about my
name. I've simply neglected to tell him I'm a princess,'' Katherine said. ''He knows I've had no previous experience as a
nanny. But the children aren't infants, so...''

''*Trey,* huh? This is getting more and more interesting.
Maybe I should reconsider the bodyguard thing.''

Katherine felt herself blush. ''No,'' she said. ''It's not...I
don't...he doesn't...he thinks I'm a nanny, and, I mean...''
She took a deep breath. ''Don't go there, Laura. He's simply

very informal. Casual. He told me he expects me to wear blue jeans to work.''

Trey had told her to dress casually, adding that he thought she looked to be a blue jeans and T-shirt type. Katherine had been thrilled he would think that, thrilled to be thought of as someone who didn't necessarily have to wear a tiara to tea. She couldn't remember the last time she'd worn something as casual as blue jeans. She didn't even have a pair in her wardrobe. That was going to change this afternoon.

''Let me have Sutherland's fax number again,'' Laura said. ''And, Katherine? I know I don't really have to tell you this again, but…please be careful.''

''Thursday night,'' Trey's mother said. ''At the country club. Have you written it into your calendar? I'll hold on while you check.''

Trey closed his eyes. ''Mom. I'll be there.'' Damn Bill, anyway. This was all his fault. Whenever Sutherland-Lewis needed to be represented at a high society function here in town—or in Los Angeles or New York, for that matter—Bill Lewis did the honors. Leaving Trey with his computers and his deadlines, blessedly far from the limelight and the curious stares that always followed him around.

Did he or did he not kill his wife? Even after three very long years, the rumors persisted.

And the irony of those rumors would have been hysterically funny, except that Helena's death still hurt far too much for him to even *think* about laughing.

And as far as the rumors went, Trey hadn't done *completely* all that he could to squash them once and for all. No, after that woman's magazine had chosen him as ''eligible bachelor of the month,'' he'd actually been grateful when the dark rumors had resurfaced, and the flock of gold diggers pursuing him had vanished.

Vanished as surely as Kathy Wind had when she'd left the estate late this afternoon.

Trey stared at his fax machine, willing it to click on. But

it was silent. It was nearly eight-thirty in the evening, and he still hadn't received Kathy Wind's references.

"I'll have my driver pick up Diana," Penelope Sutherland decided. "We'll stop at your place at seven for a small glass of wine before heading over to the club. Tell your housekeeper to dress for the occasion, please."

Trey sighed. "Anita will already have gone home for the night."

"What kind of housekeeper leaves when you need her most?"

"The kind with a family of her own. And I don't think answering the door and pouring wine qualifies for 'needing her most.'"

"I don't know why you put up with her—"

"Mother, don't." Trey cut her off before she started in on lecture number 612 on "Reasons to Hire a New Housekeeper." Penelope didn't like Anita, couldn't understand that Trey *liked* the fact that the friendly, vivacious Mexican-American woman dressed and acted so casually. Trey's mother didn't get it. She didn't understand that he didn't want to live in a mausoleum filled with silently grim servants who bowed and scraped and kowtowed. He'd had enough of that when he was growing up, thanks.

It was dark outside, and the window reflected his blurred image. Poor little rich boy. He turned back to his desk, to stare at his fax machine, which was still silent, damn it.

"Thursday at seven," he said. "It's in my book."

"You should call Diana to confirm."

"*You're* picking her up," Trey countered. "*You* call Diana."

Penelope sighed. "If you don't call her, it's not going to be a real date."

"Guess what, Mom? It's *not* a real date."

"Trey, you know how much I loved Helena." Penelope Sutherland *had* loved Trey's wife like a daughter. She'd been best friends with Helena's mother since grade school. "But enough is enough. It's time to move ahead with your life. Time to have some fun again."

Fun? With Diana St. Vincent? "Yeah, look, Mother, I've got to go. I'll see you Thursday, all right?"

Trey rolled his eyes as he hung up the phone.

Diana St. Vincent, the heir to the James Company fortune, was smart, she had an unerring fashion sense, she was socially connected, *and* she was loaded. But she was also cold as hell. Trey had known her for several years, but he still couldn't even imagine what she did for fun.

Unless, of course, his mother was talking in vaguely polite euphemisms, and by fun what she really meant was *sex*. It was time for Trey to have some sex again.

And yes indeed, after three years, there certainly were times, every now and then, when Trey could imagine maybe, just maybe, having sex again.

Oh, yeah.

That was quite possibly the biggest understatement of the decade.

And tonight—God help him—was one of those nights when his imagination was running wild and he couldn't seem to stop thinking about sex.

And not the pleasant, politely proper sex he'd shared with Helena during their eleven and a half years of marriage. He'd loved his wife, but when they'd made love, he'd always, *always* held himself back. She was so well-bred, so gentle and refined. He'd always been afraid he might shock her.

No, tonight he couldn't stop thinking about raw, ragingly passionate, heart-stoppingly, gut-wrenchingly, completely insane sex. The kind where it's almost like an out-of-body experience because you can't tell where you end and your lover begins. The kind where you lose yourself in the sheer potent ecstasy of a single kiss and—

Trey opened his eyes, suddenly astutely aware that the fantasy lover he'd just been imagining in his bed was none other than the candidate for the position of temporary nanny, Kathy Wind.

Oh God, where had *that* thought come from?

Kathy was pretty enough, and sure, she had a body that would probably cause a small sensation if she wore a bikini onto a beach. But that woman probably didn't even *own* a bikini. She seemed far, *far* from the raw, screaming sex type.

She was warm cocoa and cookies, soft and sweet, wrapped in a fleece blanket in front of a crackling fire.

She was little-sister material, while Diana St. Vincent...

It *was* likely that beneath Diana's cool facade burned searing passion.

She was a beautiful woman. Thick black hair, porcelain perfect features, a body to die for and the ability to show it off in a very classy way. Diana St. Vincent probably owned a dozen bikinis. And she'd made it clear that Trey's advances would be more than welcomed.

But he knew that any intimacies he shared with her would have a very steep price. Marriage.

And the thought of marrying Diana St. Vincent left Trey stone-cold.

She didn't care about him. Not one bit. Like all of the others—even like Helena—she couldn't see past his bank account to the man beneath.

And he wasn't going to do *that* again. He'd rather spend the rest of his life alone than be conned that way again. And alone was most likely the way he'd remain because most people—both men and women—couldn't get past his huge fortune. They were either completely intimidated and stayed away, or they wanted a piece of it, and were willing to do anything to get it.

What were the chances of his ever finding a woman who said, "The hell with your money. Burn it for all I care. All I want is Trey the man."

No, all the women he'd ever met had been far more in love with Trey-the-wallet.

It wasn't too hard to understand why. It wasn't as if he were a warm, friendly, open, expressive person.

In fact, many, many people had labeled him icy cold, both socially and at work. Especially at work.

The truth was, *he* wouldn't want to work for himself. And he wouldn't blame Kathy Wind at all if she simply never faxed her references—if she turned and ran, and he simply never heard from her again.

That would be a damn shame. Stacy had liked her. Stacy had actually stopped into his office about an hour ago to find out if Kathy's references had checked out. Dear God, was that a miracle? The idea that Stacy might actually *like* her nanny…?

Except Kathy wasn't their nanny yet.

Trey closed his eyes, praying to whomever might be out there listening. Please, please, *please* don't let Kathy change her mind. If Stacy liked her, Doug would like her, too. His children desperately needed someone with such a warm, sweet, completely sincere demeanor in their lives.

They needed cocoa in front of the fire.

And as for Trey… He'd keep his thoughts pure from now on, at least when it came to Kathy Wind. It was absurd, really, what he'd been thinking. But he could explain it easily enough. He was tired and obsessing over the fact that he wanted her to fax her references, that he wanted her for this job.

Somehow all his various wants and needs had gotten crosswired. That was all. No big deal.

With her direct honesty and appealing sincerity, Kathy would fit right in. She would become the little sister he'd never had.

The fax machine turned on with a whir and a mechanical burp, and Trey sat up. He crossed the room and…

Yes.

Kathy Wind's references.

There *was* a god.

Chapter 3

"No wonder you're not married. Just look at your underwear."

Katherine didn't even lift an eyebrow. She just kept on unpacking her things.

"How do you expect to catch a man wearing underwear like this?" Stacy held up one of Katherine's sensible white panties.

Katherine gave her a long, level look. "I tend to keep my underwear beneath my clothes. It has nothing whatsoever to do with my ability to catch men." Should she even *want* such a thing.

"Not true." Stacy spun the panties around on her finger. "My father's single, right?"

Katherine knew where this was heading. "This doesn't—"

"And he's a total babe, right?"

"Stacy, really, I'd prefer not to—"

"It's a simple yes or no question, and we both know the answer is yes. Yes, he's a babe. As least as far as old guys go. This is an undisputable fact. I mean, just *look* at the man. He could be a movie star.''

Katherine conceded. ''All right. Yes. Your father's quite handsome. But I don't see what this has to do with—''

''Your underwear?'' Stacy finished for her. ''But it does. Answer *this* for me. You're going to be living in this house for about a month and a half. In the same house Trey lives in. Has the thought even occurred to you that you should hit on him?''

''Hit on your *father?*'' Katherine couldn't help but laugh as she hung the few dresses she'd brought in the spacious closet. ''No, it definitely hasn't occurred to me. Good grief.''

''So in other words what you're saying is that you look at him, and you see an extremely attractive man that you *know* is single and completely filthy rich, and it hasn't even *occurred* to you that he might be even *potential* husband material?''

Katherine tried to lower the heat under the frying pan she was currently sitting in. ''It's just not that simple, Stacy. Not everyone is looking for a husband.''

''You are.'' Stacy didn't leave any room for doubt in her voice. ''Look at you. Puppies and babies. You love 'em, right? You probably even have little pink flowers on your nightie.'' She started opening the dresser drawers to find the nightie in question, but Katherine leaned against the dresser, holding the drawers shut.

Stacy was undaunted. She gave up trying to open the drawers, but didn't give up on the conversation. ''You want a ring and a wedding gown and Prince Charming. You want happily ever after.''

Katherine watched as Stacy flopped onto the big four-poster bed that sat in the middle of the official nanny's bedroom. ''Is that so awful?'' she asked the girl.

''For you?'' Stacy made a face. ''No way. If it's what you want, well, good luck. I hope someday you even have twins. Your problem isn't that you want to get married. Your problem is that you look at guys like Daddy—like Trey—and you automatically assume they're out of your league. *And,* this is where we get back to where we started, it's all because you wear really boring underwear.''

"Well," Katherine said. "Okay. You've truly lost me there.'' Maybe it was time to go find Douglas.

Stacy sat up. "Look at it this way. You're standing here, right? Wearing that old dull underwear. And Trey walks in. And you have a conversation, but nothing happens. Nothing sparks because your underwear is so sensible. The entire time you're talking, you're thinking, I'm the nanny, there's no way he'd go for someone like me.''

For a thirteen-year-old, Stacy was amazingly astute. Still… It was *definitely* time to go find Doug. "I think this conversation has—''

"Now imagine what might happen if, instead of that dull old boring white underwear, you were wearing something with a green-and-peacock-paisley print? Something made of silk and lace? Something fabulously interesting.''

"Stacy, that's enough. Stop.''

"I'm about to make my point. This entire conversation has been leading to this very moment. You're not really going to shut me up now, are you?''

Katherine looked into the girl's widened brown eyes. She knew she was being manipulated, but she shook her head. "Make your point. God help me.''

"You know that old saying—God helps those who help themselves? That's what *I'm* trying to do here. I'm trying to help you help yourself.''

"Is that your point?" Katherine asked. "Because if it's not, cut it. *Now.*''

"Okay." Stacy stood up. "Here you are. Wearing your nanny clothes the way you are.''

Katherine looked down at the skirt and top she was wear-ing—it was one of her favorite and most comfortable outfits. Nanny clothes. Right.

"But *this* time," Stacy continued, "what if you're wearing some really amazing underwear underneath? Trey comes in, and you're right, he doesn't see your underwear, he doesn't have a clue you've got it on. But *you* know. And the entire time you're talking to him, you're thinking about how good you look in that underwear. And all of a sudden he's *not* out of your league because *you* are as good as it gets. And instead of being nervous and shy, you give him a little attitude, a little extra something in your smile. And before he knows it, he's asking you to dinner. And *that's* why you should burn all that boring underwear *right away.*''

Katherine just stood there, gazing at Stacy. ''Well,'' she finally said. ''I'll take it under advisement, thanks. Any ideas where Doug might be?''

''Don't you want a chance for a rebuttal?'' The girl really was remarkably bright. And her point really did make quite a lot of sense.

Given the assumption that Katherine would *want* Trey Sutherland to ask her to dinner.

And that was a very big assumption.

Katherine was here to find Bill Lewis—not to ''catch'' Trey Sutherland. Or even dine with him.

''No,'' Katherine said. ''I'll pass on the rebuttal, thanks.''

Stacy shrugged. ''Suit yourself.'' She'd been carrying a skateboard when she first came in, and she took it with her, setting it down on the floor in the hallway.

As Katherine watched, the girl stepped onto it, and giving herself a push with one foot, headed down the corridor, the wheels making a soft whirring sound against the wood. ''Isn't that more of an out-of-doors activity?'' Katherine asked.

Stacy shrugged again. ''This place is so big, and Trey doesn't care. Doggie's probably in the playroom,'' she added as she rolled away.

Katherine gave an experimental whistle.

The playroom was empty—or at least it *appeared* to be empty.

But wherever Doug had gone, it couldn't have been far. The TV was on, and that same videotape was playing. *Lady and the Tramp.* An excellent choice for a boy who liked to pretend he was a dog.

She turned off both the TV and the tape, and whistled again. Louder this time.

And there he was. A little pointy chin. A delicately heart-shaped face. Two brown eyes. Peeking out at her from behind the draperies.

As a boy, he was too painfully shy even to face her. But dogs simply weren't shy. And as a dog, he could watch her rather intently.

Katherine sat down on the floor, glad she'd taken the time to change into her new blue jeans, glad she'd bought the ones that were stonewashed and already faded and soft. She opened the bag she'd brought with her, and took out the squeaky toy she'd picked up on her way to the estate.

It was a cartoon-looking pig, with a really goofy smile, holding a soccer ball, of all things.

She held it out, squeaking it, and like any self-respecting dog, Douglas bounded toward her.

Katherine lifted the toy up, out of his reach. "Sit," she said firmly, holding out her other hand, forefinger pointing, as if she were addressing a real dog.

Doug sat back on his haunches, looking fixedly at the toy.

Katherine slowly lowered the toy, holding it out for him to sniff. She reached out with her other hand and lightly touched his head, ruffling his hair, scratching behind his ears.

He looked at her then. He met and held her gaze—something he was too timid to do without hiding behind this game of make-believe.

"My name is Kathy," she told him. "Remember me from yesterday? I'm going to help take care of you for the next few weeks."

He didn't say a word, but then again, she hadn't expected him to. Dogs didn't talk.

He was such a sweet little thing. And he was a *little* thing, just a scrap of a boy, really. He'd only been three when his mother died. There was no way he could possibly have understood where she had gone, *why* she had gone away.

"Come here, puppy." He was so small, Katherine could easily pick him up. And she pulled him into her arms. "Every puppy needs some snuggling, don't you think?"

He didn't put his arms around her neck, but he didn't resist, either. He leaned closer, and she just sat with him on her lap, content to hold him as long as he let her.

Which, considering that he was in truth a small boy, was longer than she would have expected, but not overly long.

He pulled free from her, the squeaky toy in his mouth. Dropping the toy in front of her, he backed away. If he'd had a tail, it would have been wagging.

"What do you want?" Katherine asked. She knew full well, she simply wanted to see if she could coax a word or two out of him.

But he didn't speak. He simply pushed the toy closer to her with his nose.

She played along. After all, she had managed to give him a hug—something she suspected she'd never have gotten away with if she'd treated Doug like a boy.

First, Stacy had come into Katherine's room to talk while she'd unpacked. Then Doug had actually let her touch him.

Today, she was going to be content with very, *very* small victories.

"Do you want to play *fetch?*" she asked Doug.

He barked happily.

Katherine tossed the little toy out into the room, and Doug scrambled for it, picking it up in his teeth and carrying it back to her on all fours.

He dropped it into Katherine's hands. "Good dog," she enthused. "What a good—"

"What is this?"

Trey Sutherland was standing in the playroom door, his face like a thundercloud.

Doug vanished. One minute he was there, and the next he

was gone. Faster even than she could blink, he was back behind the drapes.

Oh dear, and they'd been doing so well.

"We're getting to know each other," Katherine told Trey.

"I'd like it a lot better if you could manage to get to know Douglas the *boy,* not Douglas the dog."

Well. Talk about chilly receptions. Trey Sutherland couldn't have sounded any colder if he'd tried.

Katherine glanced at the lump behind the drapery. "We should have this conversation elsewhere."

"I don't have a dog—I have a son. The conversation's over. There's nothing more to say."

"You may have nothing more to say, sir, but *I* haven't even started." Although Katherine rarely had cause to use it, her royal upbringing in Wynborough had included learning to put plenty of frost in one's voice. But she didn't use it again, at this moment. Instead, she opted for earnestness. "Perhaps we could move to the privacy of your office?"

As she'd suspected, earnest took her a whole lot farther than frosty would have.

"That is," she added with a smile, "if you're up for the five-mile hike."

Some of Trey's own chill dissipated. "It's not that far. But if you want, we could go somewhere closer."

Her own room was nearby, but it would hardly be proper to invite him there, even though she had a suite that included an outer sitting room. She might have suggested it innocently enough a half hour ago—before Stacy started in with all that talk about her underwear. But now...

She was aware of that underwear right now—plain and white and nothing special beneath her jeans and turtleneck sweater.

Did she honestly think Trey Sutherland was out of her league?

Hardly—in terms of power and wealth and social standing. In fact, they were nearly perfectly matched. He was one of the richest men in the American Southwest, and she was Wynborough royalty.

However, in terms of romance, passion, lust and burning desire… Well, there was no doubt about it. When it came to attractiveness, Trey Sutherland was a fifteen on a scale from one to ten, and she, on her very, very best day, was merely a four. It wasn't that she was *un*attractive. She simply was…nothing special.

Exactly like her underwear.

Good grief.

She forced a smile, and knew without a doubt that it had—like that blasted underwear—positively no attitude.

"No, let's go to your office," she said to Trey. "A brisk hike while I gather my thoughts might be perfect. I'll be back later, Douglas," she announced, with one last glance at the lump behind the drapes.

Trey was smiling crookedly as he led the way into the corridor. He didn't smile often, but even his halfway, crooked almost-smile had ten thousand times the charisma hers ever did. And when his mouth was set in his default expression—a slightly tense, slightly grim line, well, then he positively smoldered with sexuality and intensity.

Katherine had never smoldered in her entire life. And it was nearly assured that she would go to her grave having never smoldered once.

Oh, yes. Trey Sutherland was *so* far out of Katherine's league, it wasn't even funny.

"How many rooms do you have here, exactly?" she asked as they headed toward the main wing and his office.

"Too many."

"Whatever possessed you to buy this place? I mean, it's absolutely lovely, don't misunderstand," she quickly added. "But—"

"But, it's huge," he finished for her. "When I first bought it, it was huge and crumbling, too. The owner was going to tear it down, but I persuaded him to sell to me. It's actually a building with some historical significance. The Beatles spent a weekend here back in 1968.''

Katherine laughed. ''And here I was thinking it was historically significant because it had been built by some Mexican bandito.''

''You're almost right,'' he told her. ''Although he wasn't a Mexican, he was American. He originally came from Syracuse, New York. And while he wasn't officially a bandito, he was definitely a cattle rustler and horse thief, and, although it's not substantiated, I suspect a few railroad payrolls padded his bank account, too. He made his fortune in Texas, and settled here in New Mexico to stay out of sight of all those Rangers he'd made as enemies during his five-year crime spree. Let me tell you, Kathy, only in America could a thief have a street named after him.''

''Some Americans *do* seem to have a place in their hearts for the legendary bad guys of the old West—although I think it's just admiration for the rebel. Respect for the men and women who have cheated the rules and won—or better yet, beaten the system.'' Katherine glanced at Trey. ''This particular thief, was his name one I would recognize?''

''Oh, yeah. His name was Sutherland. Henry Sutherland. And yes, he was my great-great—I don't even know how many greats—grandfather.''

''Oh, my.''

Trey smiled. ''He was a gambler and lost his entire fortune—including this house—by the time he was forty. His son, Ford, was a gambler, too, and when *he* was twenty, he made enough money to buy back the house, but the owner carried a grudge and wouldn't sell. Apparently Henry had played fast and loose with other women, including the new owner's wife. He spent at least one illicit afternoon that came back to bite him hard on the rump.''

''Oh, dear.''

''You bet. Ford met an untimely end at the hands of a gunslinger who may or may not have been Billy the Kid— local legend says yes, but it's never been proven and probably never will. He's buried up on the hill, overlooking the house. I bought that land, too, about ten years ago. Ford's money was lost, but about forty years later, his grandson made a fortune selling bootleg liquor during Prohibition. This Sutherland's name was Ellery, and *he* tried to buy this house back, too—probably to use as a speakeasy. He got as far as a verbal agreement with the owner…who died before it could be put into writing. A nephew from Chicago inherited.

"He had plans of his own for the house, and wouldn't sell. He turned it into a hotel, which is why there are so many bathrooms, and why the Beatles stayed here, too. It was a solid, prosperous business until the 1970s when the nephew died, and left the place to his two sons. The sons lived in L.A., and put the place in the hands of a manager who couldn't even begin to handle the upkeep with the budget he was given. So the place started to crumble.

"My father—his name was Arthur—he tried to buy it next, but he had cash flow problems when the stock market crashed, and he couldn't swing the deal. He died a few years later."

"I'm so sorry."

"He might've survived the cancer, but he didn't survive the chemotherapy. He got an infection, and… Still, sometimes I think his wanting this house was what kept him alive so many extra months."

"So you bought the place, when?"

"Not long after that. The year Stacy was born." Trey pushed open the door to his office and flipped on the light. "I didn't really want the damn thing. But when I heard it was going to be torn down—somehow that just seemed wrong. I actually had fun fixing it up."

Trey Sutherland and fun weren't two concepts Katherine could visualize together very well.

"Now I love the place. I really liked looking at all these old photos of the way the house used to be," he continued. "Then, ripping out all the god-awful green shag carpeting and peace-sign wallpaper was reaffirming on all levels."

"Oh, dear."

"Yeah. 'Oh, dear' is right." He crossed to a bar, built into the wall. "Soda?"

"No, thanks, I'm fine."

So. Now they were here. In Trey's office with the door tightly shut behind them. Katherine slipped her hands into the back pockets of her jeans, hoping the stance made her look relaxed and casual. If such a thing were even possible.

"Thank you for telling me about the house," she ventured. "It's fascinating. And now, after all that time, a Sutherland finally has it back."

He carried a can of soda toward his desk. "Yeah—it's almost as if you can hear the collective sighs of all those generations of haunted spirits. I've gotta hope if they're walking these halls, maybe my being here makes them rest a little easier." He changed the subject without missing a beat. "It's probably good that we're taking some time to talk about Doug—and Stacy, too. You wouldn't know it at times, but Stace can get really fierce when it comes to Dougie. If he's at all threatened, she's like this little she-bear, ready to rip out the attacker's throat." He gestured toward his leather-covered chairs. "Sit. Please."

It was impossible to sit with her hands in her pockets, so Katherine pulled them free before she slowly lowered herself onto the edge of one of the chairs.

"She gave Doug his nickname, you know," Trey continued. "Helena and I called him Dougie, and she thought we'd named the new baby 'Doggie.' She was only seven, so I guess it made sense to her. Anyway, the name stuck, and unfortunately, it's probably at the core of the kid's current problem."

"I truly don't think Doug has a problem," Katherine told him. "I think—"

"He eats breakfast from a dog dish," Trey said flatly. "If that's not a problem, I don't—" He stopped himself. "Okay. Look. Helena died three years ago. Three *years*. The kid should be starting to come around, but instead I see him slipping further and further into this world of make-believe he's created for himself." He shook his head. "I'm afraid that one of these days, he's just never going to come out."

"He's six," Katherine pointed out. "There's not much reality in most six-year-olds' lives. Although I studied psychology in school, I'm no expert, sir, and yet—"

"Trey," he said. "Not 'sir.'"

"Hard habit to break," she murmured. "Nearly as hard to break as the habit of interrupting people all the time."

"I'm sorry." His apology was swift and completely sincere. "I'll— Please." He finally sat down in the other chair. "Continue."

"It seems to me that pretending he's a dog is simply Doug's way of dealing with any new—and potentially frightening—situation. He's painfully shy, yet here he is, forced to go one-on-one with a new nanny for what? The four thousand, five hundred and something time since his mother just vanished from his life."

"Twelve," Trey said. "The twelfth time."

She was appalled. "In three years?"

"Almost four actually, since we hired a nanny when Helena first got sick. Mae loved the kids and Helena, too, but she left when…" This time he interrupted himself. Apparently there were some details he didn't feel comfortable sharing.

Such as perhaps the fact that this loving nanny had left because she had seen or heard too much, and feared for her own safety?

Katherine chided herself for having such an unruly and uncalled for thought. Trey hadn't murdered his wife, contrary to all the rumors. And there *were* rumors. She'd heard them at the hotel, heard them while shopping in town. It was believed that Trey Sutherland had committed the perfect murder.

But that was just talk, and here Trey had just told her Helena had been sick.

He was sitting there grimly, fingers pressed against his forehead as if he had a headache, his broad shoulders slouched back in the chair, and Katherine couldn't bear to press him with curious questions about Helena's death. She would go to the library, read what the newspapers had to say about it, and then, if she had any questions, she'd speak to him. But until then, they had Doug and Stacy to discuss.

"The other nannies were…" Trey shook his head as he glanced over at her. His eyes were truly a remarkable shade of blue. "Some quit after only a few days, some just simply didn't work out from our end, most of them couldn't handle Stacy and Doug. None of them stayed more than a few months."

"That's got to have been dreadfully tough on Doug and Stacy. I'm not blaming you, mind you," she added hastily. "I'm not going to pretend that I know you in any kind of depth, but what I *do* know is that you love your children."

"But…?" Trey asked, correctly hearing that invisible little word dangling there.

"But twelve nannies in even four years would have to be trying on any child, let alone a sensitive one like Doug," she pointed out. "In my opinion, Trey—" She'd managed to say his name instead of sir, but it had come out sounding too soft, too intimate and she froze.

He was watching her, giving her his full attention, and being the focal point of all that grim intensity was rather overwhelming. But then he smiled slightly, and the harsh lines of his face softened, and he was somehow, some way even *more* handsome, his eyes even more blue. "Thanks," he said. "I know it's not easy for you to call me that."

She tried not to be affected, but her voice came out far too whispery and soft. "In my opinion, Doug's dealt with all the chaos and change in his life extremely well. He has no reason to trust me, and in fact, here we go again, right? I'm only going to be here for the short term. If Doug's been paying attention and I think he probably knows everything that goes on in this house, including a few things you don't think he knows—he *does* know I'm not going to stay. He has no reason at all to risk becoming attached to me. Considering that, and considering everything else—including his shyness—I'm more than willing to become friends on his terms, first. And if that means playing make-believe games with him, I truly think that's fine. So unless you specifically tell me that you don't want—''

''No,'' he said. ''It's obvious you've thought this through. I'm still leery, but you're right about Doug being shy.''

''Doug's shy, but Doggie's not,'' Katherine said, referring to the boy's alter ego. ''I see no reason he shouldn't use that to empower himself.''

''The dog thing drives me nuts,'' Trey admitted. ''That's the hard part about being a single parent. You have to deal with everything—even the things that make you crazy. When Stacy was really little, like two or three, she had this thing with her socks—the seam had to line up across her toes in a certain way, and if they didn't, it was a tragedy. The shoes couldn't go on her feet, life virtually had to screech to a halt. I swear, if you wanted her to leave the house at a certain time, you had to start her with her socks and her shoes a good forty minutes beforehand. It drove me mad, but it didn't bother Helena one bit. She thought it was funny—she was so patient with both the kids and...'' He glanced away, and when he looked back he tried to force a smile. ''Let's just say patience isn't one of my strengths.''

Katherine couldn't stop the rush of compassion. There was no way on earth this man could have killed his wife. Absolutely no way. Obviously, he loved Helena still. ''Well, now that I'm here, I'll do what I can to help.''

''I suppose it's too soon to try to talk you into staying on permanently...?''

Katherine laughed and stood up. ''I'd better get back to the children.''

She started for the door.

''Kathy.''

She turned back.

Trey had stood up, and silhouetted the way he was against the window and the bright-blue November afternoon, he looked even taller and broader than usual. ''Thank you.''

''You're very welcome.''

He reached up, loosening his tie and unbuttoning the top button of his shirt. ''I was hoping we could set up a time to talk each day—maybe in the evening, in between Doug's and Stacy's bedtimes. You could keep me filled in on what's going on with the kids.''

Katherine found her voice. ''That sounds…very smart.''

He shrugged out of his jacket, draped it on the back of one of his leather chairs, then rolled his sleeves up to his elbows. ''Say…nine o'clock here, in my office? Doug's usually unconscious by eight forty-five, but Stacy usually doesn't get to bed until ten-thirty or eleven. There are shows she likes to watch on TV.''

''That sounds perfect.'' Good grief, *she* sounded like an idiot. *That sounds smart. That sounds perfect.* What it *really* sounded was incredibly, foolishly disappointing.

Her heart was still pounding, though. When he'd first said he was hoping to set up a time for them to talk each day, she'd actually been dumb enough to think it was because he enjoyed her company. But no. She'd forgotten herself for a nanosecond, forgotten she was wearing that dull white underwear, forgotten that Trey was, indeed, completely out of her league. Not to mention that he was still in love with his dead wife. Dear Lord, she was *so* foolish.

''See you tonight, then,'' he said.

''All right.'' She turned to leave, extremely glad he couldn't read her mind, but again he stopped her.

''Kathy, hang on.'' He crossed the room toward her. ''You've got…''

She was completely confused as he reached around behind her. He smelled almost sinfully good at that close range, but she still nearly jumped a mile into the air as his fingers brushed the seat of her pants. What was he *doing?*

''Hold still,'' he ordered almost sternly, then touched her again and—

There was a small tearing sound, and Trey handed her a small cardboard tag that had been attached to the back pocket of her brand-new jeans.

''Oh, dear,'' she said.

He smiled. Not one of those forced, rueful half smiles he was so good at. This one was genuine, and at close range, it packed quite a wallop.

Katherine knew she was blushing, and she blushed even harder when she realized that in order for him to have noticed that tag, he had to have been looking directly at the seat of her pants. He'd been checking her out again. Imagine that. Even though she was wearing her boring white underwear.

''I didn't mean to embarrass you,'' he said.

She took the piece of cardboard from him and their fingers touched. His were warm and big, with neatly trimmed nails. She glanced up into his eyes—she couldn't help herself—and saw that his smile had faded.

He took a step back, away from her, as if suddenly aware he was standing much too close.

''I'm sorry,'' he said. ''I have this tendency to point out unzipped flies and spinach between teeth, too. I tuck labels back down into the shirts of strangers. It's gotten me into trouble on more than one occasion.''

''I think I probably need someone like you following me around,'' Katherine admitted. ''I once spent an entire day with my shirt on inside out and not *one* person told me. I finally realized what I'd done at bedtime. I was mortified.''

''Maybe no one noticed,'' he suggested. ''Most people just don't bother to look that closely at other people.''

Most people didn't look at other people the way Trey Sutherland did. He didn't just look, he examined, studied, memorized. Which was why he'd spotted that tag on her pants. He probably hadn't been checking out her rear end after all.

Katherine wasn't sure whether to feel disappointed or relieved. She motioned toward the door. ''I should…''

He nodded, taking another step backward. ''See you at nine, then.''

''Not for dinner? I mean, I'm sure the children will expect to see you.''

"Oh," he said. "No, I, um, I have a conference call scheduled and…"

"Oh," Katherine said. "That's too bad."

"Yeah, I, uh…I'll see you…later."

That was completely strange.

Katherine found herself standing in the hallway outside the closed door to Trey's office. What had just happened? Had she just imagined that Trey had suddenly gotten very, *very* tense? And if it wasn't imagined, what had she done? Had it been something she'd said, or perhaps her body language? Her eagerness for him to join her for dinner?

It was absurd even to think he'd want to have dinner with *her,* but surely he'd want to see his children. Wouldn't he?

Katherine walked down the stairs and back toward the playroom.

Yes, it *was* absurd to think Trey Sutherland would want to have dinner with her.

Regardless of *what* kind of underwear she had on, the man *was* completely out of her league.

Chapter 4

"Stacy, what do you want on your sandwich?" Kathy backed out of the refrigerator, holding a pile of cold cuts. As she turned around, she slammed directly into Trey.

He saw it coming, but couldn't get out of the way fast enough.

"Oh, dear, sorry!"

"No, I'm sorry," he said.

She'd lost her hold on some of the slippery plastic bags, and now they were pinned between them. Trey grabbed for the bags with his left hand, juggling his morning mug of coffee in his right.

He should have just let them fall. Instead, he grabbed the swiss cheese and a packet of ham—along with Kathy's right breast.

"God, I'm sorry," he said again.

She made it to the counter and dumped the cold cuts there. She was laughing, thank God, although her cheeks were tinged pink with a blush.

She looked about eighteen years old this morning, with her

hair pulled back into a ponytail, face scrubbed freshly clean of makeup, dressed in an oversize sweatshirt and jeans.

"Well," she said. "*That* certainly woke me up."

"Sorry." Damn, *he* was blushing, too. He couldn't remember the last time he'd actually blushed. Was it back in sixth grade or maybe third…?

He refused to think about how soft her body felt, or the fact that the accidental full body block had been the closest he'd been to a woman in far too long. He refused to acknowledge the sharp flare of sensation and emotion. He didn't want to analyze whether that sudden turmoil in his chest was the result of longing or need or even attraction—he'd already decided that his feelings toward Kathy were brotherly.

He quickly changed the subject. "And as long as I'm apologizing, I'm sorry I had to cancel our meeting last night."

"No problem," she said briskly. "Thank you for leaving a note."

"I had to go into the office—I didn't get back until late. I think it was around two-thirty," Trey explained. He didn't want her thinking he'd blown her off for anything other than work. "We've got a deadline for a big software project for an important client. We're down to the wire—I've got teams working around the clock. There was a problem and the project manager was home celebrating her tenth wedding anniversary, so I went in instead."

She looked up from making Doug's sandwich to smile at him. "That was so sweet of you."

Sweet. God. He didn't think he'd ever been called sweet in his entire life. He shrugged. "Anyone who can stay married for ten years these days deserves a night off."

"I'm *never* getting married. It's definitely overrated." Stacy was wearing her standard black, and this morning she'd accessorized it with an equally dark scowl. She got on her skateboard and rolled with her bowl and a box of her current favorite nuts-and-twigs-type cereal to the kitchen table.

"Is it possible," Trey said to his daughter, "for you to leave that thing at the door?"

She didn't answer him. He hadn't really expected her to.

She rolled back to the counter and glared at the orange juice as she poured herself a glass.

Mornings were by far one of the roughest times of the day. Like Trey, neither Stacy nor Doug were morning people, and the rush to get ready for school could be fraught with real peril.

"So, Stacy," Kathy said exuberantly, "what do you want on your sandwich? Roast beef or ham?" It was possible that her British accent made her sound extra cheerful. Or maybe she simply *was* bright and upbeat in the morning.

Stacy didn't look up from the table where she was slumped over her bowl. "I don't want lunch."

"Too bad," Trey said. "You're going to have lunch whether you want it or not." As soon as the words left his mouth, he *knew* it had been the wrong thing to say. But he couldn't seem to be in a room with his daughter these days without triggering some kind of disagreement. He couldn't so much as *look* at the kid without feeling this flare of frustration and despair. "Give her ham and cheese," he told Kathy grimly.

But Kathy was still being cheerful, ignoring the tension that filled the room. "How 'bout it, Stacy? Ham and cheese today?"

"I'm a vegetarian."

"But last night you ate Anita's stew—"

"Today," Stacy said rudely. "I'm a vegetarian *today*."

Lord, help me. Trey realized from Stacy's belligerent expression and from Kathy's sudden wide eyes that he'd spoken aloud. "Sorry," he said. Damn it, all he was doing this morning was apologizing. "Fine, Stace. Take a cheese sandwich."

"I'm vegan." At his blank look, she added, "No cheese." *You idiot.* She didn't say the words aloud, but they certainly were implied.

"Great. Take a salad." He tried to mimic Kathy's upbeat style as he turned to her. "Do we have lettuce?"

"Absolutely." Kathy's smile was warm and welcoming after Stacy's icy look. "One salad, coming up."

Doug skittered into the kitchen on all fours and Trey felt his neck and shoulders get even tighter. He was about to bark out an order for his son to get to his feet and walk, when Kathy stepped very firmly on his toe. "Ow," he said instead.

Then he watched as Doug stopped short at the sight of his favorite bowl—a plastic dog dish bearing the word Rover—out on the floor, filled with unappetizingly hard pellets of kibble.

Well, now, *that* was interesting. Trey had never tried pushing Doug's game to the extreme, actually trying to feed the kid dog food.

The look on Dougie's face was comical. Or, at least, it would have been had Trey found anything at all funny about the fact that his son was more comfortable as a canine than a human.

"Good morning, Douglas," Kathy said to him cheerfully, Mary Poppins in a sweatshirt. "Are you going to be a dog this morning or a boy? I bought the boy a special treat, but in order to have it, you've got to sit at the table and eat with a spoon."

Sure enough, she'd set a place at the table for Doug, in front of which was a pitcher of milk and a box of sugary cereal.

Doug's eyes widened, and then—for the first time in weeks, at least as far as Trey had heard—he actually spoke. "Lucky Charms!" He pushed himself onto his feet and ran for the table, sliding into his seat.

And then, maybe even more miraculously, Stacy actually lifted her head from her own breakfast and smiled. Of course, her smile was for Kathy, who was smiling back at the girl and giving her a thumbs-up.

Clearly, they'd been coconspirators in this Lucky Charms plot.

Kathy was wearing black nail polish—a definite sign that

she'd spent at least part of the evening in his daughter's company. Trey was pleased. Or at least he *hoped* he was pleased.

He leaned closer to Kathy, lowering his voice. "You didn't leave the kids home by themselves to go buy that, did you?"

She gave him her oh-dear look. "Of course not. I had it delivered." She leaned closer. "Sorry about your toe."

She smelled amazingly good, a mixture of clean soap and some softly, delicately fragrant lotion. From this proximity, he could count the freckles that were scattered across her nose and cheeks. They took her adorableness to a completely new level. Why on earth would she ever want to cover them with makeup?

"How do you get the grocery store to deliver that late at night?" he asked. Her eyes were a very light shade of gray-blue, with a very thin ring around the outside of the iris so dark it was nearly black. Her lashes were thick and lush and—

Trey took a step back, suddenly aware they were still standing much too close.

"You don't," she answered, putting the lid on the plastic container that held Stacy's salad. "But if you're creative, you order a pizza and then when it arrives, you tell the pizza delivery boy that he'll get a twenty-dollar tip if he drops a box of Lucky Charms at the house before ten o'clock."

"I'll pay you back," Trey told her, leaning back against the counter and taking another sip of his coffee. "In fact, I meant to tell you to keep a list of your expenses."

"Of course." She gave him another smile. "You look very nice this morning. I assume the suit means you're going into your office?"

"Thanks, and yeah." He ran his hand through his hair, feeling absurdly pleased at her compliment. "I've got meetings all day."

She efficiently zipped Doug's purple lunch box shut. "What time should we expect you home tonight?"

"I'll be back by nine," he said. "In time for our meeting."

"Oh." Kathy's smile faded. "Not for dinner?"

"I have a meeting that's going to run late."

He'd disappointed her. She was trying hard not to show it, but he had. Clearly she'd had expectations—probably based on the fact that most families shared at least one meal together during the day.

But the Sutherlands weren't most families. Not by a long shot.

"We need to go," Stacy implored. "Doug, go brush your teeth. Quickly. You've got dog breath." She gave Kathy another of her rare smiles as Doug vanished down the hallway. "He thinks that's a compliment." She rolled toward the door. "I'll be out in the car."

"Take your lunch," Kathy said. "And don't forget to say goodbye to your father."

"Goodbye, Trey," Stacy intoned. "Be sure to make lots and lots of money today because God knows the four billion we already have isn't enough."

"In my country," Kathy said, "we generally save our insults for the middle of the conversation. Greetings and farewells tend to be insult-free. A simple 'enjoy your day' will do quite nicely, please. And—call me old-fashioned—but everyone needs a hug in the morning."

Stacy's smiles were long gone. She turned the hostility she usually reserved for Trey onto Kathy, full power. "*I* don't." The conviction in her words was countered by the way she hesitantly glanced at Trey.

"That's ridiculous." Kathy softened her words with a smile that included Stacy in the joke. "I've never met anyone who couldn't benefit from a hug."

Stacy narrowed her eyes, and Trey felt himself tense. That was never a good sign. Stacy had a temper that was too much like his own. She had moods like his, too. In fact, she was just too damn much like him across the board, poor kid.

But to his surprise, she looked from Kathy to Trey and back again, and then smiled. But it wasn't a nice smile. It was a calculating smile. Trey braced himself.

"So, okay," his daughter said. "If everyone really *does* need a hug in the morning, then you guys go first."

Trey looked at Kathy, who met his gaze with what he was sure was an equal look of shock.

Um…

Kathy blushed—what a surprise. And she laughed. "But I'm not family."

"Oh," Stacy said. "I see. So you didn't *really* mean that *every*one needs a hug. You meant, only *some* people need hugs. And I'm telling you that *I'm* not one of—"

"No," Kathy said in her, I may sound friendly but I'm not taking any lip voice. "That's *not* what I'm saying. I'm actually in dire need of one, this being my first full day at a new job, not to mention the fact that I'm thousands of miles from my home and my family. I was simply expecting to get my share of hugs from you and Douglas, that's all."

"We're hug-challenged," Stacy told her. "Sutherlands are pros at the air kiss—we embrace with as little body contact as possible. And when we want to get turned on, we shake hands, mostly because it reminds us of making a business deal."

Stacy crossed the kitchen and gave Trey an exaggerated air kiss about three feet from his cheek. "Enjoy your day," she said tightly. "Try to limit yourself to only three hostile take-overs today, okay, Dad?" She grabbed her skateboard and went out the door. The screen door banged shut behind her.

"Oh, dear," Kathy said. "I'm sorry, I—"

"She's right." It wasn't even seven-thirty, and Trey already had a pounding headache. "As a family, we're…not very affectionate."

"Well," Kathy said, "if that's something—as a family—that you're not particularly happy with, then it might serve you well to figure out a way to change. Air kisses certainly serve their purpose, but they shouldn't be for family." She pushed open the kitchen door and leaned out into the hallway. "Doug! Even if you've cleaned them one at a time, you've *got* to be done with your teeth by now. Hurry, or we'll be late.''

Trey finished his coffee as he watched Kathy hustle his son out the door.

"See you tonight," she called to him, polite to the bitter end.

Maybe Kathy could teach them all how to hug. The thought was remarkably appealing but completely absurd. It was more than likely they were all beyond hope.

But then Trey remembered. This very morning, after Kathy had been here less than one day, Stacy had smiled and Doug had spoken.

His new nanny was a miracle worker. If anyone could achieve the impossible, it would be Kathy Wind.

The light was on in Trey's tower office.

Katherine could see it from the arched windows that looked out onto the center courtyard as she gently closed the door to Dougie's bedroom.

Doug was, without a doubt, the least talkative child she'd ever met. Besides his two words at breakfast, she'd gotten one "yes" and two "no, thank yous" out of him all day. But he'd handed her a pile of books to read as bedtime stories— all about dogs, of course.

She finally reached the stairs that led to Trey's tower. In the spring and summer, when it was warm, it would be quicker simply to cut through the courtyard and—

She wasn't going to be here in the summer. Or in the spring, for that matter. Unless Trey's business partner, Bill Lewis, truly *was* her missing brother. Then there might be cause to visit from time to time.

She found herself hoping that he was.

Katherine had spent the bulk of her day in the Albuquerque library, reading all the local news about the mysterious and elusive Mr. William Lewis. She'd studied the few blurry newsprint photos, trying to find a resemblance to the royal family in the man's face. He was the right age, that much was certain. He seemed to be about the right height and build, and about the right coloring.

According to the social pages, Bill Lewis seemed to frequent an upscale restaurant and nightclub called The Rat Pack. And he was a member of the Albuquerque Archaeological Society and the local Explorers' Club. He'd also done extensive fund-raising—many years in a row—for the New Mexico branch of the Big Brothers-Big Sisters Organization.

Tomorrow, Katherine would spend her day making phone calls, trying to find someone who might know where Bill Lewis was. Perhaps one of his friends from the Explorers' Club. At this point, since Trey seemed to think Bill had gone off somewhere traveling, that was her best bet.

If Bill truly were Prince James, her long-lost brother, he'd already done quite a bit for which she and her family could be very proud.

And if he weren't, well, then she'd simply been on a wild-goose chase, as Laura had called it. At the very least, she told herself firmly, refusing to be so negative as to allow her time with the Sutherlands would be *completely* wasted, she would have this pleasant little vacation from the demands of her position. And it *was* a vacation not to have to be Her Highness, Princess Katherine every time she ventured from her bedroom. It was a vacation, regardless of the tension among the various Sutherlands.

Katherine honestly liked Stacy. Beneath the girl's facade of rudeness was an incredibly intelligent, quick-witted, extremely sensitive young woman, dying to get out. Douglas was the sweetest little thing—Katherine was already completely in love with both the boy *and* the dog he pretended to be. And as for their father…

While Katherine was in the library, she'd read about Trey Sutherland and his wife, Helena, née Browning, too.

Helena had been truly beautiful—one of those coolly gorgeous, sleek high-society American blondes. She and Trey had made the perfect couple.

Katherine had read news of their wedding announcement,

news of the births of their children. She'd looked at a series of articles on Trey's booming computer software business, a piece on his merger with Bill Lewis, along with all the numerous mentions of the Sutherlands in the social pages.

And finally, she'd found and read Helena's obituary. It was extremely lengthy; it included a picture and outlined a long list of the woman's charitable works, yet mentioned absolutely nothing of her cause of death.

Nothing at all.

As if, one day, she'd simply just stopped breathing, cause unknown.

Katherine took a deep breath herself, and knocked on Trey's office door.

"It's open."

Trey's voice came from behind her, and she turned to see him walking down the stairs from his bedroom. He was still wearing the expensive Italian suit he'd had on this morning. His tie was loosened, though, and the top button of his shirt was undone. It didn't make him look sloppy, just rakishly, handsomely disheveled.

"Go on in," he said.

But she hesitated, and he reached across her to unlatch the door and push it open.

She walked into his brightly lit office, feeling just a little dumb. There was no need for her to be so nervous. This was *only* a business meeting, after all. It probably wouldn't last more than five minutes. She'd give him a quick report on Stacy's and Doug's day and then she'd be out of there.

In fact, there was probably no need even to sit down.

"I'm not sure exactly what to tell you," she said briskly. "Doug and Stacy and I are still getting to know each other."

"Can I get you something to drink?" Trey crossed to the bar. "A glass of wine?"

Wine.

"Oh," said Katherine. "No. I, um…thank you, but, I really only have wine on special occasions."

He turned to face her, looking like Central Casting's ideal

for the perfect dream date. He practically oozed money, power and charm. And then, of course, there were his movie-star good looks.

But this wasn't a date. And it certainly wasn't a dream.

And there was no way she was going to have a glass of wine, and start letting her imagination run even more wild than it already was. No, thank you very much.

"This isn't a special occasion?" he asked. "The end of your first full day at a new job?" He motioned toward the other side of the room. "Please. Sit down. God knows it's been a long enough day."

Katherine saw that there was a soft-looking sofa and several only slightly less cushy chairs comfortably grouped together in the far corner of his office. Had he been motioning toward that, or toward the more formal chairs in front of his desk?

Not wanting to presume anything, she remained standing, exactly where she was.

"I'll have a ginger ale," she told him, since he seemed determined to get her a glass of *some*thing. She watched the way his jacket stretched across his broad back as he poured it. "No offense, but special occasion or not, I've got to get up early again in the morning. Even worse, I've got to get Dougie up. You know, I've never met a six-year-old who didn't automatically wake up at dawn, ready to go."

"Doug doesn't like school very much." Trey handed her the glass of soda, and she took it from him, careful that their fingers not touch.

"That's too bad. Especially considering that he's got, what? Eleven more years to go?"

"Yeah. And then four in college. We've tried everything short of pulling him out and home-schooling him." Trey led the way to the sitting area. "But I really think he needs the social connection—you know, exposure to other kids."

He set a bowl of pretzels on the coffee table in front of the couch. "Please help yourself," he continued. "And forgive me for crunching my way through this meeting, but I worked through dinner, and lunch was a hell of a long time ago."

It probably also didn't help that he'd had only a little sleep last night. If, as he'd told her this morning, he hadn't gotten home until two-thirty, and was up and dressed and ready to go shortly after seven... Trey had probably only had about four hours of sleep last night.

Katherine sat down on the edge of one of the chairs, since it looked as if he were intending to sit on the couch. "If you like, we could talk in the kitchen. I could get you some dinner...?" Was that something a live-in nanny would be expected to do? She wasn't sure. Still, on closer inspection, it was clear that Trey was completely exhausted. Whether it was her job or not, she would have gladly made the man a sandwich, or microwaved some of that incredible macaroni and cheese Anita had made for her and the children's dinner.

"No," he said, sinking back onto the couch. "Thanks, but I just want to sit in one place for a few minutes. I had a really tough day. It started with a bang, when I had to fire a man who wasn't working out. He didn't take it well and I came damn close to calling security. And that was over twelve hours ago."

Katherine couldn't keep from asking, "Aren't you past the point where you have to endure tough days?" If what she'd read in the newspaper were true, Sutherland-Lewis was worth a seriously huge amount in American dollars.

He sat up and took a sip of his wine. "I didn't mean to sound as if I were complaining. I work because... Well, because it's what I do. I'm good at programming, and I'm good at running this business. It seems crazy to spend my time doing anything else."

Did "anything else" include spending time with his children? Katherine didn't dare ask that aloud. Besides, he'd only missed two evening meals. It might have been coincidence that they'd fallen two days in a row.

"Stacy was asking me about Thanksgiving dinner," she told Trey.

He ran his hand over the thick stubble of five o'clock

shadow on his chin and looked less than happy. "Oh, God, that's already next week, isn't it?"

"Is it?" she asked. "I wasn't exactly sure since it's an American custom. Stacy thought it was next Thursday. A week from tomorrow?"

"Yep." Trey sighed. "My mother's going to Hawaii to visit some friends, so it'll just be the four of us. Although..." He took another sip of his wine, almost as if he were fortifying himself. "I've wanted to talk to you about this, and this seems as good a segue as anything." He set down his wineglass and met her eyes. "You've asked me about dinner a couple times now, and..." His voice trailed off, but he still held her gaze. "I can't seem to be in a room with Stacy without some major blowup happening. And when we fight, Doug gets upset and we *all* get indigestion and...I've been staying away at dinnertime on purpose."

"Oh, dear," Katherine said softly.

He nodded. "Yeah. I've talked to some people—some professionals—who think it might be a good idea to give Stacy that space, but I honestly don't know. You've seen how she is, how terrible she can be. I don't know what to do anymore. Staying away seems so much like giving up, but..." He shook his head. "This sounds awful, but it's gotten to the point where I find excuses so that I don't have to come home."

He pressed his fingers against the bridge of his nose as if he had a dreadful headache as he sat back on the couch. "I can't believe what I just said. It really sounds awful when you say it out loud, doesn't it?"

Katherine didn't know what to say. So she opted for the truth. "Yes," she told him. "And since you already know that, you've also got to believe deep down inside that staying away from your children couldn't possibly be the solution to this problem."

"So what do I do? Grab her and wrestle her to the ground and *force* her to stop being so damn rude? God, Kathy, there are times that all I have to do is *look* at her, and my blood pressure starts to rise."

"But that's part of the problem," she said. "Don't you see?" She laughed as she realized it. "You've trained yourself to instantly get into this mental boxer's stance every time you so much as see Stacy." She sat even farther forward. "This morning, for instance. The first thing you said to her—do you remember?"

Trey rubbed his eyes. "God, I don't know. Was it something like 'What on earth are you wearing today?' or 'The only way you're wearing *that* outside of this house is over my dead body?'"

"Close enough," Katherine said. "It wasn't about her clothes, but you *did* criticize her, Trey. For riding her skateboard in the kitchen. You didn't say good morning, you didn't greet her in any way at all. You just told her that you wished she would leave her skateboard at the door, and your frowning expression and tense body language communicated that she'd messed up for the four millionth time this week."

"So what are you saying?" he asked. "That I'm never supposed to criticize her?"

"If you don't want her to ride her skateboard in the house, make a rule and have her keep her board in the garage," Katherine advised. "And then if she slips up and forgets, you tell her good morning because she's your daughter and you love her and you're glad to see her, and you tell her about the funny dream you had last night because you know it will make her laugh, and then you say, 'Oh, by the way, it looks as if you forgot about that rule we made, so please take the skateboard outside, okay?' And you smile so she knows it's not the end of the world."

"Easier said than done," Trey muttered.

"I once read this really great book about something called anchoring," Katherine told him. "It's something people do automatically, kind of along the lines of having a song that makes you feel really good because you first heard it when something wonderful happened. You know, 'Oh, honey, they're playing our song?' Well, people anchor things to bad experiences, too. I think the example I remember reading had to do with husbands and wives. The honeymoon's over, and they have a fight—apparently most people fight about money. A volatile topic, right? The issue's not solved in just one day, and they both come home from a tough day at work, and little Jimmy got into trouble at day care to boot, and instead of kissing each other hello, they start right in again, fighting about money. If they do this often enough, the money problem can be solved, but *still* they'll start to fight the instant they walk in the door, because they've anchored the very *sight* of each other with all that anger and pain and frustration and tension. These are two people who made vows to love and honor each other, but now they've subconsciously trained themselves to feel absolutely dreadful whenever they see each other's faces.''

"Oh, God." Trey looked stunned. "That's what I've done, isn't it? With Stacy."

Katherine nodded. "I think so. You said the very sight of her makes you tense. That probably goes both ways. And even if it doesn't, she's so sensitive, at the very least she's picking up on your tension. But this isn't all your fault. She's not perfect. I've watched her calculate what response will upset you the most, go for it, and then sit back to watch the fireworks.''

"So what do I do?" He answered his own question. "I just have to stop. I have to look at her and not get angry. I have to look at her and think, 'This is my daughter and I love her,' not 'This is my daughter and I want to wring her neck.'''

That wasn't going to be easy. But Katherine knew that Trey Sutherland wasn't the kind of man who was daunted by a difficult task.

"You also might want to hold back the criticism for a while," she suggested. "Whenever you see her, tell her something good, even if it's just that you're glad to see her." She smiled to soften her next words. "And you might try smiling at her occasionally, instead of glowering the way you do.''

Trey gazed at Kathy. "God, you must think I'm awful.''

"No. I think…'' She looked down at the floor for a moment before meeting his gaze. Her eyes were warm, and that now familiar faint tinge of pink was spreading across her cheeks.

Somewhere between this morning and right now, she'd let her hair out of that ponytail. It hung around her shoulders, a gorgeous shade of chestnut, thick and rich and shiny, and probably very, very soft to the touch.

Trey picked up and held tightly to his wineglass with his right hand, slipping his left beneath his right arm. Running his fingers through a female employee's hair would be considered bad form, even if he *did* only think of her as a sister.

"I think you're wonderful for wanting to improve your relationship with Stacy," she said softly, "and for deciding to take action, to work to make it better. So many people don't even try."

Kathy thought he was wonderful. Maybe it was only the result of a full glass of wine on an empty stomach, but her words made Trey feel ridiculously good. Or maybe it was the sudden hope he was experiencing that made him feel so damn positive. For the first time in years, he actually thought about tomorrow and felt that there was a chance—a very slim chance—that he and Doug and Stacy might actually survive the tragedy of Helena's death with their family still intact.

He finished the last of his wine and set his empty glass on the table. "What do I have to do to make you stay on permanently?" he asked.

He'd surprised her. She shook her head as she smiled at him, clearly thinking that he was only kidding around.

"Please." He leaned forward in an attempt to prove his sincerity. "I'm not joking, Kathy. Think about what it would take for you to stay, oh, say, seven years. Until Doug goes into high school. Think about financial compensation, as well as other things. How many days or nights off you'd need each week. How many weeks of vacation. Housing—you know we could make a private apartment for you right here, in one of the wings of this house. And you know, if the time came that you wanted to get married, your husband could live here, too."

Kathy was completely taken aback. "Mr. Sutherland...Trey, I—"

"I know you said you didn't have a boyfriend, but if there's someone special back home, I'll fly him out and find him a job."

"There's no one," she said.

"Whatever he does, I know I can find him a position in Sutherland-Lewis and—"

"There's no one special," she said again, louder this time. *"Truly."*

Trey smiled at her. "Sorry," he said. "I have the tendency to go into steamroller mode when I really want something. And I can't help it—I really want you."

She broke eye contact at that, looking down at her hands clasped tightly in her lap, and he realized that his word choice had been extremely poor.

"To work for me," he added quickly, but again, as it had several nights ago, the image of Kathy tumbled back on his bed, her gorgeous brown hair spread out on his pillows, flashed instantly to mind.

Wrong, wrong, wrong. Where the *hell* had that thought come from? The wine? Maybe, but he hadn't had anything at all to drink the other night.

Trey looked away, afraid she would see an echo of that shockingly intimate image in his eyes. He was trying to entice her to stay permanently, not scare her away for good.

And the way she was sitting there, so proper and polite, knees glued together, back ramrod straight, shoulders back, as if she were wearing one of those old-lady suits she'd worn to the job interview, she would be horrified to know that he'd been thinking about her not only naked, but naked with her long legs wrapped around him as he took her hard and fast and—

As Kathy would say, "Oh, dear." Oh. Dear.

Trey stared at his wineglass. Sister, remember? She was

adorable, yes, but his feelings for her were brotherly. At least, they were most of the time.

He risked a quick glance at her. Yes, so she *did* have long legs. She had very, very *nice* long legs.

And those very, very nice, very long legs had never been wrapped around anyone in the manner of which he'd been thinking. Those very nice legs belonged to a very nice, very *young* woman who was completely not in his league.

He was jaded, he was bitter, he was cynical, and he wanted to lose himself in a completely physical relationship that didn't touch his heart or his soul. He wanted savage, pounding, tempestuous no-commitment sex.

And sweet Kathy Wind, well, it didn't take all those degrees he'd earned from NYU and Harvard to know what *she* wanted. She no doubt wanted sweet, gentle lovemaking, a heart-stoppingly slow communion of mind, body, heart and soul. She wanted whispered words of love and forever. She wanted happily ever after.

Except happily was just a myth, and ever after was a lie.

Damn it, he'd been feeling almost decent, but now he'd gone and depressed the hell out of himself.

At least he no longer had the urge to nail Kathy to the wall simply because she was soft and warm and female, with pretty hair and an even prettier smile.

God, he was a royal mess.

He looked up and found her watching him.

"Are you all right?" she asked quietly.

"I'm tired," he said. "I'm sorry, I... Do me a favor, Kathy?"

"Of course."

"Just think about it," he said. "You know, about staying here permanently."

Eventually he would convince her he was dead serious. And then he would win. Because everybody had a price. And sooner or later he would figure out what Kathy's was, even if she didn't know it herself.

"I'm afraid that thinking about it won't do very much good," she told him apologetically. She had such pretty eyes.

"Think about it anyway," he said. "Make your demands as decadent as you can imagine."

Kathy laughed. "You truly have no idea how decadent I can be."

"Actually," he said, "considering that one of your references was Wynborough royalty, I do have some idea. And, you know, I've been meaning to ask you about that. How does one go about meeting a princess?"

The pink was back, tingeing her cheeks. "It's easier than you might think," she said. "Meeting them was...purely an accident of birth."

"Did your mother or father work for the royal family or something?"

"Or something," she told him. She stood up, clearly ill at ease and not wanting to talk about herself any further. "I should probably go check on Stacy. It's time for her to go to bed."

Trey rose to his feet, too, glancing at his watch. He'd had no idea it had gotten so late. "Just so you know, the princess spoke extremely highly of you."

It was funny, actually. Kathy looked as if she wanted to shrink down to almost nothing and escape from the room by crawling beneath the crack in the door. "I'm so glad," she managed to say. "If you'll excuse me, sir."

Somehow he'd flustered her so much that "sir" was back.

He walked with her toward the door. "I have another early-meeting tomorrow morning. I'll be out of the house before you get the kids up. With luck, I'll be back before five."

She looked up at him, her eyes wide and hopeful. "Oh, good. We'll expect you for dinner, then?"

Um.

His complete chagrin must have been written all over his face, because she laughed softly. "I guess not."

"There's a charity dinner tomorrow night. In a moment of

complete insanity, I promised my mother that I'd go. I'm sorry. There's no way I can get out of it this late in the game.''

"Friday then?"

She looked so sweetly hopeful, Trey felt like a total villain.

"It's going to take me a few days to clear my schedule," he admitted. "There are a few things I can't change, and Friday's dinner meeting is one of them."

The hope in her eyes was significantly subdued, and Trey knew she no longer thought he was quite so wonderful as she had only minutes earlier.

"I'm going to do this," he told her. "I'll come to dinner. Soon. I promise you."

"Don't promise me," Kathy told him. "Promise yourself."

Chapter 5

"There. Now you look perfect."

Katherine stood in the shadows in the upstairs landing, and watched as the extremely beautiful dark-haired woman finished adjusting Trey's bow tie.

Trey was wearing a tuxedo and Katherine was very sorry, but whoever she was, the dark-haired woman was wrong. He didn't need his tie to be exactly straight to look perfect.

The expensive wool-blend jacket and pants had no doubt been tailored to his form precisely. Dressed in a business suit, Trey was drop-dead gorgeous. But in a tuxedo... It was definitely drool time.

Katherine had been eight years old when she'd seen her first James Bond movie. And ever since then, a handsome man in a well-cut tux had the power to turn her knees to bread pudding.

She couldn't have moved if she'd wanted to. And part of her—the very naughty part of her that knew she was eavesdropping and didn't particularly care—didn't want to move.

Down below, the dark-haired woman was still completely

invading Trey's personal space. She was standing much too close, yet he didn't seem to mind.

No, indeed, and Katherine didn't know many men who *would* mind if someone as beautiful as this luminous woman moved close enough to kiss.

Her thick, black hair was to die for, her body gorgeous, her face a perfect oval with delicate features that were perfectly matched.

Unlike Katherine's face. Her own eyes belonged to some sensible English schoolteacher, her nose was decidedly Germanic, and her much too generous mouth looked as if it belonged on a Muppet.

Growing up in a house filled with beautiful women—and all three of her sisters and her mother *were* heart-stoppingly beautiful—Katherine thought she had learned never to compare what she saw when she looked in the mirror to anyone else.

Obviously, she needed a refresher course.

The dark-haired woman who was brushing imaginary lint off of Trey Sutherland's extremely broad shoulders was, no doubt, wearing extremely fancy underwear. Hence her complete confidence.

Yes. Sure.

The woman was wearing a very form-fitting black dress that was cut low enough to reveal the tops of her extremely lush breasts. That same dress hugged her flat stomach and softly flared hips and tight rear end and—

And the last crazy shard of her fantasy—the one in which Katherine had a *Sound of Music* type love affair with her handsome employer—was smashed. There was no way in Hades she could compete with a woman like this one.

As a rule, it was foolish and self-depreciating to make comparisons, but rule or no, this was a total no-brainer.

The dark-haired woman was older than Katherine, more sophisticated, coolly, elegantly in complete control.

''Your mother's already out in the car,'' she murmured. She was standing so close, her enormously perfect breasts were brushing against Trey's chest. "This could be our last chance to be alone all night."

She was giving him every body language signal in the book, all but using semaphore flags to let him know that she wanted him to kiss her.

But instead of taking her into his arms, Trey took a step back, away from her. "We shouldn't keep her waiting."

He didn't want to kiss her. He didn't even particularly like her.

Katherine felt a flare of triumph that she instantly squashed. She had to laugh at herself. Logical, practical Princess Katherine—caught up in a childish fantasy.

And just because Trey didn't like the woman didn't mean that he wasn't going to go home and have mad, passionate sex with her later tonight. Katherine knew that men usually didn't have mad, passionate sex with women they sincerely liked. She knew because men usually liked *her*.

And she needed to remember that she wasn't here in Albuquerque to have a desperately romantic love affair with the darkly brooding Trey Sutherland. She was here to find Bill Lewis, to find out if he might be her long-missing brother.

Katherine watched as Trey led Miss Gorgeous to the door. And as that door closed behind them, she sat down on the top stair and sighed.

Elbows on the knees of her jeans, she rested her chin in the palms of her hands.

She knew she wasn't the most experienced woman in the world, but despite that, when it came to desperately romantic love affairs, she knew precisely what she *wasn't* looking for.

She wasn't looking for complicated. And she definitely didn't want impossible.

And, since that was the case, she should be doing her best to keep every kind of distance possible between herself and Trey Sutherland. She shouldn't be sitting here at the top of the stairs, positively *mooning* over the man.

Because even if some miracle happened and Trey—perhaps after suffering some otherwise minor head injury that tem-

porarily impinged on his common sense—were to decide that
he was as wildly attracted to Katherine as she was to him,
any relationship they began would be horribly, dreadfully,
painfully complicated.

He was, after all, still in love with his dead wife.

And, adding even more complications to the tangled web
of their lives, the man had no idea who Katherine truly was.

Although, in many ways, she found her hidden identity to
be particularly wonderful. Trey didn't have a clue that she
was a princess, yet—amazing!—he liked her. She *knew* that
he liked her. *And* he thought that she was doing such a good
job caring for his children that he wanted her to stay for seven
years.

Katherine had never had a job before—*duties,* but certainly
never a job she'd earned and was being compensated for—
and it was intensely gratifying to know that on her first time
out she was doing so wonderfully well.

Trey's feelings—his appreciation and fondness—for her
were genuine. She knew that. He liked and respected *her.*

For the first time in her entire life, Katherine knew for
certain that someone liked her for who she was inside and not
because she was a princess.

And if that miracle occurred and Trey actually fell in love
with her…

Yes, it would be complicated and impossible, but oh, how
wonderful, too.

When Katherine had been twenty, she'd let herself get
swept off her feet during a holiday in Rome.

Richard Anderson had been an American, a student visiting
from New York, whom she'd met when she slipped away
from her sisters and their bodyguards to take a very public
group tour of the catacombs. She'd worn sunglasses and a
hat, and, as usual, no one had recognized her as Princess
Katherine of Wynborough.

Rich had approached her in that easygoing manner of most
Americans, and asked her to take his picture with his camera.
They'd started talking and something had sparked. He was

breathtakingly handsome and very charismatic, and she had been woefully young and easily smitten. Particularly since he seemed so equally charmed by her. She'd agreed to have dinner with him—in part, because it had seemed so unlikely he knew she was a princess. In retrospect, she'd realized that he wasn't exceedingly intelligent, and he spent an awful lot of time talking about himself. But he looked like a scruffier, younger version of Tom Selleck, and she'd loved the way he'd gazed into her eyes, the way he'd made her feel as if she were the only woman on the planet.

They were both on holiday for two long weeks. She'd spent each day, all day, with him, and it hadn't been long before they spent a good portion of their nights together, in his extremely low-rent hotel room.

Katherine had felt wonderfully carefree and bold—until she found out that Richard had known precisely who she was all along. He'd taken that first tour after following her from her hotel. He'd pursued her because she was royalty, not because he particularly liked her.

He'd proposed marriage and she'd turned him down, too badly hurt by his deceit. He didn't love her. His intentions were only to snare himself a rich royal wife, or, barring that, at least to carve a royal celebrity notch into his belt.

In retrospect, Katherine knew she had used him just as completely as he'd used her. She hadn't spent all that time with him because he was clever and witty and brilliant. No, she was ashamed to admit it, but she'd been with him because of his handsome face, his hard, lean body, and his powerful charisma.

And after the initial hurt had worn off, she'd realized she was in fact quite relieved to have had such a good excuse *not* to marry the boy.

Still, since then, she'd dreamed of finding a man who would love her purely for herself. Not for her title or her wealth or the power she had, simply for being the daughter of the ruler of such an influential little country.

And—as long as she was dreaming—she wanted that man

to have a face like Trey Sutherland's. And a body like Trey
Sutherland's. And she wanted him to be intensely brilliant,
and dryly funny, and sweetly warm and hopelessly kind deep
down inside.

Like Trey Sutherland.

Katherine sighed.

And then sat up, listening hard.

Was that…?

Yes, definitely. That was the sound of crying she heard.
Coming faintly from the direction of the children's wing.

Katherine scrambled to her feet and ran for the playroom.

"It's open."

Katherine pushed open the door to Stacy's bedroom and
peeked inside.

The girl was sitting on her bed, clarinet in her lap, music
scattered about her. "So," she said. "Now I'm in big trouble,
right?"

"May I come in?"

"What, am I supposed to say no, and then you *won't* come
in?"

"If you say no," Katherine told her, "then I'd ask you to
come down to my room so that we can talk there."

"And what if I don't want to talk?" Stacy stood up and
put her clarinet in its stand with a savage thrust. "What if it's
the talking I object to, not you coming into my room, huh?"

"Then we talk later," Katherine said evenly. "But you
know as well as I do that this isn't going to go away until we
talk about it, so we both might as well just grit our teeth and
get it over with right now, instead of dragging it out until
Lord knows when."

"What did I do that was so awful?"

"May I come in?"

Stacy rolled her eyes. "Yes. God. Come in. Most people
wouldn't even knock—they'd just barge right in."

"Why should I show you any less respect than I'd wish
for you to show to me?"

"Because I'm a kid."

"That's a load of crap," Katherine said briskly, watching Stacy's eyes widen. Good, she'd gotten the girl's full attention. "One of the things I'm going to be helping you do over the next few days is to compile a list of characteristics you and Douglas absolutely require in a caretaker. And I think—because you value your privacy so highly—that finding someone who believes that younger people should be treated with as much respect as adults should be prioritized rather highly on that list. Don't you think?"

"Well," Stacy said. "Yeah."

"What *you* need to keep in mind as well," Katherine told her, "is that any person worth hiring will have their own list of requirements as well—things they'll expect from you and Doug."

"Well, good luck for that, because neither of us are exactly angels."

"No one will expect you to be angels. But they *will* have other expectations. Do you want to know mine?"

Stacy shrugged.

"I expect honesty and kindness," Katherine said quietly. "The two things I will *not* tolerate—ever—are cruelty and dishonesty. Now, dishonesty is very straightforward. I'll expect the truth from you at all times, no matter what, no exceptions. Cruelty's a little bit harder to draw boundaries around, because there are times—and I believe that's what happened today—when a person may be unintentionally cruel."

Stacy's posture was instantly defensive. "Yeah, well, you know that old song, 'You've gotta be cruel to be kind…?'"

"There are times when that might be true," Katherine countered, "but I'm certain the songwriter wasn't thinking in reference to a six-year-old, and I think you know that as well."

Stacy was silent and staring fixedly at the floor.

Katherine sighed. "Stacy, I know that you love Doug. Why

would you possibly have told him those awful things about
your father and...is her name Diane?''

"Diana." Stacy's mouth was a grim line. "St. Vincent. The
royal bitch. Grandma Sutherland wants Trey to marry her. I
thought it was time for Doggie to know, that's all."

"By telling him that Diana was going to be your wicked
stepmother?'' The only movie Doug watched nearly as much
as *Lady and the Tramp* was *Cinderella*. Katherine was still
amazed at Stacy's lack of sensitivity. She'd just spent forty-
five minutes trying to calm Doug down and convince him that
no stepmother would ever lock him in the tower.

"If somebody doesn't do something soon, Trey's going to
marry her!"

Katherine kept her voice low and even to counter Stacy's
shrillness. "Don't you think your father would come and talk
to you first if he were even *thinking* about getting remarried?''

"No." Stacy slumped into a chair that was in the corner
of the room in a fluid move that was so reminiscent of her
father. "I think he would tell us after the fact. He thinks I'm
a baby—at least he treats me like one." She ran her hands
over her face—another very Trey-like move. "God, she was
over here again tonight. I *hate* her. It's so *gross* the way she
rubs herself against him.''

Katherine sat down on the edge of Stacy's bed. "And you
think that makes it all right for you to frighten your brother?''

"I had no idea Doggie would go ballistic that way."

Katherine just looked at her, one eyebrow slightly raised.

"Well, all right, maybe I sort of knew—but maybe this is
worth screaming about. You know, if Trey *does* marry her,
we're both going to be shipped off to boarding school before
the flowers in the wedding bouquet even wilt," Stacy added
fiercely.

"Your father would never do that."

"My father doesn't want us around, he just doesn't want
to admit it," Stacy countered. "He'd be relieved to have
someone else make that decision for him."

"Your father has never let anyone make a decision—especially not a major decision like that—for him in his entire life."

"He married my mother because his parents wanted him to. That's pretty major, wouldn't you say?"

"Stacy, I simply can't believe that. I'm sorry, but in this day and age, most people don't get married just because their parents want them to." Katherine quickly corrected herself. "At least not in *America*."

"Some do. My two grandmothers were best friends. They were both loaded, and they told Trey and Helena that if they got married, they'd give them about a ton and a half of money. I've heard Trey tell this story, and he always says, 'So I conveniently fell in love with Helena.' He *admits* it. Just ask him. Diana the Ice Bitch is loaded, too, but he doesn't need the money anymore." Stacy sat up, leaning forward in her intensity. "I figure what he needs this time is the sex."

Katherine was glad she was sitting down. "Stacy, this is hardly an appropriate conversation for a thirteen-year-old to be having about her father."

"He's a guy, right?" Stacy said. "I've read magazines and books—I see movies. Guys need sex, and he's been alone for a really long time. It's *got* to be on his mind."

"Women need sex, too, but I don't think we should be talking—"

"I figure he's going for the convenience again." Stacy wouldn't let up. "Grandma Sutherland's practically shoving Diana into his bedroom. Unless we do something, he *is* going to marry her. I've told her about the ghosts, but I think she thought I was just trying to scare her."

"Weren't you?"

"Well, yeah, but that doesn't make the ghosts any less real. I can feel 'em sometimes, usually in the hallways at night. I can just picture Diana marrying Trey, moving in here, then freaking out when she realizes the place is haunted. She'll want to move, and Trey won't and..." She shrugged. "They'll end up divorced after only a few years. I'm just trying to save them the future aggravation."

Oh, was *that* what she was doing now? "I thought that the ghosts of Ford and all the other various Sutherlands were resting easier since Trey bought back this house."

"Ford's around some of the time," Stacy said, completely seriously. "But he's just hanging out. He's not doing any of the haunting. Helena's ghost handles that department."

Helena. Her mother.

"She died in this house, you know," Stacy told her.

"I…didn't."

"Part of her's still here—that happens a lot with the spirits of people who've left the world suddenly. Violently."

Suddenly and *violently?*

Stacy was sitting back in the chair again, but she'd pulled her knees up to her chest and encircled them with her arms. She looked very small and very vulnerable, despite the fact that her words were clearly meant to make Katherine uncomfortable.

And instead of asking the girl exactly how her mother had died, Katherine soft-pedaled the question. "That must have been very hard for you, when your mother died."

"I don't want to talk about that." Stacy sat up. "I want to figure out how we're going to keep Trey from marrying the Ice Bitch."

Katherine wouldn't give up. "If you ever *do* want to talk about—"

"I know." Stacy sprang out of the chair. "You could seduce him."

What? "Excuse me, but I don't think I—"

"Yeah," Stacy said. She started pacing, unable to sit still. "Of course. That's it. If he's looking for convenience, well, you're even more convenient than Diana St. Vincent. I mean, you're here *all* the time—"

"Let me make one thing perfectly clear right now, miss. I have absolutely *no* intention of seducing your father at your behest!"

"Oh, come on, it's not like you don't like him. I've seen you looking at him, you know, checking out his butt."

Katherine couldn't hold her laughter in any longer. "I beg your pardon! I have *never,* ever checked out his butt!" At least, not while Stacy and Doug were in the room.

Stacy was laughing, too. Katherine took that to mean the girl wasn't completely serious, thank goodness.

"What if he invited you to one of his stupid business parties?" she asked Katherine. "Would you at least go with him?"

"If I did, who would be here with you and Doug?"

Stacy didn't hesitate. "Anita. She stays late every now and then."

Katherine stood up. "I think it's time for you to go to bed."

"You didn't answer my question. Would you or wouldn't you?"

"The question is moot," Katherine told the girl. "He's not going to ask me, because he's dating Diana." She moved toward Stacy, enveloping her in her arms, giving her a swift hug and releasing her before she had the chance to go all stiff and unresponsive. Everybody *did* need a hug at least once a day, even Stacy. Katherine believed that absolutely. "Good night, you raving lunatic."

Stacy laughed. "Kathy, it's a *good* plan. You're just too—"

"Sane?" Katherine finished for her. "You bet I am. See you in the morning."

She shut the door behind her, leaning back against it for a moment.

Yes, indeed, it definitely had been a bona fide three-aspirin night.

And it wasn't over yet.

Chapter 6

"See you Tuesday night, darling," Diana St. Vincent said after brushing her lips against Trey's, as she stepped inside her seven-and-a-half-million-dollar, very modern, architectural train wreck of a house.

"Tuesday night?" Trey repeated, but the door was already closed. "I don't think so." He turned to the street, where the driver of his mother's car was waiting attentively.

What had his mother signed him up for now?

Cursing silently, he headed toward the car. His head was aching, the food had been far too rich, and that plus the company tonight had given him total indigestion.

The driver opened the back door, and Trey climbed inside. "No," he said to his mother. "Whatever you've got planned for Tuesday night, no. I can't make it."

"You've got to," she said, slipping a compact back into her evening bag and snapping the bag shut. "It's that reception for Bill Lewis, remember? He's being awarded Benevolent Businessman of the Year for his work with the Big

Brother organization. Since he's dropped off the face of the earth—again—*you've* got to be there to accept his award.''

Trey swore pungently. "What time?''

"The dinner starts at seven. Cocktails at six.''

"What time will they be giving the award?''

"Well, last year it wasn't until quarter to nine, but—''

"Then I'll be there at eight-thirty,'' Trey told her.

"I'll tell Diana—''

"Alone,'' Trey said very firmly.

His mother sighed. "Trey. You know what it will look like if you show up without a date.''

"I don't give a damn what it will look like. Diana's definitely getting the wrong idea,'' Trey said. "She seems to think we're just short of announcing our engagement. And something tells me you're not helping any.''

Penelope crossed her elegant legs as she made a face poohpoohing his concerns. "Relax and go with it, dear. She's perfect for you.''

"God, I hope not.''

"Oh, don't be that way. You've got to admit I called it right with Helena, didn't I?''

Trey was silent. He had fallen in love with Helena, but she had married him for his money. Or maybe, more accurately, she *wouldn't* have married him if he *hadn't* had money. He'd had this conversation with his mother before, and she hadn't understood why he'd been so upset when Helena had told him the truth—that their marriage had been more of a business merger than he'd ever imagined. Of *course* Helena would have taken his wealth into consideration before agreeing to marry him, his mother had said. No woman in her right mind *wouldn't* have allowed herself to be swayed by a fortune of that size. Trey should be grateful he'd had all that money in his favor—it had helped him win a woman as lovely as Helena.

He'd dealt with the hard, cold truth—that his marriage to Helena hadn't been the purely emotional, irrational love match that he'd believed. He'd come to accept the fact that

Helena *had* loved him in his own way. He couldn't have left her—he loved her too much, and besides, they'd already had Stacy. So he'd tried his best to make the marriage work.

But it had always hurt just a little—knowing that Helena never would have married him if he hadn't been rich.

"I'm not marrying Diana," he finally said. "I'm not marrying anyone. So just back off. Please."

Penelope sighed again, deeply, dramatically. "I know *you* don't care, but…people start gossiping whenever you're seen out alone."

Gossiping. Speculating whether or not he'd actually killed the wife that he'd adored. It was so absurd. He could ignore it, most of the time, but Trey knew that even though the rumors were in part his mother's own fault, the talk bothered her immensely.

"Okay," he said. "I'll bring someone. Don't worry about it."

Like a pit bull, Penelope wouldn't let the conversation go without tearing it totally to shreds. "Who?"

"I don't know. Someone." It came to him in a flash. "Kathy."

God, that was brilliant. He could get Anita to stay late. Kathy was sweet enough. She would gladly do him a favor to save his butt, and she'd probably appreciate an evening out of the house as well. They could have dinner at home with the kids and then…

"Oh." His mother had gone into heavy drama queen, closing her eyes and pinching the bridge of her nose with two delicate fingers.

"Oh," she said again, "no. Trey, dear Lord, please, please, *please* don't tell me you're doing something as tacky and unoriginal as having an affair with the new nanny."

Trey laughed aloud as the driver pulled up in front of his house.

"What is she? Eighteen and buxom? From Sweden?"

"Twenty-five. And from Wynborough. And relax. I find her about as sexually stimulating as Mary Poppins." He paused. "Although, now that I think of it, under those starched dresses, Mary Poppins probably dressed like a dominatrix."

Trey got out of the car fast—before his mother could smack him. But then he turned back.

"Mom, I know all you really want is for me to be happy, but don't play matchmaker anymore. Give me a break, all right?"

His mother sighed, her concern completely real this time. "I'm afraid if I give you that break you want so badly, you'll lock yourself in your office and never come out. Helena was the one who died, Trey. Not you. I know you loved her, but—"

Trey gestured toward the house. "It's late. I better get inside."

"Uh-oh," she said. "I'm getting too personal, aren't I? You better run away."

He headed down the path. "Good night, mother."

"Give kisses to Anastacia and Douglas for me," she called after him.

"I will," he promised. And for the first time in a long time, he could imagine actually being able to pass on his mother's kisses to his children. For the first time in a long time, he was making plans to extract himself from the safety of his office, to have dinner, regularly, with his kids.

His mother was wrong. He'd already unlocked the door to his office. He *was* ready to come out and rejoin the world. He just wanted to do it slowly. Surely. He wanted to get his kids back before he reclaimed the whirlwind social life that Helena had loved so much. And he *was* going to get his kids back. Thanks to Kathy Wind and—

A light was on in his office.

He frowned. That was odd.

As his mother's car pulled away, he hurried inside.

Exactly how had Helena Sutherland died?

Suddenly, Stacy had said. Violently.

It was definitely time for Katherine to find out. And while the far too well-behaved princess never would have the chutzpah to approach Trey Sutherland and ask, brave Kathy Wind, in her blue jeans and turtleneck, had exactly what it would take.

She would ask him tomorrow, she decided. She would leave a note on his desk tonight, asking him to set aside some time for them to talk. He'd told her he would be out during dinner tomorrow night, too. She'd let him know in that same note that she'd even be willing to meet with him late at night, after he got home, if that were the only option.

Unless, of course, he wasn't planning on coming home.

She thought of Diana St. Vincent, of how close the woman had stood to Trey, of the possessive way she'd swept her hands across his broad shoulders and chest.

No, it was most likely that *tonight* would be the night Trey wouldn't come home.

Katherine would word the note carefully, giving him several options as to when they could talk.

But they *would* talk. And while Princess Katherine might have been too polite to look a man in the eye and inquire as to how his wife died, Kathy Wind had no such limitations, and no fear.

Yes, Katherine was finding out that Kathy Wind wasn't afraid of much. Right now, as a matter of fact, she was in the process of boldly searching Trey's office for any clues as to Bill Lewis's whereabouts.

Katherine had figured that as long as Trey was out for the evening and the kids were snug in their beds, she might as well check to see if Bill had called in over the past few days. Provided, of course, that Trey kept a record of things such as phone calls, and provided that Bill had called while Trey was at home, not at his office downtown.

And as long as she was in Trey's home office, she checked out his Rolodex, found Bill Lewis's address and phone number. It matched the one she'd already had for Bill. No surprises there.

She glanced at the files that were out on the top of Trey's desk. There seemed to be nothing personal. Just information about Sutherland-Lewis's current clients, projects being worked on, a personnel file for one Bruce Baxter, one of Trey's employees, that she quickly closed after seeing what looked to be an extremely dreadful evaluation, including the words *termination recommended*. There were no files on Trey's desk to give her even the smallest hint as to where Bill Lewis might have gone.

She found a pile of pink phone message slips, and quickly riffled through them. Trey's mother had called him here at his home office and left messages on his machine three times over the past few days, but there was no mention of his business partner.

She spun in a slow circle as she gazed around the room.

Trey had a number of file cabinets that lined the far wall of his office. She approached them, feeling as if opening the drawers might be going just a bit too far, but curious just the same. Did he keep any personal information in there, or were the files within purely work-related?

She opened the top drawer, immediately feeling guilty and evil. But the files were similar to the ones on his desk. All projects or clients. Nothing personal. And nothing at all about Bill Lewis.

The second drawer was the same, as were the others.

She closed them with her hip, turning to look back at the office. It was much too clean. There were no piles of papers, no stacks of handwritten notes, no piece of paper labeled "Bill's phone number in the Bahamas" stuck to a corkboard.

Okay, so maybe being a superspy wasn't so easy. Maybe James Bond didn't just break into an office and have the information he was searching for conveniently pinned to the wall. Maybe he knew where to look while she didn't.

She went back to Trey's desk, and sat down in his chair and tried to think like James Bond. There was always the possibility that the information she was looking for wasn't here. And if *that* were the case, not even Mr. Bond himself could have found it.

She tried the desk drawers. The top one was locked. The center drawer held pencils and pens, a stapler, rubber bands, a pack of breath mints, and a tiny plastic toy dinosaur, its fiercely bared teeth made far less menacing by the fact that it was entirely bright-orange and lying rather impotently on its side. It made her smile, though. Who would have thought intensely business-minded, workaholic Trey Sutherland would keep a plastic dinosaur in his desk drawer?

Katherine closed both the drawer and her eyes and sat, letting her head rest against the comfortable leather of Trey's very cushy desk chair. It reclined slightly, and she sighed, breathing in the lingering scent of the man's delicious-smelling cologne.

"Thinking about taking over as president of the company?"

Katherine rocketed up and out of the chair as Trey closed his office door behind him. His face was expressionless. Had he been watching her for long? She surely would have noticed if he'd opened the door before she'd sat down, before she'd peeked inside his desk drawer, before she'd closed her eyes.

Wouldn't she have?

"I…was going to leave you a note," she stammered. "I wanted a chance to talk to you tomorrow and…" Oh, dear. She sounded *so* lame. He was going to think she was some kind of corporate spy or…or worse. A thief, perhaps. Or a blackmailer or—

"Kind of hard to write a note with your eyes closed, isn't it?" He crossed to the bar, untying his bow tie with one swift yank.

"I'm sorry," she said, moving guiltily out from behind his desk. "I shouldn't have been sitting behind your desk. But the chair looked so comfortable and oh, it *was,* and I…I was exhausted and—"

"Relax," he said. "What do I look like, one of the three bears? I don't mind if you sit in my chair. Hell, you can have my porridge, too, my pleasure.'' He took a glass down from the cabinet. ''But since I don't have any porridge handy, how about something to drink?''

Her heart was still hammering so loudly it seemed impossible that he couldn't hear it. A drink, he'd asked. ''Um. Yes. Please. A glass of wine—if you don't mind.''

He glanced at her, his tired eyes suddenly almost cuttingly sharp. ''Is this a special occasion?''

''I think,'' she said, her voice still a little shaky, ''since you haven't fired me for being in your office uninvited, that it could very well be.''

He laughed at that. Good grief, when this man laughed, he was off-the-chart handsome. And dressed in a tuxedo the way he was… It made it very hard to think like a proper superspy. In fact, Katherine had to look away for fear he'd catch her drooling.

''I hope since you seem to be glad I'm not going to terminate you for trespassing, that the note you were going to write wasn't one telling me you *want* to quit.''

She looked up to find that he was standing right in front of her, holding out a delicate-looking tulip-shaped glass filled with white wine. He smelled as delicious as she'd remembered.

''Oh, of course not,'' she said.

He gave her both the wineglass and a slight, crooked smile. ''Well, that's a relief.'' He gestured toward the chairs in front of his desk. ''Please, sit down.''

''I wanted to set up a time to talk to you,'' she told him as she sat. It wasn't really lying if she simply left out the fact that she'd also come here searching for any clues that would lead her to Bill Lewis, was it? She truly hated dishonesty. ''I wasn't expecting you back so soon, or even…''

She wasn't expecting him back at all. She didn't say the words, but Trey knew what she was thinking. He took a sip of his drink as he leaned back against his desk.

''If there's ever a time I don't intend to come home at

night, I'll let you know in advance," Trey said quietly. "But I don't see that happening in the near future."

She blushed slightly—just a faint tinge of pink across her cheekbones. But she met his gaze steadily as she lifted one eyebrow. "I assume that means there'll be no wedding plans made in the near future either, then. That's something you might want to reassure your children about. We had…a small incident this evening."

A small incident. Kathy was as good with understatement as he was. "God, I'm sorry," he said. "What did Stacy do this time?"

Trey had guessed correctly. Stacy had been behind that proclaimed "small incident." He could see the truth in Kathy's eyes. She had such an open, honest face, she wouldn't have been able to hide the truth if her life had depended on it.

"What she did doesn't really matter," Kathy said evenly, diplomatically. He'd clearly startled her when he'd first come in, but now she had her control back, locked down in ultra-Mary Poppins style—gentleness as soft as down, over firmness as solid as tempered steel.

"What matters is that Stacy's very upset at the idea of your remarrying," she continued. "I'm afraid she's not particularly fond of your current lady friend. Of course, it's not her role to dictate who you should or shouldn't see socially, but regardless of that, it's clear some dialogue between the two of you on this topic is needed."

Trey had been holding his tongue, determined not to interrupt her even though he'd wanted to badly. "Are you done?"

Kathy blinked at him. And then she smiled. "Yes," she said. "And thank you very much for not interrupting me." God, she actually had dimples in her cheeks.

"She's not my lady friend," he told her. "Diana, I mean. My mother's been trying to set me up with her, but, frankly, I'm not ready for anything serious, and even if I were…" Even if he were, he would look for someone who wanted a short sexual fling, not someone lobbying for marriage. He shrugged. "There's no chemistry. It would never work."

Why was he telling her that? She was the nanny, not his shrink.

But she was nodding, in complete agreement. "There really has to be chemistry, doesn't there? Some kind of magnetic pull that happens—even though you may not want it to."

The kind of pull that was making him slowly gravitate toward her, even right now when he was trying to sit absolutely still. The kind of pull that he'd felt from the first moment Kathy Wind had walked into his office and—

Trey stopped himself. That was absurd. Yes, what he'd felt—what he was feeling right now—*was* a kind of chemistry, but it was all about friendship. He'd *liked* Kathy instantly. It had nothing whatsoever to do with sex.

He would never have an affair with his kids' nanny—not, as his mother had put it, because it was tacky and unoriginal, but because it would be cruel and deceitful. She was so young and sweet, harboring visions of happily ever after. And he had already learned the hard way that there was no such banana in the fruit bowl of life.

"So. What happened with Stacy?" he asked, hoping she'd tell him only because he wanted her to stay a little bit longer, not because he particularly wanted to know what awfulness his daughter had done this time. And he wanted her to stay because he *liked* Kathy, he reminded himself. Liked. As in both of them fully dressed and sitting three solid feet away from each other, using their mouths to make conversation. He wanted her to stay because her company was so refreshingly sweet and sincere after an evening spent with Diana St. Vincent.

Kathy sat back in her chair. She didn't seem to be in a hurry to leave, and he felt himself relax a little.

She sighed. "Stacy showed a typical thirteen-year-old's lack of judgment and said something about wicked stepmothers to Doug without thinking it through. His reaction was a bit…stronger than she'd anticipated."

Trey had to smile. "When you say it like that, it sounds as

if it almost happened peacefully and calmly. But I know my kids. How long did the yelling last?''

She smiled back at him. A big smile, complete with the dimples again. ''Long enough. But don't worry. I *did* manage to get things back under control. But that's not what I wanted to talk to you about.''

''It's not.''

''But it's late, and if now's not the best time to—''

''Now's great,'' he said. Damn, there he went again. He *did* interrupt all the time. ''Excuse me.''

''I'm getting used to it.''

He swore softly. ''I'm sorry.''

''I was joking. Good grief. You don't really do it that much.''

He sank into the chair opposite her, his legs suddenly tired. ''It's arrogant and rude.'' God, when did he become arrogant and rude? What had happened to kind and considerate? Gentlemanly? Compassionate?

He looked up at her. When he'd first entered the office, she'd told him she was exhausted. And she *did* look tired, slight shadows beneath her eyes. ''Look, if you want to set up a time to talk tomorrow and—'' He interrupted himself this time. ''Damn, I've got that dinner meeting, so I probably won't be back until after eleven.'' He ran his hand through his hair in frustration. ''Day after tomorrow? What's that, Saturday? Maybe late morning?''

''I'd love to talk now. We're both here, and we both seem to be relatively awake.''

''All right,'' he said. ''Now wins. What's our topic of discussion?''

She leaned forward slightly, setting her wineglass down on the edge of his desk. She'd only taken a sip or two. Clearly the special occasion had only been a little one. ''Actually, I have a rather difficult question to ask you.''

As she looked over at him, her eyes were so serious, he started to get nervous again. A question. Like maybe if she could leave before the Christmas holidays instead of sticking it out until January?

"I would normally consider this to be none of my business," she continued, "but I had a conversation with Stacy this evening that I found very disturbing, and if I'm going to have any chance at all of establishing a relationship with her, I think I need to know... Well, I may as well just ask." She took a deep breath. "Exactly how did Stacy and Doug's mother die?"

Ah. *That* question. Trey knew it had to come sooner or later. He rose from the chair, turning away from the gentle, steady grayness of her eyes. "I guess you've heard the rumors, huh?"

He crossed to the bar.

"Yes. And while I think it's important that I be aware of those rumors—because the children are surely hearing them, too—I want you to know that I don't believe them. Not one bit." She laughed softly. "But I guess you already know that. If I did believe them, I wouldn't be here right now, would I?"

Trey had already had too much to drink tonight, what with the pair of gin and tonics he'd had at the party. He poured himself a plain soda and added a double twist of lemon purely so that he'd have something to do with his hands.

"Helena died of cancer. It all happened much too fast. She was diagnosed, and three months later we buried her." He told Kathy the abbreviated, Cliffs Notes version of his family's tragedy with his back still to her. No details, no emotion. He turned to face her. "It was devastating for the children."

"As it must have been for you as well," she said softly. "I'm sorry."

"She had a tumor in her stomach and one in her brain, both inoperable, and painful as hell," he found himself telling her despite his intentions to withhold the terrible details. "There were probably more, it had probably metastasized throughout her entire body, but she opted out of exploratory surgery. What was the point, right? She had a zero chance of survival.''

"I'm so sorry," Kathy murmured. It was funny. When most people said those words, they were simply making noise. But Kathy meant it. She *was* sorry. He could see it in her eyes.

"Helena also decided not to go into a hospice," he told her. "She wanted to be near the kids, right until the end, but even back then I wasn't sure that was the right choice. And with hindsight, I *know* it wasn't. She was in so much pain. She tried to hide it from Stacy and Doug, and it took all her energy. It was very hard for her. It was hard for the kids, too. I'm sure they didn't understand any of it.''

His guard was down as he gazed at Katherine, and she could see the years-old toll of his pain and grief. He was a man used to being able to fight and win despite insurmountable odds, but this had been one battle in which he hadn't stood a chance. He looked so vulnerable, so lost, even now, and her heart broke for him.

"She died here?" Katherine asked him softly. "At home?"

And just like that, shutters went down. "Yeah." He turned away, and all Katherine could think was that it must have been more awful than he could stand to think about, even years later.

Somehow he managed to force a smile. "So. Now Stacy thinks she's seen Helena's ghost wandering the halls.''

Stacy had said Helena had died suddenly, violently. It must have been frighteningly sudden for a ten-year-old girl to lose a parent like that. And her mother's awful pain must have seemed horribly violent. Even though Helena had tried to hide it, Stacy was old enough to have gotten hints.

"I don't know what Doug thinks," Trey continued, moving to the windows to look out, "because he won't talk to me.''

He looked so utterly lonely standing there, drink in one hand, the other hand rubbing the back of his neck as if he ached down to the bone.

"Give Doug a little more time," she told him. She had an

idea for how to get Dougie talking again, but she didn't want to say anything to Trey yet—didn't want to get his hopes up. Her plan involved regular trips to the dog pound after school, where apparently volunteer workers were needed desperately to help care for the strays living there.

"His birthday is coming," Trey said. "He's going to be seven. I have no idea which of his classmates are his friends, which kids to invite for a party. I don't even know if he *has* any friends."

"His teacher says he's very quiet," Katherine reported, "but there are a pair of little girls, Molly and Hanna, who play with him all the time."

"They probably don't have a dog of their own at home."

She laughed. She couldn't help it.

Trey turned and looked at her, and for one awful moment, she absolutely could not read the expression on his face.

But then he smiled. Crookedly. But it *was* a smile.

"I'm glad you find us amusing," he said. "Most people run away from us, as hard and as fast as they can."

"I absolutely adore your children," Katherine told him.

"Aha," he said. "So if you suddenly take off, I'll know *I'm* the one you're running from."

"Don't be silly," she said.

He smiled again. "Silly. Now that's a word I don't get called every day." He looked down at the glass in his hand. "I'm really glad you like the kids."

"I like you, too," she told him. "Very much, as a matter of fact. Mr. Sutherland."

He just looked at her.

"I didn't want you to get the wrong idea," Katherine explained. "It seemed to make what I said a little less forward sounding when I called you Mr. Sutherland, didn't it?"

He laughed.

"I'm glad you find me amusing, too," she told him. "A little laughter can be very good for the soul."

He settled back against the windowsill, just smiling at her. It was funny. This entire conversation had taken such a bizarre twist. It was almost as if they were flirting—except for the fact that she'd made it very clear that she wasn't coming on to him in any way.

And he seemed to realize that this dance they were doing was only a friendship dance, because now he was making a point of staying by the window, clear over on the opposite side of the room.

"Please," he said. "Call me Trey all the time. I promise I won't get the wrong idea. As long as *you* don't get the wrong idea when I ask you to save my ass and be my date for some boring awards ceremony that I've got to attend Tuesday night."

Katherine couldn't believe it. Trey Sutherland was actually asking her…out? *"Boring,"* she said, her heart beating just a little bit harder. "When you put it like that, how on earth could I say no?"

"My business partner is getting some honorary something-or-other, and I've got to be there to accept for him, the slacker. And for some reason, my mother thinks there'll be less gossip about me if I don't show up to these things alone." He carried his glass back to the bar, set it on the counter. "I figured we could have dinner with the kids and Anita, then throw on a tux and a sequined gown, and hit the award dinner in time for some fancy French pastries, scoop up the award and be back home before ten-thirty. What do you say? Will you go with me as purely a good deed—save me from having to endure Diana St. Vincent's company twice in one week?"

It wasn't a real date. He'd just made sure that she knew it wasn't a real date. Still… "Have you been talking to Stacy?" Katherine had to ask him.

"Stacy?" He was confused.

"Never mind," she said. "Just a coincidence. Of course I'll go with you. Anything to keep Diana St. Vincent from grabbing your rear end."

He laughed at that. "That's not what I said."

"Maybe not in so many words, but it was implied." She

hesitated. "But I'm afraid I don't have anything formal to wear." Certainly nothing with sequins.

He took his wallet from his pocket, held out a credit card. "I've been meaning to give this to you. I had the bank issue a card to my account in your name. Just sign the back of it. Do you have time between now and Tuesday to pick up something formal to wear?"

She took the card. It had the name Kathy Wind printed on the front in little gold letters. Oh, dear.

"If you don't have time, there are some on-line boutiques that have next-day delivery. Stacy'll show you how to sign on to the internet."

"Trey, I don't need this. I can buy my own clothes." Katherine tried to hand him back the credit card.

"No, this is on me. Go wild." He went across the room, toward the door. "And go to bed. I've kept you up much too late."

She slipped the card into her back pocket. She'd hang on to it, but it didn't mean that she'd use it. "I don't suppose there's any chance at all that your business partner will show up at this award ceremony?"

"As far as Crazy Bill's concerned, there's always a chance."

"Because, I was talking to my si—" Oh, dear, she'd almost said *sister*. "Friend. My friend, Princess Alexandra. On the phone. This morning." Good grief, could she sound any more uncool? She could practically see James Bond standing behind Trey, shaking his head in disgust. She took a deep breath and smiled. "Alexandra thought she may have met your business partner, Bill Lewis, at one time. She wanted me to pass along a message to him, so I was hoping that when he returns, you might let me know so I could give him that message?"

"Sure," he said. "Small world, huh?"

"Very." He had no idea.

"I'm going to be up and out early again tomorrow," Trey told her. "So if I don't see you, have a good day."

"I will," she said. "Thanks. And you, too."

As she left, she flashed him another smile.

I like you, too, she'd said. *Very much, as a matter of fact.*

The feeling was completely mutual.

And Tuesday night was going to be fun. For the first time in years, Trey was actually looking forward to an evening in town.

With Kathy Wind.

His friend, he reminded himself. *Friend.*

Chapter 7

Doug was silent as they hurried into the shopping mall.

Katherine had promised to take him to the dog pound today, but their plans had changed when she'd gone to pick the
children up after school.

Stacy had gone AWOL.

From what Katherine could gather, the girl had found Doug
in the kindergarten through fifth grade hallway after the last
bell had rung, shoved a note for Katherine into his pocket,
and had left the school through the back door.

"Gone to the mall," the note had said in scribbled letters.
Stacy hadn't specified which mall, how she was getting there,
whom she was going with, or what time she would be home.

After an interminable stop in the headmaster's office, Katherine finally had the location of the mall closest to the school's
grounds. The Friday afternoon traffic was miserable and, of
course, she'd gotten lost. And then it seemed to take forever
to find a parking spot. Katherine used the time to pray that
they'd find Stacy right away. The thought of having to call

Trey and tell him that she'd lost his daughter just a few days into this job was too awful to bear.

It was odd. Katherine had thought she and Stacy had been getting on quite well. At breakfast, the girl had been nearly animated as they'd argued the issue of exactly which movie was Leonardo DiCaprio's best. And while they hadn't agreed, their debate had been friendly and fun.

Or so she'd thought.

Now this.

It seemed so obviously and openly rebellious. It was almost as if Stacy were testing her—seeing how far Katherine would let her go.

And there she was. Stacy Sutherland. Standing alongside a small group of teenagers who were sitting at one of the tables in the food court.

Katherine grabbed Doug's hand and pulled him with her into a nearby clothing store. Her instant melting sense of relief was immediately sharpened by a rocket-fuel flare of anger. And she knew when she approached the girl, it would be better to appear calm and completely in control rather than blithering and blistering. She needed to be matter-of-fact.

She caught her breath, pretending to look at a rack of winter skirts, but in truth letting her blood pressure return to as near normal as possible.

A very large man had followed them into the store, oddly out of place among the women's clothing. He had closely cropped hair, and he held himself like a soldier. Like Gabe Morgan, the head of the Royal Wynborough Bodyguards.

As Katherine watched, the man took a silk dress and a shimmery gold blouse from the racks, and carried them to the back of the store to, what? Try them on?

Katherine laughed, but then found to her horror that she was very close to dissolving into tears.

Doug, in a burst of empathy, gave her a hug. "You okay?" he asked, his brown eyes enormous in his elfin face, for the first time actually uttering two words in a row that weren't *Lucky* and *Charms*.

Katherine bent down and hugged him as fiercely as he was hugging her. "Yes," she said, kissing the top of his head. "I'm okay now. Thank you so very much."

She took several deep breaths and was actually able to smile by the time she and Doug went back out into the mall. And she knew precisely when Stacy saw them coming. The girl's shoulders tensed, as if she were bracing herself for World War Three.

But Katherine just kept on smiling. She fully intended to lay down every little last detail of the law with the girl, but not here and now. And certainly not in front of Stacy's friends.

"Good afternoon," she said, managing to sound quite cheerful and not at all put off by this unplanned, frantic expedition to the mall. "I'm so glad we found you. I wanted to make sure you had a little bit of spending money."

The look on Stacy's face would have been well worth filming. Her defensive look crumbled into confusion and finally a rather stunned disbelief. She'd expected to be yelled at.

"I…had a five in my pocket," Stacy said.

"Oh," Katherine said, giving her another smile. "Good, then." She glanced briskly at her watch. It was already after four. There was no way they could get all the way across town to the dog pound at this late hour. It closed early on Friday afternoons. "What do you say we meet by the main entrance at five?"

The three boys and four girls sitting around the table didn't look particularly clean-cut and studious, but then again, neither did Stacy with her badly dyed hair and dark liner around her eyes. Two of the boys were old enough to have facial hair—or at least something resembling facial hair—growing in strange little tufts beneath their lower lips. The other boy had very long, very light-blond curls and narry a single prospect for facial hair in sight. He was smoking a cigarette— possibly to make up for the fact that, unlike the other boys, he actually looked his tender age of thirteen or fourteen.

"You from England?" he asked, squinting at her through his smoke.

"Wynborough." She smiled at him, prepared to introduce herself and ask his name. "I'm—"

"Crazy," he interrupted. "You're definitely crazy. Or dumb." He nudged one of his friends. "They gotta ship in their hired help from overseas," he said. "No one local's dumb enough to work for a murderer."

Two of the girls laughed.

"Shut up, Craig." Stacy's shoulders tightened, and Katherine knew that these boys and girls weren't her friends. On the contrary. They were completely antagonistic. And horribly rude.

"*You* shut up, freak." The boy—Craig—flicked his still smoking cigarette butt at Stacy. "What? You afraid I'm gonna tell your *nanny* that your daddy killed your mommy? She'll find out soon enough. Like when your old man comes after *her* some dark and stormy night."

"Come to think of it," Katherine said, turning to Stacy. "There's a lot to do at home—I think we should probably leave *now*."

Stacy ignored her completely, bristling instead at Craig. "That's *not* true. Don't you dare say things like that in front of my brother!"

Craig just laughed. "What, you think he doesn't know? Look at him, he's a freak, too." He leaned toward his friends. "My little sister's in his class at school, and she says he doesn't talk. He just barks like a dog. A total freak." As they laughed, he turned back toward Stacy. "I think he saw it happen, and it turned him into a retard."

Stacy was livid. She was bigger than Craig, too, and Katherine knew that she had to say or do something fast before Stacy pulled the awful boy out of his chair and thrashed him soundly.

Not that he didn't *need* a sound thrashing.

And Craig wasn't letting up. He was talking directly to

Doug now. "How'd your daddy do it? Did he use a knife? Bark once for yes, freak, twice for no."

But instead of hauling off and hitting him, Stacy turned around. She grabbed Doug's hand instead of Craig's hair, and pulled her little brother away from there, as fast as she could move.

Katherine fixed Craig with her best royal glacial stare. She stood there, perfectly still, until he finally looked up.

"Stacy's mother died of cancer," she told him very, very quietly. "You go home tonight, and you think about that when your own mother lets you know how much she loves you in dozens of little ways. You think about her not being there, think about what it would mean to you if you lost *her*. And then you think twice about being cruel the next time you see Stacy."

Craig sneered and told her to do the anatomically impossible.

Katherine didn't move. "As awful as you try to be, your mother probably still loves you. Imagine losing that."

She could hear them laughing as she walked away, but it was forced laughter. She doubted that she had gotten through to Craig, but maybe one of the others had listened. Maybe *they* would think twice before being so dreadfully cruel to Stacy.

And maybe Bill Lewis would actually show up for this award ceremony on Tuesday. Maybe every one of their problems would have easy, simple solutions. Bill would turn out to be the missing Prince James. Stacy and Trey would break their pattern of fighting and listen to each other when they talked. Craig would search his heart, realize how cruel he had been to tease Stacy and Doug, enter the priesthood and devote his life to helping starving children in Africa. And she would find the man of her dreams, find a love as powerful as Trey's had been for Helena, and live happily ever after.

Right.

Stacy and Doug were nowhere in sight. She hoped they'd have the wherewithal to meet her at the main entrance.

She moved swiftly through the crowds and…

There he was again.

The man who held himself as if he once had been a soldier.

He was pretending to look in a bookstore window, but Katherine knew better.

He was following her.

He was doing it quietly and inconspicuously, but he *was* following her.

He was no doubt a bodyguard, sent from Aspen, sent to see that she stayed out of harm's way. She didn't recognize this man, but that didn't mean a thing. There were many royal bodyguards, many she hadn't met, many she *had* met whom she wouldn't recognize in a mall in Albuquerque.

Katherine had asked Laura Bishop to talk to Gabriel Morgan, who'd been sent to keep an eye on the princesses while they were in the United States, to convince him that she would be perfectly safe while in Albuquerque without a bodyguard.

Obviously, Gabe had decided Princess Katherine had needed a baby-sitter after all.

Katherine glanced again at the man, and he turned away. Good, he wasn't going to acknowledge her. She didn't mind him following her quite so much, as long as he stayed nearly invisible.

She hurried toward the main entrance, and, *yes*, there were Stacy and Doug.

As she drew closer to Stacy, she could see the girl's face was tight with anger. She was carrying Doug as if he were a toddler, his arms around her neck, legs locked around her waist. Still, as Katherine approached, she realized that despite Stacy's tense face, she was singing to Doug. Softly. Soothingly. *How much is that doggie in the window.*

"What did you say to them?" Stacy said, interrupting her song. "You know, they only get worse when a grown-up butts in."

"Why were you even talking to them in the first place?" Katherine knew knowing why wouldn't do a bit of good, but she couldn't stop herself from asking.

"Where's the car?" Stacy asked impatiently. "Because, like, he's getting really heavy."

Poor Doug had streaks of tears on his face.

"You okay?" Katherine asked him.

He nodded. He looked about as exhausted as she felt. What a dreadful afternoon this had been.

"How about we get out of here?" she asked him. "How about if you walk? On two legs?"

He nodded again, and Stacy let him slip down to the ground.

"It's a bit of a hike to the car," she told Stacy briskly. "Shall we get started?"

"I'm in trouble, aren't I?"

"That depends on your definition of *trouble*," Katherine said. "If trouble means you and I are going to sit down and have a lengthy chat, then, yes, indeed, my dear, you are."

She pushed open the door, and they all went outside. Katherine. Stacy. Doug.

And several moments later, the royal bodyguard followed, a little more visible than Katherine would have liked him to be.

But this was just one of those truly rotten days. The way things were going, he would follow her home, all the way into the Sutherland's driveway.

Stacy stared straight ahead out the windshield of the car. "Are you going to tell my father that I went to the mall without asking you first?"

My father. Not Trey.

Katherine pulled up to the traffic light, watching for the little blue Toyota in the rearview mirror. It wasn't the kind of car she would have expected one of the royal bodyguards to drive, but then again, it was far more inconspicuous than those big black sedans they usually cruised around in.

There it was. Four cars back.

"I give your father brief reports every evening," she told the girl.

"Can you maybe make this one briefer than usual?" Stacy asked. "He's going to have a cow if he finds out I went to the mall alone. I don't know why it's such a big deal to him, but it is."

Katherine glanced at her as the light turned green and she accelerated into the intersection. "Maybe he knows the kind of people who hang out at the mall."

Stacy rolled her eyes. "Craig and his butthead friends hang out at my school, too. Trey doesn't seem to have any problem with my going *there*. He doesn't let me go to the mall because he thinks I'm still a baby. He doesn't think I'm old enough, if you can believe *that*. It's one of the four billion things we fight about. And then he turns around and hammers me for not having any friends. How does he expect me to make any friends if I can't go hang out at the mall after school?"

"I think one of the hardest parts of being a parent is probably learning to let your children grow up," Katherine told her. "My father still has trouble with it and my sisters and I are all in our twenties. Your father has it even harder, because he doesn't have your mother to help him."

Stacy was silent for a moment. "Doggie doesn't really remember her, you know, but I do. She had long blond hair and green eyes. I don't look anything like her. She was so pretty. And she always pretended to be so happy."

Katherine glanced into the back seat. Doug was fast asleep. "Pretended?"

"She wasn't really happy," Stacy said. "I know because I used to hear her crying when she thought no one was around."

She was silent for a moment, and Katherine waited, hoping she'd go on. But the girl shook her head. "So what, am I grounded now?"

"No," Katherine told her. "But if you ever go *any*where again without telling me first, there *will* be hell to pay. Count on it."

She turned onto the road that led to the Sutherland estate. Sure enough, the little blue car followed. "I spoke to Anita earlier today, and since your father won't be home for dinner again tonight, I thought we could just order a couple of pizzas. Is that okay with you?''

Stacy shook her head. "Wait a minute. Isn't this the part when you yell at me and tell me how inconsiderate I am?''

Katherine pulled into the driveway, up to the gate. "I think you already know that what you did today was inconsiderate. And I prefer not to yell. It hurts my throat.''

As she lowered the window to key in her access code, the blue car went past without even slowing. Thank goodness.

"You know, Stacy, I really admired the restraint you showed at the mall. I know you wanted to smack that awful boy. I was very proud of you when you didn't.''

Stacy had that I'm-in-the-twilight-zone look on her face again, probably because instead of yelling at her, Katherine had complimented her, told her she was proud.

"I just…'' she began. "I wanted to rip out Craig's lungs, but…more than that, I wanted to get Doggie out of there. I don't want him hearing those things.'' She laughed, but it wasn't because she found the situation funny. "It's probably way too late for that, isn't it? He probably hears all kind of nasty things at school. God, you hear things like that often enough, you start to wonder if maybe it's not true.''

Katherine pulled up to the garage, pushed the remote door opener. Glancing back at Doug who was still sound asleep, she asked, "You don't think it's true, do you? That your father killed your mother?''

"Of course it's not true,'' Stacy scoffed. "I mean, they used to fight when they thought I couldn't hear them, but everyone's parents fight, don't they? Besides, Helena died of cancer.''

There was something in the girl's voice, something in her tone that was odd, as if she didn't quite believe her own words.

Katherine pulled the car into the garage. "I'm here,'' she said, "if you ever want to talk.''

"Yeah," Stacy said. "Thanks." She got out of the car quickly.

"Stacy," Katherine called after her. "One more thing. Now that you know my rules—that I want to know where you are *before* you go there..."

The girl stopped but she didn't turn around.

"Please don't disappoint me," Katherine said quietly.

Stacy nodded, and vanished into the house.

Chapter 8

There was laughter coming from the playroom.

Trey stood in the hallway, just listening. Stacy was talking about a funny movie she'd seen several nights ago, and although Doug hadn't said anything that Trey had overheard, he was laughing.

A quick look inside the room revealed that Doug was sitting at the playroom table, drawing—certainly a human enough activity.

Stacy and Kathy were playing a game of Monopoly on the floor in front of a crackling fire.

Kathy was stretched out on the rug, on her stomach, chin propped on her hands, supported by her elbows.

The firelight made her thick brown hair glisten, and her eyes danced as she laughed at Stacy's story. Her smile did the strangest things to his stomach and—

Trey quickly moved away from the door, back against the wall before she looked up and saw him.

Who was he kidding here?

Yeah, sure, he thought of Kathy Wind as a friend, as a cute

kid sister. But she was definitely someone *else's* kid sister, not his.

The woman was gorgeous. Blue jeans and big boxy over-shirt and all. She was the embodiment of hope. She was living proof that life went on. She was sweet and warm and...

And she was an employee who was doing a *really* good job with his kids. Was it any wonder that he should think she was special?

That was all the funny feeling in his stomach was. Grati-tude. Gratitude and a sincere appreciation of her beautiful, warm smile.

She came out of the playroom, almost walking directly into him.

"Oh," she said. "Hello. I didn't expect to see you this evening. Is everything all right?"

It was. Trey nodded. "Yeah, I'm... Everything's fine."

She gestured back to the playroom door. "You should come in. Stacy and Doug and I are eating up here tonight. We're going to watch a movie while we have pizza. It should arrive any second, really. We ordered plenty, if you have time for a slice?"

She smelled amazingly good. It was her hair. He had to stop himself from moving closer, breathing more deeply.

"I don't," he said. "I'm already late. I just..." he shrugged "—I wanted to see how Stacy and Doug were doing."

And he had to admit he wanted to see Kathy, too. He liked it when she smiled at him, liked her direct gray gaze, liked feeling warm after too many years of being so damn cold.

But it wasn't about sex, it was about friendship. Maybe if he kept on saying that to himself, he'd start to believe it.

"Can't you just poke your head in and say hi?" she asked.

"I don't want to kill Stacy's good mood," he said honestly. "She tends to take one look at me and—"

The doorbell rang.

"It's a cop-out, I know," he continued.

"I've got to get the door," Kathy said. "You know, Stacy

got an A on her science test today. Maybe if you just lean in and congratulate her for that...?"

Trey watched her as she hurried away down the hall.

Just lean in.

The doorbell rang again, and he didn't have to lean in. Because Stacy came out into the hall.

"Kathy, are you getting the door?" she bellowed, then stopped short at the sight of Trey.

"Hi, Stace," he said, forcing a smile. "Yeah, she's, um, getting it. Hey, word's out you aced a science test today. Good job."

She shrugged. "It was stupid. I would have had to be a complete idiot to get anything less than an A."

"Well, then, congratulations on not being a complete idiot."

It was a lousy attempt at a joke, but she didn't even blink. "Yeah, right." She turned and went back into the playroom.

Trey felt like collapsing against the wall, completely spent. God, when had a simple conversation with his daughter become an intensive physical and emotional workout?

It was late, he had to go. Taking a deep breath, he stuck his head in the playroom door. "Hey, Doug. I just wanted to stop in and say, well, hi."

Doug stared at him expressionlessly.

"So, hi," Trey said, mentally rolling his eyes at how completely lame he sounded. What was wrong with him? He was literally sweating from the effort of saying hello to his own kids?

Doug lifted his hand in what might have been a vague wave.

"See you guys later, I've got to go," Trey said, and then left without allowing himself to hear whatever it was Stacy muttered in his wake.

He took the stairs down two at a time, slowing only as he saw Kathy approaching, carrying several pizza boxes and a big bottle of root beer. She'd balanced paper plates and cups and napkins rather precariously on top of the pizza boxes.

"Can I help you with that?" Trey asked.

She smiled. "I've got it, thanks." She slowed to a stop slightly above him, turning to look back down at him. "How did it go?"

"I don't know," he admitted.

Her smile deepened. "You're still alive. I'll take that as a good indicator."

"We exchanged words at a normal decibel level," he told her. "So I guess that's a victory, huh?"

"Absolutely," she said. "Definitely."

There it was again. That feeling of hope. "I wish I could stay and have pizza," he said.

"We wish you could, too."

We. Not I. She hadn't called him Mr. Sutherland, but she might as well have.

But what did he expect? That she would fall madly in love with him, tremble when he was near, like the heroine in *Jane Eyre?*

No, when Kathy looked at him, she only saw her employer. If she saw him as a man at all, it was as a man who was a viable candidate for the Lousiest Father of the Year Award, a man who'd lost the ability to connect with his own children.

If she felt anything for him at all, it was pity.

"You'd better hurry," she said. "Or your meeting's going to run really late."

She was right, but still he hesitated. "When you say good night to Stace and Dougie, tell 'em I love 'em, okay?"

Her eyes got even softer. "I always do."

She started up the stairs again, and Trey went down. He took his overcoat and his briefcase from where he'd left them by the door and went out into the sharp coldness of the night.

Somehow, someway, he was going to come up with a deal that Kathy couldn't turn down. Somehow, someway, he was going to make her stay long past January.

He was an expert negotiator. He'd find out her price, and he'd make her an offer she couldn't refuse.

It was crazy, it was insane, but he couldn't shake the idea

that she was the best thing that had ever happened to this family.

He couldn't remember the last time he'd wanted anything more.

In fact, *he* was the one who was on the verge of trembling, he wanted her so badly.

To work for him, he reminded himself. Just to work for him.

Until the end of time.

Stacy had left a Victoria's Secret catalog in Katherine's room.

Underwear.

There were pages and pages of underwear, absolutely none of it plain. Even the bras and panties that were white were exotic.

Katherine tossed the catalog onto the floor, moving in front of the mirror to look at her reflection.

Stacy had been right about her nightie. It was flannel with a little flowered print, and it went all the way to the ground, and buttoned right up to her chin. It was not even remotely sexy.

She unbuttoned three, and then two more of the buttons, going for some obvious cleavage like the models in the catalog. She moistened her lips and mussed her hair, trying to give it a windswept, romantic look, but really only succeeding in looking messy. She let her nightie slide off one shoulder.

No, it was just no good. All she looked was silly.

All she looked was—

She heard a thump, and then a soft wail from Doug's bedroom, several doors down.

She ran for the door, flinging it open and hurrying down the hall. The little boy slept so restlessly, she'd imagined on other nights that it wouldn't take much for him to roll right out of bed. That was surely what had happened.

His door was ajar, and she pushed it open farther.

Trey was already inside. Doug was on the floor, crying

softly, and Trey knelt next to him. He must have just arrived himself, he was only just gathering Dougie into his arms.

Katherine crouched beside them. "Is he all right?"

Trey was running his fingers through the boy's hair, check-ing his head, making sure he hadn't raised a bump when he'd fallen. "Believe it or not, I think he's still asleep."

He smelled like cigarette smoke, the scent of rich cuisine, and coffee—the lingering aromas of the club where he'd had his dinner meeting.

"Are you sure he's okay?" she asked. "My little sister once fell out of bed and gave herself a black eye. She didn't even wake up, but in the morning, she had this enormous bruise. It would have been so less severe if we'd iced it right when it happened."

Trey moved slightly so that the light from the hallway fell onto the child's face. Katherine pushed Doug's hair back from his face, her fingers accidentally brushing Trey's.

"Sorry," she murmured, then instantly felt silly. What was the big deal? So she'd touched him. There was no need for a formal apology. Good grief.

She glanced up at him, prepared to exchange a friendly smile, but he wasn't smiling.

He was looking at her as if he'd just noticed she was there. His gaze dropped to the neckline of her nightgown, to the way it had slipped down exposing one bare shoulder, to her...

Cleavage.

Oh, dear.

She hiked her nightgown back up on her shoulder, and realized instantly that the adjustment had only made the un-buttoned front opening dip down farther between her breasts.

He looked up almost jerkily, as if suddenly aware that he'd been staring at her.

"You were in bed," he said. His voice was raspy, whis-pered, as if he suddenly needed to clear his throat.

"Not quite," she said, resisting the urge to clutch the neck-line of her nightie closed, knowing that doing so would only bring further attention to it. It wasn't unbuttoned *that* much. Serena wore blouses that she'd unbuttoned nearly as far.

"I can sit with him now," she told Trey, glad that the dim lighting helped hide her embarrassed blush. "If you could just help me get him back into his bed..."

Trey lifted him easily, pulling up the covers and tucking the bedraggled stuffed dog that Doug still slept with next to him. "I come and sit with him a few minutes every night before I go to bed," he said quietly as he sat down next to his son. "I don't mind staying for a while."

Trey gazed down at Doug, now completely fast asleep, trying his damnedest not to look at Kathy. Still, he was hyper-aware that she was standing right next to him. Much too close. Maybe it was only his imagination, but he could swear he felt her body heat.

He desperately wanted her to leave.

Because he desperately wanted her to stay. He wanted to pull her close and lose himself in the sweetness of her lips, in the lushness of her body. He was burning to touch the smoothness of her skin, the softness of the full breasts he'd gotten a tantalizing glimpse of beneath her thin nightgown.

It was completely insane.

He was in his six-year-old son's bedroom. His intense response to this woman's nearness was completely inappropriate, on every level imaginable.

But it was completely overpowering, completely overwhelming. And it knocked all those lies he'd been force-feeding himself clear out of the water.

Sister.

Friend.

What a joke.

The truth was undeniable. He lusted after his kids' nanny. He had from the first moment she'd walked into his office. Come to think of it, Mary Poppins had always turned him on, even back when he was ten.

She was still standing there, hesitating.

He would not let himself look up at her. Would not.

"As long as you're sure," she said softly. "Because I honestly don't mind staying for a while."

"I'm sure," he somehow said, still keeping his focus safely on Doug's face.

He would have been successful. He would have managed not to look at her again.

But she leaned forward, smoothed Doug's hair back from his face, and kissed him sweetly on the forehead. And in doing so, she gave Trey a completely unrestricted view down the front of her nightgown.

He could have closed his eyes. He probably should have. But he didn't. He let himself look at her perfect breasts. And he let himself want her, knowing full well that he shouldn't, knowing that he wasn't going to do a damn thing about it.

"Good night," she said as she straightened up.

She obviously, innocently had no idea what she had just done.

"Good night," he whispered, holding his breath until he heard her walk away, until he heard her close her bedroom door.

God.

He was in big trouble here.

Chapter 9

Maybe this wasn't such a good idea.

The dog pound was not a particularly cheery place, with its rows and rows of small cages that reminded Katherine of a jail for animals. The lights overhead were glaring and fluorescent, the worn tile underfoot cheap, industrial and forty years old.

The supervisor giving them a quick tour of the facility was clearly overworked, obviously rushed as she explained their jobs as volunteer dog walkers.

"The nearest park is five blocks away, I'm afraid. But a quick tour around the block is really all the dogs expect. Head south, though. North, the neighborhood gets a little…intense. Unless, of course, you're with one of the bigger dogs. Any questions?"

Katherine looked at Doug.

He looked back at her, eyes wide.

"Does it matter which dogs we walk first?" she asked.

"Check the sign-out sheet for each animal." The supervisor was already walking away, her friendly face apologetic as a co-worker waved frantically for her attention on the other side of the big room. "If they've been walked within the past day or two, try to choose one who hasn't been out recently."

Doug had moved across to the rows of cages, and he crouched in front of one, his hands on the chain links, nearly nose to nose with the dog inside.

It was an older dog of indistinguishable breeding. A mutt. It was a big dog, with big floppy ears and very gentle, very wise old eyes in a pointy, friendly face.

"This guy here doesn't have a sign-out sheet," Katherine called after the supervisor.

"Oh, those don't need to be walked," she called back. "That entire area is, well, it's our version of death row, I'm afraid. The puppies, against the other wall—they need the most attention. They're the ones most likely to wind up being adopted."

Death row.

Oh, dear.

Katherine could tell from Doug's face that he didn't understand. That was probably a good thing.

"Mrs. Freeman asked us to walk the puppies," Katherine told him, "instead of these adult dogs. Puppies need more exercise because they're growing."

Doug looked back at the old dog, who rather creakily rose to his feet. He wagged his tail very slightly, reaching out to touch the boy's fingers with his nose.

Doug laughed. The dog's tail wagged harder.

"Great," Stacy said. "He falls in love with one of the ones who're about to be killed."

Doug went very still, his eyes wide.

Katherine tried to intervene. "Stacy—"

She crouched down next to her brother. "Don't you know what death row is?"

He shook his head.

"Thank you, Stacy," Katherine started again. "But I think—"

"Don't you think he should know?" She turned back to

her brother. "It's awful, Doug. All of these dogs in this part of the room are scheduled to be *killed*. They call it 'put to sleep,' or 'put down' so that it doesn't sound so bad, but it doesn't have anything to do with sleeping. They never wake up again. The dogs are killed because nobody wants to take care of them anymore."

Doug looked up at Katherine with horror in his eyes. "Oh, Kathy," he said. "Oh, please, we can't let him die."

It was a sentence. A complete sentence. Even Stacy was so surprised, she sat back on her heels.

And Katherine knew—even though she hadn't planned it this way—that she was going to bring home more than one surprise for Trey this afternoon.

Trey wasn't getting anything done.

He was sitting in his tower office, staring at his computer screen, thinking of…

Thinking of things he shouldn't be thinking of.

He'd purposely stayed upstairs this morning until he'd heard Kathy and the kids leave the house.

He stood up and stretched his legs, crossing to look out the window. As long as he wasn't getting any work done, he might as well work out a plan of action—figure out what he was going to do about the fact that he had it bad for Kathy Wind.

The thought still made him laugh out loud.

How the hell had *that* happened?

What the hell was he going to do?

Kathy wasn't the kind of woman who had sex purely for the sake of having sex. If he let her know that he was attracted, she would expect more from him than just a few brief, explosive weeks of passion.

But maybe—if they became lovers—she would stay past January.

The thought was a ridiculous one, and Trey pushed it aside. There was no way he would use her—or anyone—that way. He hated the way women like Diana St. Vincent had such obvious motives for wanting to be with him. They wanted his wealth, his power, his social standing. It didn't matter who he really was, just as long as he had Trey Sutherland's wallet in his back pocket.

No, his motives for wanting to sleep with Kathy had nothing to do with the fact that she was the best nanny he'd ever known, or the fact that he would do damn near anything to make her stay.

Anything within reason.

The truth was that he wanted Kathy Wind because he wanted Kathy Wind. The only thing he'd be using her for was the sex.

Of course, that was bad enough, wasn't it?

But Trey knew he couldn't give her anything more than that. And he knew she'd end up getting hurt.

The dead last thing he wanted to do was to hurt her.

What he had to do was simply enjoy his attraction to her. Acknowledge it as something that was forbidden, and enjoy the time he spent near her, letting himself look but not touch. God knows it had been forever since he'd wanted to touch a woman. It was nice knowing his libido was finally starting to thaw.

But like all things, defrosting took time. Going from the freezer to the oven worked for Anita's favorite Corning Ware, but emotionally, he could very well shatter from such extremes.

Unless, of course, Kathy knocked on his door and announced that she wanted pure, raw, screaming sex from him, with absolutely no strings attached, just genuine, mutual physical pleasure with no exchange of words, no chance of miscommunication.

If she did that, he would immediately lock his office door behind her and start taking off her clothes with his teeth.

He rolled his eyes. Yeah, like hell he was going to "enjoy" sitting back and simply letting himself look at her.

But what else could he do?

Rat-tat.

The sudden knock on the door made him nearly jump into the air.

He had to laugh at himself. There was no way that was Kathy. It was probably Anita with the mail. Or the gardener with a question about the tree that had died out back. Or...

He opened the door.

It was Kathy.

Her red flannel shirt was buttoned nearly to her neck and tucked into her jeans. She looked neat and efficient. And sexy as hell. God, he wasn't going to be able to look at her ever again without a picture of how she'd looked in that nightgown flashing into his mind.

"May we come in?" she asked.

We. Trey realized Doug was standing next to Kathy, Stacy right behind them.

"Sure," he said. He cleared his throat, then stepped back to let them enter. "Please. Hey, Doug. Stace. What's up?"

"Actually," Kathy said, leading his son into the room, "Doug has something to say."

Something to say. Yeah, right. Trey had been on the phone with a specialist just this morning. He'd finally given in and made arrangements to test the boy, see if he was in some way autistic, to cancel that possibility out before they tested him for various and frightening kinds of mental illness.

Kathy squeezed Doug's shoulder and he stepped toward Trey.

"Daddy, Kathy took us to the dog pound today."

Oh my God. The kid actually spoke. An entire sentence, clearly ennunciated, not just his usual mumbled single-syllable answers to yes-no questions. Trey reached for the chair behind him. He had to sit down.

Somehow the meaning of Doug's words penetrated, and he laughed slightly. "The dog pound. Wow." He looked up at Kathy. He knew everything he was feeling was splattered across his face, but he couldn't have hidden it if he'd tried. "Wow."

She nodded, smiling at him, her eyes luminous.

Trey looked back at Doug. "Did you have a good time?"

The boy shook his head vehemently. "No. It was awful. They have a death row, and we found out that Poindexter was going to be put to sleep *tomorrow*."

Poindexter. He looked up at Kathy, but she was watching Doug.

"And Kathy told me that Dex was very, very old, and might not live very long," Doug continued, "but I said I didn't care, and she told me that if I got to keep him then I would need to be a boy most of the time and not a dog the way I like to pretend, because Dex would need me to be a boy so I could take care of him."

Brilliant. Kathy was incredibly, amazingly brilliant. Trey wanted to laugh. He wanted to cry. And he wanted to hug Kathy, but Doug was standing there so seriously, so intensely, that all Trey did was nod. "Well, yeah," he said. "She's certainly right about that."

"And Kathy said that even if Dex couldn't stay here with us, she'd pay for him to live happily ever after in a kennel and that we could find one nearby so I could see him every day, and that I had to ask and make sure that was okay with you, but oh, please, Daddy, he's so lovely, can't I keep him here instead?"

A dog. Here at Sutherland estate.

Doug was looking at him so hopefully. Even Stacy was leaning in the open door, waiting to see what he had to say.

"What kind is he?" he asked.

"A butt-ugly one," Stacy said.

"A mixed breed," Doug told him earnestly. "I think he's got at least a little German shepherd and a little Irish setter and a whole lot of everything else including yellow lab."

Trey stared at his son. What kind of six-year-old knew the different breeds of dogs?

"He's pretty big," Doug admitted.

Trey couldn't believe he was actually sitting here having a conversation with his son. The kid had said more in the past two minutes than he'd said in the past two years. "Friendly, though?" he asked.

Doug nodded. "Oh, yes."

Trey looked at Kathy. "No history of aggressive behavior?"

She shook her head. "None. His owner was a little old lady who had a massive stroke and went into a nursing home four months ago. There was no one to care for the dog and no money for a kennel. It was, literally, only hours before he was scheduled to be destroyed. I couldn't see leaving him there. And I meant what I said to Doug. If you don't want a dog in the house, I'll gladly foot the bill—"

"What, are you kidding?" Trey said. "He sounds great." He looked at Doug. "Is he as great as he sounds?"

Doug nodded, his eyes enormous.

"I've always wanted a dog," Trey continued, "A *real* dog. And it looks like we've got ourselves an excellent one."

Doug launched himself into Trey's arms and hugged him fiercely. "Oh, thank you, Daddy." He lifted his head. "Can I go tell him that he can stay?"

"Yeah." Trey had to laugh, imagining his once-silent son talking—nonstop—to a dog named Poindexter.

"Come on, Stacy!" Doug nearly knocked Katherine over on his way out of the room, but she didn't mind. After all, he *was* running on two feet.

Trey still sat back in one of his leather chairs, looking as if he weren't sure which direction was up. As Katherine gazed at him, he lifted one hand to his forehead, covering his eyes, rubbing slightly as if he had an enormous headache.

Oh, dear. As much as he liked that his son was talking again—and Katherine knew how very much he liked that—it was possible that he *hated* having a dog in the house.

She moved toward him. "I'm really sorry I didn't call you first. I realize what an imposition this must seem and—"

"*Imposition?*" He looked up at her, disbelief in his eyes. "You've got to be kidding." In one graceful movement, he stood, heading toward the window. "I was so afraid...." His voice shook and he stopped. "When he came in and actually told me that you took him to the dog pound..." He laughed, but it was more a burst of emotion. "I was floored. I was completely blown away. I'd pretty much given up on him, Kathy. God, I'd honestly thought I'd lost him."

He turned to face her, and she realized with a jolt of shock that he had tears in his eyes. "And then, to have him back, just out of the blue like that..."

He laughed again and one of his tears escaped. He wiped it away with the heel of his hand and Katherine couldn't stand it. She went toward him and wrapped herself around him, ignoring the fact that in general, employees did not hug their bosses.

But he held her just as tightly. His arms felt heavenly around her, and she knew the truth—this was as much for her as it was for him. She was tremendously close to weeping herself.

He smelled impossibly good—his cologne, the soft laundry smell of his shirt, his own unmistakable, subtle yet undeniably male scent. It was dizzying. She could hear his heart pounding, hear his ragged breathing as he both laughed and cried.

"How can I thank you?" he said hoarsely, his breath hot against her ear. "You haven't even been here a week, and I've got my kid back. How the hell am I ever going to be able to pay you enough for that?"

"It was really just luck—"

"Luck, my ass." He pulled back to look at her. "If that chair hadn't been there, I would have fallen over. God, I'd almost forgotten what his voice sounds like."

Katherine couldn't move. At six feet away, Trey Sutherland was impossibly handsome. At six inches, with tears in his gorgeous eyes, he was capable of triggering serious heart failure.

"Just a little bit of your magic," he said, his husky voice catching, as he lifted her chin to look into her eyes, "and he's back. Are you some kind of sorceress, Kathy Wind? Somehow you've managed to put us all completely under your spell. What am I going to do about you?''

She laughed. It was either that or kiss him, and she knew she shouldn't do that. Still, the way he was looking down at her, the way his arms seemed to tighten around her, the way his gaze seemed to caress her face made her sway toward him and lift her mouth and—

He whispered an exorbitantly high number into her ear.

Katherine froze. "Excuse me?''

"A year,'' he said. "If you'll stay past January. With a twenty percent raise at years three and six.''

She stepped back, pulling out of his arms, understanding flooding her. He was talking salary. That incredibly high number was a *yearly* salary. "You can't be serious!''

"I am. What do you say?''

Her mouth was hanging open, and she closed it. She laughed in amazement. She shrugged somewhat inanely. "I say…no.''

It was his turn to be completely stunned. *"No?''*

"I'm flattered,'' she said. "Of course. But—''

"Double it,'' he said.

Katherine turned away. Good grief. This was getting out of hand.

"My offer still stands about the apartment,'' he continued. "I'll get you a car, too. Medical insurance. All your living expenses will be handled. You can invest the money and after seven years, you'll be able to retire.''

She turned back to face him. He was serious. He was actually dead serious. "There's just no way anyone in their right mind would pay a nanny that much.''

"So maybe I'm out of my mind.'' Trey looked completely sane, standing there backlit by the window that overlooked the courtyard. "If double's not enough, name your price,'' he said.

"Stop! You're making me extremely uncomfortable!'' It was almost absurd. She'd been standing there, in his arms, ready to surrender to the onslaught of his kisses. But *that* hadn't made her uncomfortable. Not one bit. Not like this.

"I don't have a price," she told him more gently. "Don't misunderstand me—I love your children." And, God help her, despite this outrageous financial attack, she knew it wouldn't take much for her to start falling in love with Trey, as well. The sheer joy she'd seen on his face when Doug had spoken to him, when Doug had told him they'd gone to the pound, was something she'd carry with her to her dying day. "But money just isn't important to me."

"Obviously not." He held out his hands beseechingly. "There's got to be something that would make you stay. There's got to be *some*thing you want."

She'd wanted him to kiss her. She'd wanted that enough to nearly initiate it herself. And, good grief, wouldn't *that* have been embarrassing. Here he was, trying to keep their relationship to that of employee-boss for another seven years, and she had been about to lay one on him.

He probably hadn't even really noticed that for a few long moments, he had held her tightly in his arms. Yes, he had given her all the signals that a kiss was coming, but that was probably instinctive on his part. Somewhere in the remote recesses of his mind, he'd realized that she was female.

But when his eyes had finally focused, he hadn't thought twice about turning their embrace into a business meeting.

She was *not* in his league, she reminded herself. She wasn't even playing the same game. She turned away. "I should go see where Doug and Stacy have gone."

"Kathy, I'm sorry if I offended you. That wasn't my intention." Trey cleared his throat. "Thank you so much for what you did today. I'd like it if you could at least consider my offer. And I'll, um…I'll see you at dinner?"

"You'll be at dinner tonight?" She couldn't keep the pleasure from her voice. "The children will be so pleased," she added quickly. Oh, dear, she should be wearing a shirt that said Loser. She gestured toward the door. "I should…go…"

She nearly tripped over her own feet as she hastily went

out Trey's office. She closed the door behind her, kicking herself. Could she have sounded any more eager?

Of course, it could have been worse.

She might actually have drooled.

Chapter 10

"I've decided to get my nose pierced."

Trey nearly dropped his fork. "Like hell you will!"

"I think that's probably the kind of decision you really need to ponder for quite some time," Katherine interjected smoothly. If she had been sitting closer to Trey, she would have given him a swift kick, but the dining room table was too big and she was too far away.

The conversation had deteriorated right from the start, right from the raspberry sound Stacy had made when Trey mentioned there had been something in the newspaper about trouble at the shopping mall she liked to visit. Kids carrying guns, he'd told them. Stacy had rolled her eyes and made that extremely rude sound and Katherine had watched Trey grit his teeth.

"She'll have plenty of time to ponder this decision," Trey returned. "As in five years. Because it's not going to happen while she's living in *this* house."

"Then maybe I should just leave!" Stacy stood up, and somehow managed to knock her glass of milk over.

It was purely accidental, Katherine could see that. But Trey didn't see the flare of embarrassed remorse in his daughter's eyes. He only saw the staunch defiance it quickly transmuted into.

"Don't just stand there," he ordered his daughter in exasperation. "Get something to mop it up with!"

Doug kept his head lowered as Stacy got a towel from the kitchen and cleaned up the spill, her movements jerky with anger. Then, picking up her half-finished plate of food and her empty glass, she purposely looked at Katherine instead of Trey. "May I please be excused?"

Doug jumped up, too, even though he'd eaten even less.

Trey opened his mouth to speak, but Katherine beat him to it. "Yes," she said. "You may. Both of you. Go on up to the playroom and finish your homework. I'll be up in a bit."

As the door to the kitchen swung shut behind them, Trey sat back in his chair and rubbed his forehead and eyes.

"Why do I do that?" he asked, tipping his head to look across the table at her. "I know she's only trying to bait me, and I sit here and watch myself fall off this giant cliff of manipulation. I react exactly the way she wants me to react. But it gets to the point where I feel if I don't say anything, I'm letting her get away with being incredibly rude."

Katherine didn't know what to tell him.

"You're right about that anchoring thing, though," he continued. He looked exhausted. "Both Stacy and I have forgotten how to simply sit in a room together without fighting."

Katherine turned to look at him. "Maybe that's it."

"What?"

She stood up. "I have an idea. Come with me."

The piano.

It was in the rear parlor—the one Trey thought of as the piano room. He'd bought the enormous grand years ago, when he and Helena were fixing up the place, when they had lots of empty rooms to fill, when he'd had the first of a still continuing series of very, very good financial years.

He'd bought the piano, and then business had continued to be so good, he never had time to play it.

He looked at Kathy. She was so pleased with herself, her cheeks flushed, her eyes sparkling, he had to smile. "You're kidding, right?"

She shook her head. "No, I most certainly am not. Didn't you say you used to play? Stacy spends hours playing her clarinet every day, you know. It's perfect. You and she can spend time together without having to utter a single word." She opened up the piano bench, searching through the music there, coming up with his jazz fake book. "Ooh," she said, flipping it open. "Was this yours?"

"No."

She lifted an eyebrow as she glanced at him, completely suspicious. "Are you by any chance lying?"

"Yes."

She set the music in the stand above the piano keys, closed the bench and patted it. "Sit, please."

He sat. Reluctantly. "Kathy, really, it's been years since I've even—"

She pointed to the music. "'Harlem Nocturne.' Do you know it?"

Trey looked at the notes and chords written out on the page and sighed. "Yeah."

"It's been one of my favorite melodies since I was a little girl," she said, settling into the smooth wooden curve of the piano's body, leaning against the closed top with her elbows, chin propped in her hands as she faced him.

"It's been so long. I don't know...." He touched the familiar silkiness of the keys lightly, not pressing down hard enough to make a sound. When he looked up, Kathy was watching him, her gray eyes so expectant and warm.

God, he wanted her.

His mouth went dry just looking at her. This afternoon, he'd nearly kissed her. He'd been completely blown away by the change in Dougie, and she'd reached for him. Just like that, she was in his arms, as soft and warm as he'd imagined.

He'd lowered his head to kiss her, and in that fraction of a second before his mouth had claimed hers, he'd realized that while a hug had a variety of meanings and interpretations, a kiss was a kiss. While a boss could hug an employee, a kiss was an entirely different matter. A kiss could push them to a place he wasn't sure either of them really wanted to go.

So instead of kissing her, he'd insulted her by offering her a salary that should have made her sign a seven-year contract on the spot. Should have, but didn't. He was still amazed.

And he still wanted to kiss her.

Badly.

Tuesday night, they were going to get dressed up, and he was going to take her into town. How the hell was he going to keep his hands off her for all that time they'd spend alone in the limo?

There was no way he could rescind his invitation. And even if he somehow *could* uninvite her, he didn't want to do that.

He was a sick bastard. He was sitting here dying, tied in a knot from desire. Yet he couldn't think of anywhere he'd rather be.

"There are some things you just never forget how to do," she told him softly. "Play for me. Please?"

How could he refuse when she asked that way? "Don't laugh," he said.

"I wouldn't dream of it," she murmured.

Trey looked at her—he didn't need the music. He just lost himself in her eyes as his fingers found the familiar keys.

And as he watched her, Kathy cringed. The piano was terribly out of tune. It sounded like hell, the intervals and chords jarringly off, metallic-sounding in their weird dissonance. He stopped after only a few bars, embarrassed by how impossibly bad it sounded. "Sorry."

She was completely undaunted. "So we'll get it tuned. It's not your fault it sounds that way. Don't stop. Please?"

"What are you, some kind of masochist? That was terrible."

"Oh, no, Trey, the piano might have been out of tune, but your playing was *beautiful.*"

"Cut the pop-psychology. I'm not six years old," he told her with a laugh. She was his children's nanny, not his. He didn't need her Mary Poppins positive attitude. He should have been annoyed by it, but somehow he was only amused. "Look, I heard what it sounded like. I'm nearly as rusty as the piano."

"If *that* was rusty," she enthused, "I can't wait to hear you in a week or two."

He laughed at her relentless approval. And he laughed at himself as well, at his reaction to her unconcealed admiration. When she looked at him that way, he would do damn near anything she asked.

Her smile widened. "This could work," she insisted.

"Yeah, like I'm ever going to be able to get Stacy into this room to play with me."

Kathy Wind was not afraid. "Leave that to me."

"New underwear."

Katherine gave Stacy a long, silent look.

The girl shrugged, pretending to be nonchalant. "That's my condition," she said. "And it's a deal breaker. I won't go down to the piano room unless you take me to the mall and pick out some new underwear for you to wear Tuesday night when you go out on your date with Trey."

"It's not a date."

"I'll let you pick out the dress," Stacy said generously. "But you've got to let me choose the underwear."

Katherine sat down next to Stacy on her bed. "It's important that you understand that Tuesday night is *not* a date. I'm doing your father a favor by going with him. That's all."

And that *was* all. He didn't see her as someone to date. She was someone to employ, at best. She didn't need to remind herself of that.

"I'm ready to shake on this," Stacy said. "All you have to do is agree about the underwear and I'll go down to the piano room and I won't make any cracks about Trey's choice of music.''

"This is blackmail."

"It's a business deal."

Katherine made up her mind. "You'll go down to the piano room and play your clarinet with your father for at least thirty minutes every day from now until Christmas."

"Every *day*? There's no way he'll have time to do this *every* day."

"Yes," she said, "he will. He truly wants the two of you to become friends again. It's very important to him, Stacy."

"I don't know." Stacy was behaving as if she weren't going to agree, but Katherine knew she would, knew she wanted to. She just couldn't make it seem too easy.

"That's *my* condition," Katherine told her. "It's my deal breaker."

"For doing this every day," Stacy said with a sniff, "I should get to pick out your dress for Tuesday night, too."

"Not a chance."

"Okay, then…I also get to cook Thanksgiving dinner this year," Stacy said. "I have complete control over the menu."

Katherine was thrilled. She'd been hoping Stacy would involve herself in the plans she and Doug had already been making. "Control of the main course," she countered. "Doug and I are planning to bake pies on Wednesday night."

"So is it a deal?" Stacy asked. "Thanksgiving dinner and underwear?"

"For that, you have to promise no complaining, no rude comments whatsoever, no mention of private body parts or anything else that might embarrass your father for all thirty of those minutes each day," Katherine warned.

Stacy thought about that, and nodded. "All right."

Katherine held out her hand. "Deal."

Stacy shook. "Deal."

Doug was in the playroom, talking to Poindexter.

Trey stood in the doorway and just listened as his son told

the dog the entire plot of Disney's *Aladdin*. In detail, using little plastic action figures to act the story out. It was funny—as if now that Doug had started talking again, he was making up for lost time.

Dex's ears were up as he lay on the rug in front of the cold fireplace, looking for all the world as if he were hanging on Doug's every word.

"Hey, kiddo," Trey said, stepping into the room when Doug stopped for a breath. "It's a beautiful day. I bet Dex would love to lie in the sun in the courtyard. Why don't you guys go outside?"

Trey was scheduled to meet Stacy in the piano room in a matter of minutes. There was a probable chance that the next half hour was going to be loud and ugly. He wanted Doug out of the house. He knew how much it bothered him when Trey and Stacy fought.

As boy and dog scrambled down the stairs, Trey followed more slowly.

He was nervous—until he heard Kathy's laughter coming from the open door to the piano room. He felt relieved, and then ashamed and a little angry that he couldn't manage this on his own. He took a deep breath before stepping into the room, pushing the negative feelings out and away from himself, well aware that it wouldn't do either Stacy or himself any good to go into this angry.

"There you are," Kathy said. Her smile lit up the entire room. It was impossible not to smile back.

"Am I late?" He glanced at his daughter who was focused on the music on her music stand, her hair fallen forward to shield her face.

"No, we were early," Kathy reassured him. "The piano's all tuned, so you're ready to go. Here are the rules. Trey gets to pick the first song—"

Stacy's head came up. "*He* does?"

"Age before beauty," Kathy said calmly, "but you're next. You'll alternate. And whatever piece the other one picks—" she looked from Trey to Stacy "—no complaining. You smile and say, 'This looks great.' Come on, I want to hear you say it for me."

Trey couldn't hide a smile as he looked at his daughter. "This looks great," he intoned along with her. She must have been biting the insides of her cheeks and she had to hold her lips very oddly to keep from smiling, too.

God forbid that she actually smile.

"If you have to speak," Kathy continued, so very seriously and earnestly, "you must say something nice to each other first. In fact, why don't you start by doing that right now."

"Kathy, I don't think this is necess—"

"We should all get into the habit of doing it anyway." She was the one who cut him off this time. "Saying something nice when you first see someone. I'll start. Stacy, I thought it was wonderful the way you helped Anita carry the groceries in from her car this afternoon without anyone having to ask you. And, Trey, I think you must have the lovliest smile I've ever seen. Please feel free to use it more often."

Loveliest smile, huh?

"Well, that's lucky, because just seeing you…" He realized what he was saying might sound too personal, too intimate, and he included Stacy in his proclamation, "*both* of you, makes me smile."

"See how nice that feels?" Kathy said softly, smiling back into his eyes.

It was insane. It was like lusting after Mr. Rogers. But every cell in his body was hyperaware of her. He wanted to bury himself in her sweetness and warmth. How the hell was he going to deal with this? Not by standing here like an idiot, smiling at her, that was for sure. But he couldn't look away, couldn't seem to stop.

"Kathy, you are really going to look great in that sexy new underwear we bought you today."

Stacy's words had the jarring, hair-raising, interruption-causing effect of a needle sliding off a phonograph record. Trey turned to look at his daughter, his mouth open, aware that Kathy had done the same.

"*Stacy!* You promised you wouldn't embarrass—"

"Trey," Stacy finished Kathy's sentence. She looked at her father. "It doesn't embarrass you to know that Kathy and I made a deal that in exchange for me coming here today, I got to pick out new underwear for her to wear with the dress she bought for your date Tuesday night, does it?"

"It's not a date!" Kathy said at the same time as Trey.

"The dress is black," Stacy told her father. "I managed to convince her to get the one that wasn't a turtleneck. I think you're going to like it. I picked out a WonderBra that's going to make the dress look amazing, and matching thong panties—both in teal velvet."

"You can't embarrass me," Kathy told Stacy, but her cheeks were nearly crimson. "I refuse to be embarrassed." She looked squarely at Trey. "It's very nice underwear, but it's nothing at all to be embarrassed about."

He had to clear his throat. "Well, sure," he said. "Teal's a pretty color."

God help him, teal *velvet* against the pale smoothness of Kathy's skin. He wasn't going to be able to think about anything else on Tuesday night. Hell, he wasn't going to be able to think about anything else right now.

"And it's not as if anyone's going to see it," Kathy continued. She leaned closer and whispered something to Stacy.

Stacy didn't bother to lower her voice. "I did *not* break my promise. *He's* not embarrassed. He's fine about it."

"My underwear's red today," Trey told Kathy. "I figured Stacy was going to bring that up next, so I might as well beat her to the punch."

Kathy laughed, as he'd hoped she would.

"Actually, I was going to thank you for letting Doggie keep Poindexter." Stacy turned her back to him. "I thought that was really great of you and I really respected the way you handled the whole situation."

She meant it. Trey knew she meant it, because she couldn't manage to look him in the eye.

And just like that the teal underwear was forgotten. Well, nearly forgotten.

"Thanks for saying that, Stace," he said quietly. "Knowing that you respect me means a lot."

Kathy started for the door. "I'll let you guys get down to the music."

As the door closed behind Kathy, Trey put a B-flat lead chart on Stacy's music stand. "I want to start with a song called 'Stardust.' It's an old jazz standard that my father used to love."

"Gee," Stacy said with a sigh. "Jazz, huh?" She sighed again. "This looks great."

Trey laughed as he sat down at the piano. And for just a second, he could have sworn he heard Stacy laughing, too.

Chapter 11

"May I have this dance?"

Katherine had been watching the couples spinning across the spacious country club dance floor, but she now turned around to find herself gazing into a pair of chocolate-brown eyes. The owner of those eyes looked just enough like Jimmy Smits to actually make her consider saying yes.

"Sorry, Hector." Trey had returned from the bar carrying two long-stemmed wineglasses. "It would be poor form for Kathy to run off with you after I battled the horde at the bar to get her a glass of wine."

"Sutherland." Hector's smile was warm. "Nice speech tonight. Short and sweet. Bill would've been proud."

Katherine's attention was on Hector even as she thanked Trey for the glass of wine. "Do you know Bill Lewis well?" she asked him. She could feel Trey's eyes on her. "I'm just...I find it odd that he didn't appear in person to accept such a high honor."

"Bill isn't much for convention," Hector told her. "And

yeah, I know him pretty well. We've been friends since college.''

She wanted to ask him more questions about Bill, but Trey was still watching her. He would begin to wonder what was going on if she suddenly started quizzing Hector like an investigative reporter.

So instead, she held out her hand. ''It was a pleasure meeting you, Mr...?''

''Gomez.'' He actually lifted her fingers to his lips. ''The pleasure was all mine, Miss...?''

''Wind,'' Trey supplied. He set down his glass of wine, took Katherine's and set that down, too, gently extracting her from Hector's grip. ''Excuse us, Hec.''

Trey didn't wait for Hector to respond. He just pulled Katherine with him onto the dance floor.

''Can I give you some advice?'' he said, raising his voice to be heard over the loud music from the band.

He held her at a distance, gentlemanly careful not to brush against her with his body. Still, it was exceedingly difficult not to be aware of the fact that her hand was tucked into his, her other hand on his very broad shoulder, his other hand warm against her waist.

It was also difficult not to be self-conscious of the fact that as he gazed down at her, he had an unobstructed view of her WonderBra-enhanced neckline.

This dress wasn't extremely low-cut. In fact, Katherine had chosen it because it fulfilled her criteria of being both properly formal *and* relatively modest. Most of the formal gowns she'd seen were strapless or had cut-out backs or long slits up the sides of the skirt. This one had rather dainty cap sleeves and absolutely no peekaboo mesh to reveal her belly button. It had a back and a soft, full skirt that went all the way to the ground. It fit snugly, accentuating her full breasts and the curve of her hips, but compared to the others it was practically dowdy.

Until she tried it on with the underwear Stacy had selected

for her. The bra rearranged everything quite a bit, and suddenly the dress and its neckline were both alarmingly sexy.

She looked up into the steady blueness of his eyes. "I suppose that depends," she answered his question, nearly having to shout to be heard. "Advice about what, exactly?"

"Hector's a nice guy—Bill's been friends with him for years, but…" He leaned closer, spoke directly into her ear, his breath warm against her neck. "He's a player, Kathy."

"Really? Upon which team does he play?"

Trey laughed.

"Something local, I guess," she said. "I must seem very ignorant, but I didn't even realize Albuquerque had a professional sports team."

"Oh, my God. You're serious." He laughed again. "When I say he's a player," he explained, again leaning closer to speak more softly, more privately into her ear. "I mean that he… Well, frankly, he plays *women*. He's a Don Juan."

"Oh." Duh. She laughed at herself. "Dawn breaks on Marblehead. Yes, I have heard that expression before—player. I just wasn't thinking along those lines. My goodness—now I feel ignorant, indeed!"

"You really didn't notice that he was practically drooling on you?"

Katherine had to laugh. Drooling. "*Was* he?"

"I was about ready to hand you a towel so you could mop yourself off."

She could feel herself blushing again. "Instead you came to my rescue by pulling me out of drooling range. How gallant."

"No," he said. "Just selfish. You look far too beautiful tonight. No way was I going to let you get drooled on."

By anyone but me. Trey didn't say the words aloud, but he knew they lingered unspoken in his eyes. Still, she was so innocent, she probably wouldn't recognize the heat for what it was, probably wouldn't realize, either, that she'd been keeping him awake at night for more than a week now.

Unless he held her too close. Then she would get a very, very big hint about the way he reacted to her nearness.

But she was much too sweet. Impossibly young. And that made the things he wanted to do with her completely out of line. Bring her to his room. Kiss her softly, gently, until she melted in his arms. Seduce her and make love to her all night and into the early hours of the dawn. To do the exact same thing the next night and the next and the next and the—

But that was not an option. It would be unbelievably cruel to treat her that way. She'd expect something from him, something he couldn't possibly give her, and she'd end up hurt. And he'd never forgive himself.

Her smile was mischievous. "How do you know I don't like being drooled on?" she asked. "How do you know I'm not something of a player myself?"

Trey laughed. He couldn't remember the last time he'd actually laughed so often at one of these high-society functions. "It was just a guess. Was I wrong?"

Katherine felt her cheeks heat slightly. She'd actually started this. What could have possibly spurred her to suggest that she might like being drooled on? It had been flirtatious, at the very least. And certainly far more self-confident than she would have believed possible.

Her underwear. Dear Lord, Stacy had been right. She was wearing brilliantly colored underwear that *did* look marvelous on her. She looked good tonight. She knew she did. And as much as she was embarrassed by the effect of her WonderBra, she liked it, too. She liked the second glances she was getting. Particularly the ones she'd been getting all evening from Trey, mostly when he'd thought she wasn't looking.

And now he was flirting back. It was obvious from his smile, the heated edge in his eyes, the way he was holding her just a little bit closer in response to her words. Of course, it was probably automatic pilot for him. Katherine knew many people who could deliver a top-rate yet completely meaningless social flirtation without breaking stride. Still, coming from Trey, it was enough to make her giddy.

His leg brushed against hers, her breasts grazed his chest, and she thought the sensation would make her faint.

"I think everyone rather likes to be drooled on every now and then," she said in a voice that came out hopelessly breathless. "Depending, of course, on who's doing the drooling."

"If you *are* a player," Trey said, his mouth very close to her ear, his voice intimately quiet, "your technique is brilliant. No one would ever suspect you were capable of a sexual hit and run."

She laughed at that. It was either laugh or melt into a boneless pile at his feet. It should be illegal for a man to have such a sexy voice.

"At the risk of disappointing you, I have to confess that I'm nothing of the sort." She could feel her voice becoming hoarse from shouting over the music, but there was no way she would dare lean into him to speak into *his* ear. He smelled far too good, and she'd end up just standing there, inhaling his cologne, completely speechless. "One of my many weaknesses, I'm afraid. I've always longed to be cosmopolitan."

Her mother and sisters had the queen and princess thing down. They could do regal and elegantly cosmopolitan without blinking an eye. And they seemed to like it, too. But always uncomfortable, Katherine made a point of standing off to the side whenever possible.

Except right now, she didn't want to be off to the side. She wanted to be right where she was. In Trey's arms.

"You know, I've always wanted to be a female James Bond, but I seriously doubt that's going to happen this late in the game."

He had no problem moving closer to her. He was very careful not to touch her, but his breath was like a warm caress. "Hmm. James Bond aspirations. No wonder you're not interested in working for me after January."

Katherine felt her smile fade as she pulled back to look at him. "I know you don't understand about that, and I'm afraid I can't explain—"

"Shhh." He lifted his hand, one finger raised as if he were going to press it against her lips. But he didn't touch her. "I was just making a joke. I wasn't trying to make you feel guilty or start a business meeting."

"Still, I feel badly—"

"Don't. I'm in awe of you. There are people in my company—top-level businessmen—who would leave their career track at the drop of a hat for the kind of money I offered you, regardless of the fact that they would have no true interest in that type of work. But you're totally unwilling to compromise your plans for the future. I respect that."

"You make me sound like Joan of Arc. I'm afraid it's not as simple or clear-cut as all that."

The song ended, but Trey didn't release her. "Nothing ever is." He looked down into her wide gray eyes. "Like right now, for example. We're here, we're dancing, we're having fun. Simple, right?" He laughed. "Not quite. Do you know that there are about 150 people watching us right now, wondering exactly who you are, paying attention to the fact that I'm not here with Diana tonight? And tomorrow or the next day, word will get out that you work for me. If we only dance one dance, they'll assume it was your birthday or some special occasion, and that our dancing was just a social nicety. But if we dance together again, even just one more time, there'll be gossip and speculation, and by Thanksgiving morning, everyone who thinks they're anyone in Albuquerque will assume I'm doing my nanny."

Her eyes got even wider and she laughed. "Oh, dear."

"And again, the solution seems simple, right? We should stop dancing so no one gets the wrong idea. But again, it gets complicated, because I don't want to stop. I'm enjoying dancing with you. You're a good dancer, and I can't remember the last time I was at one of these things actually having fun. And…" And it was even *more* complicated than that, because he really wanted what everyone watching would assume he'd just take.

The band started playing again.

"Who cares what people think?" Kathy said.

"Yeah, that's always kind of been my philosophy, but—" he shook his head "—they're going to be talking about you, too."

"Maybe," Kathy said with a smile that she couldn't hide, "they'll think *I'm* playing *you*."

Trey had to laugh at that. "More likely they'll think it's the other way around."

They were dancing again. Kathy was somehow back in his arms and they were moving in time to the music. And everyone was watching.

"Are you a player, Trey?" Her voice was soft in his ear.

How had this happened? Suddenly the entire mood had changed from lighthearted to extremely intense. He was holding her much too close. Her breasts were soft against him, her thighs brushing his. He looked down and caught a flash of teal at her shoulder.

Teal. Velvet. Underwear.

For a moment, he couldn't speak.

"You're good-looking enough to get away with it," she murmured, "but somehow you just don't strike me as the type." She laughed. "Listen to me, the voice of wisdom. As if I could tell just from a few brief conversations whether a man is sincere or not. I have to admit, my track record's dismal."

Her track record. She *had* a track record. That didn't really surprise him. After all, she was twenty-five years old and beautiful, but at the same time, he would have had no trouble believing she was still a virgin.

"I've always tried to be honest about where a relationship can or can't go," he told her, breathing in the sweet scent of her hair.

"As long as both people are clear about the possibilities, or the lack of them—"

"Then there's no chance of a misunderstanding," he finished for her. Then laughed. "Actually, there's never *no* chance of a misunderstanding. But it lowers the odds a whole lot.''

She was giving him her full attention, gazing up into his eyes. He could feel her fingers at the nape of his neck, touching his hair, and it took every ounce of restraint he had not to lean forward those last few inches and kiss her.

''Of course, there's no real way to be absolutely certain that possibilities for something more lasting won't develop from *any* given relationship,'' she whispered. ''There's no way to predict that something that starts as attraction won't develop into something more powerful—even for someone who professes that it won't.''

''What if it only develops into a more powerful attraction?''

''Well, at least then you've tried,'' she told him so seriously. ''That's so much better than letting opportunities for true love pass you by.''

True love. But of course. It made perfect sense that sweet, innocent, beautiful, passionate, vibrant Kathy Wind would be searching for true love.

But she wasn't going to find it in Albuquerque. At least not at the Sutherland estate.

Trey took her hand and pulled her with him off the dance floor. He knew damn well that their conversation had been in code. She had told him without a doubt that she was interested in him, that if he kissed her, she would kiss him back. And if he invited her to his room...

But that wasn't going to happen. Not tonight, not any night.

Because Kathy was looking for true love. And Trey had nothing true left in his heart.

Katherine smiled her thanks at Trey as he held open the door to the house. She went inside, forcing herself not to look back over her shoulder, to check to see if her bodyguard had parked his blue subcompact across the street.

She'd spotted the man with the military haircut that she'd

first seen at the mall. She'd seen him in the parking lot as she
and Trey had come out of the country club.

Trey had driven them to the award presentation in his sports
car instead of using his limo and driver, and she'd been extremely nervous that he would spot the blue car following
them as he drove them home.

She'd seen the blue car off and on as she'd taken the children to school and back. But she'd expected neither Stacy nor
Doug to notice it.

Trey was an entirely different story.

There wasn't much that went on around him that he missed.

There was no way to explain the presence of a Royal Wynborough bodyguard without revealing who she was, and she
wasn't ready to do that yet.

And her reasons had nothing to do with locating Bill Lewis.

She wanted Trey to kiss her. Several times tonight, she'd
thought he'd been about to. But they were in public, so she'd
waited.

Until now.

Until they were home.

She wanted him to kiss her, to feel what a kiss was like
with no royal title surrounding her like a force field. She
wanted to be kissed by a man as a woman—not as a princess.

And maybe it was only the false confidence brought about
by her brilliant teal underwear that made her inaccurately believe she was in his league, but she was convinced Trey was
going to kiss her. Maybe even tonight.

The house was quiet. Anita sat reading at the kitchen table.
She smiled and put on her jacket as they came into the room,
and took her leave almost immediately, clearly in a hurry to
get home to her own family.

It was only eleven o'clock, but it seemed much, much later.
It seemed like 2:00 a.m. The dead of night. Dark and silent
and filled with possibilities that wouldn't exist in the light of
morning.

Trey tossed his keys onto the counter.

"This is kind of weird, huh?" he said, glancing at her.

''I've seen you home, but it's my home, too. It's hard to get a sense of closure this way. Maybe I should say thanks for coming with me and shake your hand.''

A handshake? Katherine didn't think so. Not after the way he'd been looking at her all night. ''And then I'll say thanks for inviting me.''

Still, a handshake might be a good start. She held out her hand, and he moved toward her with another of those half smiles that made him look impossibly handsome and charming, both unbearably sexy and little-boy sweet.

His hand was big and warm with long, elegant fingers, neatly manicured nails. It engulfed hers completely.

He smiled again as he released her hand. ''And still we're standing here.''

But now they were standing a whole lot closer and he was looking directly into her eyes.

''I had a wonderful time,'' she told him breathlessly, forcing herself not to step away from him, forcing herself to boldly hold his gaze. She *wanted* to be this close. She wanted to be even closer, so she took a step toward him, saw the realization in his eyes that she wasn't moving away, going upstairs.

Please God, don't let her be wrong about the signals she'd been picking up from him all evening. He liked her, he was attracted, he was interested. The things he'd said to her during their last dance, *that* had to have been more than just a high-society flirtation.

''You're a marvelous dancer and I always enjoy your company,'' she told him. ''I know this wasn't a real date, but maybe...''

''Maybe what?'' His voice was husky and that disconcerting heat was back in his eyes. And Katherine blessed both Stacy and her underwear for giving her the nerve to be so forward. Because she knew he wanted to kiss her. She *knew* it.

And, as if she were having an out-of-body experience, she

watched herself reach up and lightly touch the smooth lapel of his tuxedo. "Maybe we could do it again sometime."

Her own words astonished her and she nearly laughed aloud.

But Trey was silent and completely immobile, and in a mere fraction of seconds, her confidence crumbled to dust.

Who was she kidding? Her underwear didn't make a whit of difference. She was still Katherine, the quiet, sensible, *plain* princess. Her hair was still ho-hum brown instead of auburn or red. Her eyes were still boring gray.

She still looked like someone's nanny—except now she looked like someone's nanny in a formal gown who was coming on to her boss.

"I'm so sorry," she said, finally unfreezing enough to pull her hand away.

But he caught her hand and kept her from running away. And looking down at his fingers laced together with hers, he smiled. "So I guess it's not just me," he said.

Katherine couldn't breathe, couldn't speak. He looked into her eyes, and from just that, from just a look, her knees went completely weak.

"You've noticed this, too," he continued. "This…attraction between us."

It wasn't a question, but she nodded. Yes. Oh, yes.

"It's dangerous, don't you think?"

She nodded again, still completely speechless. She wasn't wrong, after all.

He touched the side of her face, and she closed her eyes. Her heart was pounding so loudly, it seemed impossible that he couldn't hear it.

"I'm not sure what we should do about this," he whispered. "I can't even stand here without touching you, without wanting…"

Katherine opened her eyes as she felt herself sway toward him, as he drew her into his arms and slowly, impossibly slowly, lowered his mouth to hers.

Just when she thought he was finally going to kiss her, he

stopped, his lips a whisper away from hers. "This is just going to be a good-night kiss," he told her. "Just one. Just a kiss. Tomorrow we can try to figure it all out, okay?"

He brushed his lips against hers, lightly, tasting her before sweetly claiming her mouth. It was a gentle, almost careful kiss, but enormously thorough, and Katherine melted against him. It was all wine and soft music and moonlight, it was the kind of kiss a lover would give after vowing never to break her heart. 'Til death do us part...

Trey pulled back, breathing hard, and she realized how very hard he'd had to work to keep that kiss as soft and gentle as he had. The heat in his eyes belonged to other kinds of kisses. Wild, passionate, soul-deep kisses that would set the very air around them aflame.

And there was no way she was going to say goodnight and walk away without a taste of *that*.

Katherine stood on her toes and reached up around his neck, pulling him down to her. And she kissed him. Not carefully, not gently. She kissed him the way she'd been dreaming about kissing him since she first saw his picture back in Colorado.

She heard him groan as he wrapped her in his arms, as his hands swept over her body. He cupped her derriere with one hand, pressing her hips hard against him, his other hand tangled in her hair as he kissed her back just as fiercely.

This was a kiss worth breathing hard for. This was a kiss neither of them would forget—probably not within the next decade, maybe longer. *This* was a kiss.

It was hot, it was deep, it was endless. She ran her fingers through the thick silk of his hair, down the smooth wool of his tuxedo, across his muscular back and athletic rear end, daring to fill the palms of her hands with the sheer power of the man. She found the edge of his jacket and slipped her hands up, wanting to touch him, wanting to find the heat of his skin.

She inhaled him, devoured him, welcoming him into her own mouth, claiming his tongue, his teeth, his lips for her own. He slanted his head to give her more of what she wanted—long, hungry kisses that made her ache with the magic of their exquisite possibilities.

He pulled free just as she worked his shirttail from his pants, just as her hand skimmed the satin smoothness of his bare back.

"My God!"

As he finally pulled free, he wasn't simply breathing hard, he was gasping for air.

His eyes weren't merely hot, they were molten.

And his gaze lingered on her mouth before he looked up into her eyes, and she knew it was all he could do to keep from kissing her again.

"Suddenly, I'm not sure I want to wait until tomorrow to figure this out," he whispered.

He touched her shoulder and she realized one sleeve of her dress had fallen slightly down, exposing the brightly colored strap of her bra. "I've got to confess, I've been thinking about this pretty constantly since Stacy first mentioned it."

Katherine let herself drown in the blue depths of his eyes. "It's just underwear," she said, but she knew better.

"You better go upstairs, before I try to talk both of us into letting me see the rest of it."

"Maybe that's not such a bad idea," she said softly.

He shook his head. "It is," he told her. "Kathy, I didn't expect this. It's one thing to fantasize, but when it's real... We've got to talk before this goes any further. There are things you need to understand before... God, I don't want you to get hurt. We need to be on the same page right from the start. And I'm afraid..." He shook his head. "Can we talk about this tomorrow?"

"Of course." It wasn't easy, but she pulled free from his arms. "I guess it's good night, then. I had a lovely time." She smiled at him before she turned away. "Especially the kissing part."

She heard him laugh as she left the room. "Yeah," he said. "Me, too."

Chapter 12

Someone was crying.

Katherine paused in the hallway, listening, wondering if it was only the wind, or maybe even just her imagination.

But no, there it was again.

Doug and Stacy were in school. She'd dropped them off just a few hours ago, and had returned home, half hoping Trey would be there.

But he must have left for his office early this morning. And his car was still gone when she'd returned.

She was both nervous and eager to see him, terrified and elated. Last night's kiss had been spectacular. But Trey's insistence that they move slowly alternately worried or made her impossibly hopeful, depending on her mood of each passing minute.

Her darker, more terrified moments were spent filled with self-doubt. *She'd* kissed him. *She'd* approached him. The chemistry she'd felt while they were dancing hadn't been real. The words he'd said to her, about their mutual attraction, were a little bit harder to shrug off, but she'd even managed to come up with an excuse for them—he'd only said it so as not to embarrass her, after she'd touched him.

Her less dark moments had doubts of their own. He *was* somewhat attracted to her, particularly while she was wearing the WonderBra. But the brunt of her attractiveness came from her proximity. She was here, all the time, living in Trey's house. She was convenient—a rather ugly word that Stacy had used as well.

But then Katherine would remember that kiss, the feel of his mouth on hers, the way he had held her, the power of his passion, and his strength as he'd made certain they not move too fast. He surely cared about her, or else he would have realized what little effort it would have taken to finesse his way into her bed. Instead, he wanted to be sure they had the chance to truly think, to talk before getting in too deep. How could that be anything but a *good* thing?

Katherine had spent half of the night trying to clarify her own thoughts. What did she want from a love affair with Trey Sutherland? Did she dare take a chance, see if something real, something strong and lasting could grow between them? It would be risky. She was already half in love with the man. And he'd always have Helena's vibrant memory with which to compare her.

And if there was one thing of which Katherine was completely convinced, it was that Trey had truly loved Helena. And he probably loved her still. That could only bring her heartache.

She heard it again. That soft keening sound. The sound of a heart breaking.

Anita had gone out to the store. Poindexter was downstairs lying near the heating vent in the warm kitchen.

Katherine was alone in the house.

Alone save for the spirits of Sutherlands past.

The hair on her arms stood on end as she listened harder. No, it was definitely *not* her imagination. Someone *was* crying. She followed the ghost of the sound down the hallway toward Stacy's room.

The girl had claimed her mother still walked these halls, and in the dreary morning light, Katherine could almost believe it. She could almost picture Helena, pale and otherworldly, wandering this enormous house, weeping.

Weeping today, perhaps, because Katherine had spent a rather good amount of time last evening kissing Helena's husband.

Perfect. Add *that* guilt onto all the anxiety and trepidation she was already feeling. Katherine shook her head, still following the sound, determined to prove it had far more earthly origins.

She stopped outside Stacy's room. The door was tightly closed. That was odd. Stacy always kept it open when she left for school.

She stepped closer. Yes, the crying sound was definitely coming from within the girl's room.

She knocked on the door, and the crying stopped. She knocked again, and, after several long moments, the door opened.

It was Stacy. Sullen and red-nosed, she glared expressionlessly at Katherine, pretending that she hadn't been weeping.

Katherine was astonished. "How did *you* get home?"

"I walked." The girl left the door open, turning her back on Katherine and crossing to her bed.

"But—"

"School sucks, so I left, okay?"

"Well," Katherine said, stepping into the room, "actually, no. It's not okay for you to just walk away from—"

"Tina Maretti tripped me in homeroom." Stacy flung herself down on her bed, gripping her pillow as if it had the power to keep her afloat in the roughest of seas. "She said it was an accident, but I *know* she did it on purpose. I fell down, and my pants split. Just like that, I was standing there in front of twenty-two kids with my butt hanging out." She closed her eyes in misery. "In front of *Craig*. God, why did *he* have to be there?"

"Oh, dear." Stacy's pants—a pair of light cotton bell-bottoms—were on the floor. Katherine picked them up. Sure enough, they'd torn right along the back seam. About ten inches. Stacy wasn't overreacting—there was no way a tear that enormous would have gone unnoticed.

"I wanted to die." Stacy's eyes filled with tears and her lower lip trembled. "Kathy, I just wanted to die."

"Oh, sweetie." Katherine sat down next to her and pulled her into her arms. "Why didn't you call me?"

"Mrs. George wrote me a pass to the nurse so I could call you and get another pair of pants," Stacy said, her tears flowing down her cheeks as she gasped for breath. "And Craig gave me his sweatshirt to tie around my waist—she must've made him do that. I knew you wouldn't be home yet because you just dropped us off, but I couldn't wait in the nurse's office. I couldn't. I know you told me never to leave school without telling you first, but I couldn't stay there!"

"It's okay," Katherine murmured. "This sounds as if it were something of an emergency."

"I can't go back," Stacy sobbed. "Not today. Not *ever!*"

"You can take today off," Katherine promised her. "I'll call the school, tell them you're here. And then it's a long weekend. By Monday, everyone will have completely forgotten."

"Craig will *never* forget! Or Tina. God, I just wanted to smack that smirk off her face! I wanted to…I wanted to *kill* her!" She lifted her tear-streaked face, completely aghast. "Kathy, what if I've got bad blood? My ancestors were all thieves and murderers."

Katherine was floored. "Murderers?"

"Daddy probably told you the polite company version, right? Cattle rustlers and gamblers? That's only half true. Ford Sutherland was a hired gun—like a hit man. And *his* father killed at least two railroad men when he robbed a train. Two we know he killed for sure. Who knows how many others? What if I've got something awful inside me, and one day when someone like Tina trips me again, I just snap?"

Katherine smoothed back Stacy's hair. The question was

completely absurd, but she answered her seriously, somehow managing not to smile. At least not very much. "You don't have bad blood. You have very, very *good* blood. Your father and mother—"

"My mother. Great. Cheer me up by bringing *her* up." She pulled away, turning her back to Katherine. "Do you mind just letting me be alone for a while?"

Berating herself for mentioning what she should have known would be a touchy subject, Katherine gazed at the girl's narrow shoulders, wishing she could give her another hug, wishing she could make the entire awful morning just disappear.

Instead, she stood up. "I'll go call the school, let them know where you are."

Stacy didn't look up.

"Maybe we could have lunch together," Katherine suggested. "Talk about your plans for tomorrow's dinner?"

Stacy turned at that. "Tomorrow?"

"It's Thanksgiving," Katherine reminded her.

"Yeah," Stacy said, rolling her eyes. "Right. Thanksgiving. Whoopie."

Trey had a whole hell of a lot to be thankful for this year.

Doug was back from his residency on the Planet of the Canines. And Trey's own musical meetings with Stacy were a raging success. Although they still hadn't gotten to the point where they were doing much talking, they had found a common bond that enabled them to be together without triggering World War Three. They'd given an impromptu recital this morning for Kathy and Doug, and after, Stacy had smiled at him. The entire day had passed—so far—without a single outburst or voice raised in anger. Their relationship was still far from perfect, but thanks to Kathy, they were well on their way.

Thanks to Kathy.

Trey had to smile as he watched out the kitchen window as Stacy taught Kathy how to skateboard. Kathy was up for the challenge, laughing as she rolled across the driveway. She was good at it. She had a good sense of balance, and she wasn't at all afraid of going too fast.

Unlike Trey. Who was terrified of going too fast.

He'd been avoiding Kathy.

Ever since Tuesday night. Ever since she'd kissed him and turned his life completely upside-down.

He'd purposely canceled their scheduled meeting last night. In fact, he'd made a point to be out of the house all day, only coming home briefly to practice with Stacy and throw a ball around with Doug.

He knew Kathy was confused. Hell, she had every right to be, the way he'd kissed her.

But he'd done a lot of soul-searching, and had come to the dismal conclusion that he couldn't risk getting involved with her.

He couldn't start something knowing that she was going to end up hurt. He liked her so much. He liked everything about her—her loyalty, her honesty, her integrity, her smile, her body....

He watched her skim past him, knees bent, arms out, her T-shirt hugging the full swell of her breasts. He closed his eyes. Don't go there. Don't *go* there!

Kathy deserved so much more than a tired, cynical, jaded man who was only looking to get laid. She didn't want him— couldn't possibly want him.

And what he wanted didn't matter.

Although now that he knew beneath her quiet, competent air was a volcano of passion, it sure as hell didn't make it easier to deal with his desire. The bottom line was that he was afraid to be alone with her. Afraid he wouldn't be able to keep himself from taking everything she so sweetly offered.

He was afraid to talk to her about it, afraid she would offer him a completely guilt-free, no-strings arrangement, all the while hoping he would somehow change his mind, hoping he would stumble into that true love she was searching for, as if it were merely something he'd misplaced.

And he knew that wasn't going to happen.

If he were going to get physically involved with a woman, she should be someone as cynical and jaded as he was. Someone whose hope had been worn down. Someone who expected nothing more than briefly shared pleasure and a body to help warm her bed at night.

That definitely wasn't Kathy. He had to stay far away from her.

Problem was, he couldn't stop thinking about her.

She jumped off the skateboard, still laughing, and looked up—directly into his eyes. She froze as she saw him watching her through the window, her smile fading. And Trey knew that he'd already hurt her, he'd already dashed her expectations by staying away all yesterday. There was no doubt about it. He had to talk to her. Soon. He had to be as honest as he could be and tell her there was no chance of this thing between them working out.

He'd vanished yesterday under the guise of a work emergency. Yes, there had been a deadline that needed to be dealt with, but it didn't really require his around-the-clock attention, especially not the day before Thanksgiving. But Kathy didn't know that, and he had been intending to return to his downtown office even tonight, after Doug had gone to bed, determined to keep his distance until the mere sight of her was no longer enough to make his blood race through his veins.

But before he left for the office, he had to talk to Kathy.

She lifted her hand in a sort of half wave, and somehow managed to smile. It was a very sad smile, though, and he realized that she'd already figured out the decision he'd come to. He'd already told her through his body language today. And suddenly talking to her tonight wasn't soon enough. He had to do it now. Apologize.

Doug was deep in discussion with Poindexter, so Trey went out the kitchen door and down the steps to the driveway. Kathy was standing off to the side, watching Stacy demonstrate her balancing technique.

"She's very good, you know," she said to him as he approached, somehow knowing he was there even though her eyes never left Stacy.

"Yeah," Trey agreed. "You're not so bad yourself."

Her shoulders were tense, and he doubted it was from fear of Stacy falling. But still, she laughed. "Me on a skateboard. Can you believe it?"

"Not your preferred method of transportation, huh?"

"Actually, it's tremendously fun," she told him. "You really should try it."

"I have. Who do you think taught Stacy?"

"Really?" She turned toward him, and her smile was completely genuine, her eyes sparkling with interest and amusement. It battered against his resolve, forcing him to look away. And when he glanced back at her, she was significantly subdued.

He was glad he was going to talk to her now, in the broad light of day. At night it would be far harder to resist taking her into his arms and—

Trey cleared his throat. "Could we... Would you mind taking a walk with me?"

She was surprised. "Now?"

"Yeah." He raised his voice. "Hey, Stace, mind if I borrow Kathy for a little while?"

Stacy stopped short, popping her skateboard up and gracefully catching it. "Is something wrong—someone in trouble?"

"No." Just Trey. And he was sure Stacy hadn't meant it *that* way.

She shrugged, still clearly curious. "I don't mind."

"Will you tell Doug where we've gone?" Kathy asked. "We won't be *too* long."

"Take your time," Stacy said.

"Come on," Trey said to Kathy. "I'll show you where Ford is buried." He stopped himself before he reached for her hand.

She followed, but once they were outside the gate, into the back, she stopped. "We don't have to go all the way up to the top of the hill. What's the point, really? This isn't going to take long.''

The breeze moved her hair across her face, and she pretended to be engrossed in tying it back into a ponytail, only briefly meeting his gaze.

''I've been hiding from you,'' he told her. ''I want to apologize for that.''

''Oh, dear.'' She laughed, but it seemed more to hide the fact that her mouth was tremulous. ''We're going to do the apology thing now, are we? Is that what this is? Well, in that case, I'm sorry, too. I came on much too strong the other evening. It was my fault entirely.''

''No,'' he said. ''It wasn't. I was there, too, remember?''

''Right.'' She nodded briskly. ''Well, if that's it then...''

She would have turned away, but he caught her arm. And instantly let her go. God help him if she wound up in his arms. ''Kathy, look, I just think it would be way too complicated. I think we'd both be better off as—''

''Friends,'' she finished for him. She smiled much too brightly. ''I understand.''

''It was just one of those crazy things.'' He was trying to convince himself as well.

''Of course.''

''You work for me,'' he tried to explain.

''I understand completely.''

''I'm sorry.''

She met his gaze steadily now, and nodded, her bearing positively regal in her graciousness. ''Your apology is accepted. Thank you so very much for talking to me about this—and not just hiding from me indefinitely.''

It had to be the first time in his life he'd ever been thanked for ending a relationship.

She was pale, her freckles standing out. ''I'm glad to have you as a friend,'' she said softly, giving him the gift of a smile despite the fact he knew damn well that he'd hurt her.

He'd done exactly what he'd hoped he wouldn't do.

And God, even though he'd done it, he *still* ached to kiss her beautiful mouth, to pull her into his arms and devour her.

Devour her sweetness. Steal her innocence. Crush her hope.

He fought like hell not to reach for her as she turned away. Fought and won.

He watched her walk back toward the gate, noble enough to do the right thing, but not noble enough to feel good about doing it. In fact, he felt sick to his stomach, felt sucker punched to the gut.

It was a feeling he suspected wouldn't go away for a long, long time.

Chapter 13

December arrived with gorgeous, clear skies and sixty-degree days. It was the kind of weather that inspired happiness, but for the past week, Katherine had merely been going through the motions.

She sat at the desk in her room, staring at the file of notes and information she'd compiled about Bill Lewis—the man who could indeed be her missing brother. She'd spoken to a number of people about him, but received almost no new information. He was personable, charismatic, one-of-a-kind, generous, a shrewd businessman—and it was not against his nature to completely drop off the face of the earth time and again.

She'd found out where Bill Lewis *wasn't*. He wasn't in Albuquerque, of that she was certain. He wasn't in the apartment he kept in New York, nor the beach house near L.A. That left the entire rest of the world as possibilities.

James Bond would be extremely unimpressed at her sleuthing abilities.

Katherine sighed as she shuffled through her papers again,

hoping to find—what? Something she'd missed? Instead, she found herself thinking about Trey.

She'd seen Trey exactly four times since they'd had their little talk, since he'd dropped the "friend" bomb on her. She should have expected that. She should have known better. Teal underwear or not, it had been insane to think he'd ever see her in a romantic light. She was the kind of woman men were friends with.

She was okay about this. Or, at least, she would be. Eventually. She knew firsthand what a little time and distance could do for an injured heart and bruised ego. And she couldn't blame Trey for something he didn't feel.

What she *wasn't* okay about was the fact that despite his attempt to clear the air between them, he'd retreated back into deep hiding. His kids weren't seeing very much of him, and that was wrong. *She* should be the one staying away from dinner, if anyone had to stay away.

But there was no way to tell him that. He'd canceled every single one of their regular nightly meetings for the past week, as well.

She hadn't even had the chance to tell him about the torn pants incident at school. Stacy seemed to have gotten over it. She'd gone back to school with little complaining. But more and more often, Katherine heard the sounds of weeping from the girl's room. It seemed to be more than mere teenage angst. She'd tried talking, but Stacy was keeping her thoughts to herself.

The phone rang and Katherine stood up, stretching her legs as she went into the hallway. She'd purposely stayed close to home since Doug had complained of a headache this morning. She wondered if it were the school nurse giving her a call now.

"Sutherland residence."

Silence. "Um, Kathy, isn't Anita there?"

It was Trey.

"Oh," she said, her traitorous pulse kicking into double

time at the familiar sound of his voice. "No. No, she's out running errands."

He swore softly, then sighed, a frustrated expulsion of air. "All right. Can you have her call me, please, when she gets in?"

It was as if they were strangers. Funny, she'd thought he'd told her that he wanted to be *friends*. She closed her eyes, picturing the way he'd looked on Thanksgiving, dressed down in faded jeans and a cable-knit sweater. The wind had ruffled his gorgeous dark hair as he'd stood there on the hillside and essentially apologized for not being attracted to her.

She opened her eyes. "Is there something *I* can do for you?" she asked, perhaps a touch too sharply.

He hesitated. "These are your hours off."

"Oh, of course," she said tartly. "You're absolutely right. I wouldn't possibly be able to lift a finger to help you unless I'm being paid to do so."

He made that noise again that was a cross between a sigh and a frustrated laugh. "I'm sorry—"

"I'm here," she interrupted. "I'm not doing anything particularly exciting. If there's something you need help with, please ask."

"I left Bob Bowen's phone number on my desk, up in my office," he told her. "I think it's under that paperweight Dougie made me in kindergarten."

"I'll get it for you," she told him. "Do you want me to call you back?"

"No," he said. "I'll call you back on my office line—save you the hassle of fighting your way through the automated answering system."

"Give me a few minutes to get there," Katherine said. "I'm on the other side of the house and I seem to have misplaced my skateboard."

He actually laughed. A real laugh. "Thanks," he said. "Talk to you in a few."

Katherine hung up and moved briskly down the hallway. She tried not to think too much as she went up the stairs to the tower. Trey's office door was closed and she turned the knob and went inside, then turned on the lights.

She hadn't been in here in a while.

She went behind Trey's desk, careful not to sit in his chair. She found the paperweight, but there was nothing underneath it. No slips of paper anywhere on his desk. Just a pile of files, each clearly marked with a client name, none of which were Bowen.

The phone on his desk rang, and she picked it up. "Trey Sutherland's office."

"Hello, is Mr. Sutherland vail bull?" It wasn't Trey. It was a woman's voice, with a southern twang so thick Katherine almost couldn't decipher the words. Vail bull? *Available.*

"Oh," Katherine said. "I'm sorry. No, he's not in right now."

"Actually, I'm looking to find Bill Lewis. Is he there by any chance?" The woman's voice sounded strained, shaky, as if she were extremely upset. A lover discarded, perhaps?

"Who's calling please?" Katherine asked, taking a pen from Trey's top desk drawer.

"Betty Jo Parker. It's very important that I speak with him."

Katherine wrote down the name. "If you can leave me your number, Ms. Parker, I'll have him get back to you as soon as he comes in."

The woman hesitated. "I think I'll try again later. Can you tell me what time you expect him?"

"Unfortunately, I can't," Katherine told her. "Mr. Lewis has been out of touch for a while. If you don't mind my asking, when was the last time you saw him?"

Betty Jo Parker's laugh sounded more like a sob. "I spoke to his lawyer just last week. But as for Bill, it's been much, *much* too long."

"Why don't you leave your number and—"

The line was dead. Betty Jo had hung up without revealing her location.

Katherine's first potential clue in weeks. A woman who had

spoken to a lawyer who had presumably spoken to Bill Lewis within the past week! And yet she'd managed only to get a name, no number. There had to be thousands of Parkers living in the United States—and that was assuming the woman had a phone listing under her own name.

The phone rang again. She picked it up, hoping it was Betty Jo, calling back. "Hello."

"What's up? The line was busy." Trey.

"A woman named Betty Jo Parker, called for Bill Lewis," Katherine told him. "I'm sorry. I thought it was you and—"

"That's all right. Did she say what she wanted?"

"Just to find Bill."

"Great. She can get in line."

"Do you know her?" Katherine asked. "She sounded upset."

"The name's not familiar. And Bill's more the Veronica than the Betty Jo type. Did you find that number?"

"I'm sorry, it's not anywhere on your desk. At least not in plain view."

He swore. "Where did I put that…? Wait. All right. I know. Caller ID. The box is by the computer. Over to the right."

"I see it," she reported.

"Do you know how to use it?" he asked.

"I think so." Caller ID. Betty Jo Parker's number would be listed on there and… Sure enough, there it was. Parker. Katherine quickly scribbled down the number. The exchange was not local, and Katherine made a mental note to determine its origin.

"Bob called at about ten last night," Trey told her. "I'm positive I didn't clear the numbers from the Caller ID box."

Bowen. It had been the call before Betty Jo's. Katherine read him the phone number.

"Great," Trey said.

She took a deep breath. "I was hoping you might have time to meet with me to—"

"I know it's been a while," he interrupted. "But I've got

to cancel again tonight. I'm sorry. Work is crazy and the kids seem to be doing really well. I'll be home around four to spend some time with them, but I've got to skip dinner again, and I won't be back until after midnight.''

''Actually,'' Katherine said, ''Stacy's been very unhappy lately. I was hoping you could try talking to her. She won't tell me what's wrong.''

''Are you sure? She's been almost upbeat around me.''

Was she sure? Right now, she had to wonder. Were Stacy's tears from normal thirteen-year-old frustration, and was she, Katherine, really only using this as a chance to get closer to Trey?

''I've got to run,'' he said in that stranger's voice, so very politely. ''Thank you very much for the phone number.''

''You're welcome,'' she said. ''Mr. Sutherland.''

She hung up the phone before he had a chance to respond. Not that she particularly expected any kind of response at all.

''Do you have a sec?''

Trey sat back down on the piano bench, surprised. Stacy had never initiated a conversation before. ''Yeah,'' he said. ''Sure. What's up?''

Stacy focused all of her attention on cleaning out her clarinet and putting the wooden pieces back in her case. ''I was just wondering what we were going to do about Kathy.''

''Kathy?'' For an instant, Trey thought perhaps his daughter knew why he'd been spending so much time at work, knew that despite his keeping his distance, nothing had changed for him. Somehow Kathy had gotten under his skin, inside his lungs. He breathed her, dreamed her. There was not a single moment of the day when he didn't want her. Even now, more than a week later, he could still taste her kisses, still smell the soft scent of her perfume as if she'd been in his arms two minutes ago.

What the hell *was* he going to do about Kathy?

But that couldn't have been what Stacy meant. There was

no way she could know. He'd been so careful to hide everything he was feeling.

Stacy looked up. "If we don't do something, she's going
to leave in a month. She's been talking a lot lately about 'the
qualities Doug and I wish to find in a new caretaker.' She's
been making lists. I don't want her to leave," she said flatly.
"And Doggie doesn't, either. Offer her a pile of money. Make
it worth her while."

"I've done that. She turned it down."

"Double it."

He had to smile. "You think like me, kid. But I did that,
too. Apparently money doesn't matter to her."

"So what we've got to do is figure out what *does* matter
to her." Stacy chewed on her lower lip, scowling in concen-
tration.

"I don't think there's anything we can do to make her
stay," Trey told her. "I think we need to be prepared to—"

"Give up?" Stacy looked at him as if he'd suggested they
take Poindexter back to the pound.

"Have you ever heard the expression 'Hold on tightly, let
go lightly?'"

"It sounds stupid. It sounds like giving yourself permission
to be a quitter."

"It's not. It means when you know, really *know* that you're
fighting a losing battle, sometimes it's best to let yourself lose
quickly and gracefully."

God knows he hadn't done that with Helena. He'd fought
like hell to keep her with him, long after she'd stopped fighting to live. And when he should have been giving her only
comfort and support and love, he'd given her anger and pain
and frustration. He'd given her argument and disagreement.
He'd shouted and cried. He'd refused to let go, and she'd left
him anyway.

"This isn't a losing battle," Stacy said. "Marry her." She
was dead serious. "*That's* what she wants. I know. We talked
about it."

Trey had to hold on to the piano bench with both hands. "Kathy told you that she wants to *marry* me?"

"Not you specifically," Stacy said with a shrug. "Just that she wants to get married. She has that classic Snow White fantasy. You know, 'some day my prince will come?' All *you* need to do is be her prince. Marry her and she'll stay. Think of the money you'd save."

Trey laughed in astonishment. "That's not exactly a church-approved reason for marriage. To keep your nanny from resigning."

"Do you like her?" Stacy shook her head. "Why am I asking you that? I *know* you like her. How could you not? But do you *like* her like her? I mean, the idea of kissing her wouldn't gross you out, right?"

Elbows on his knees, deep in his own personal twilight zone, Trey put his forehead in the palms of his hands. "I can't believe you're asking me this."

"She thinks you're hot."

He lifted his head to look incredulously at his daughter.

She laughed at the expression on his face. Great, at least *some*one thought this was funny.

"She didn't say that, either," Stacy explained. "But I *know* she's thinking it. I can see it everytime she looks at you. Marry her, Daddy. You'll have to make her fall in love with you, but that won't be so hard. She's really into romance. A few slow dances, some kisses in the moonlight and she's yours."

Trey couldn't believe the conversation he was having with Stacy. He couldn't believe they were even having a conversation at all.

He couldn't believe she'd actually called him *Daddy*.

The truth was, they were sitting here, talking, because of Kathy. Kathy had found them a way to spend time together without fighting. Kathy had brought Doug back to him, too.

Trey *didn't* want her to leave. As tough as it was to be around her, constantly wanting her the way he did, the thought of her packing up and moving out was even harder to bear. Still, marriage was absurd.

"Has it occurred to you that I might not want to get married again?"

"Why wouldn't you?" Stacy asked. "You're lonely, and she's only the absolutely nicest human being on the face of the earth—not to mention she's beautiful. Have you noticed that she's beautiful?"

"Yeah." He'd noticed.

"You'd be insane to let her get away."

"But I'm not in love with her." As Trey said the words, something stirred uneasily inside him. He stomped it down. He *wasn't* in love with Kathy Wind. He was completely, desperately in lust with her, but that's all it was. It started with the same letter, but it was very different.

"So...fall in love with her," Stacy said as if it were as easy to do as picking up a gallon of milk on the way home from work.

"Love doesn't work that way, and you know it." And he wasn't ready for love. He didn't want that giddy feeling that came from walking on a high wire. He didn't want to rely on another person for his happiness. He didn't want to give his heart away again. He'd done that once, and he'd buried his heart when he'd buried Helena. Or so he'd thought. But here it was, on the verge of becoming permanently lodged in his throat. God, he didn't want that. He'd rather live his life unhappily than risk that kind of pain.

Trey stopped breathing. What had he just been thinking? He already *was* completely unhappy.

The only times he'd truly been happy in years had been because of Kathy. Dougie talking again. Playing music with Stacy.

Just talking to Kathy, watching her smile. God, when she smiled at him...he felt a contentment he'd never had with Helena. He felt a connection, a—

What the hell was he doing to himself, limiting himself this way by forcing himself to stay away from her? Kathy had wanted to explore possibilities. But he'd been so hell-bent on making sure she didn't end up hurt, he didn't see how badly he was hurting himself in the process.

Because what if...?

What if she did have the power to truly bring him to life again, not just sexually, but emotionally and spiritually? God knows she didn't want his money. But what if, *what if* she truly wanted *him?*

"Why don't you ask her out again?" Stacy asked. "I can baby-sit Doggie. I'm old enough, you know."

Trey smiled at his daughter. "Yeah," he said. "I guess you are, aren't you?"

"I want two things for Christmas this year," Stacy told him. "I want your permission to go to the mall by myself. And I want you at least to take Kathy out on a date."

"It would be a whole hell of a lot easier just to buy you that pony you always wanted."

"I'm not a kid anymore." Stacy closed her clarinet case. "I don't want a pony. I want Kathy to stay. I want us to be a family again."

Trey's throat felt tight. He cleared it. "I thought we were doing okay lately."

"Why settle for okay when we could have great?"

Trey looked at his daughter, sitting there so grown-up, so perceptive, so mature. If they hadn't stopped fighting constantly, he never would have known. He never would have been able to see past the sullen troublemaker.

Maybe Kathy Wind *was* magic.

"She's worried about you, you know." Somehow his voice came out evenly. "Kathy is. She thinks something's upsetting you. She asked me to talk to you about it, see if you could use, I don't know, some help?"

Stacy stood up. "I'm fine," she said shortly. Apparently she wasn't ready to talk so candidly about herself. "You wanna help me? Marry Kathy and make sure that she stays."

* * *

"I tried calling her back," Katherine told her younger sister, "but there was no answer, no voice mail, no machine."

"Betty Jo Parker from Nevada," Serena mused.

"I really can't leave here right now," Katherine said. "Otherwise I'd go talk to her myself."

"I've always wanted to go to Nevada," Serena decided. "I'll slip into my Batgirl suit and go check her out, see if I can track down this lawyer she mentioned. Little does Bill Lewis realize, but the trap around him is tightening! With you cleverly hidden in the home of his best friend, and myself ready to pounce on his former lover—"

"I don't know for certain she's his lover." Katherine tried to interject a bit of calm reality into Serena's enthusiastic fantasizing. "She just seemed extremely upset, so I thought that's what she might be."

"Maybe she's pregnant." Serena gasped. "Dear Lord, Kathy, do you realize that this woman could well be carrying an heir to the Wynborough throne?"

"Let's not get ahead of ourselves here," Katherine cautioned. "We don't know that any of this is—"

"Mother and Father will have twin heart attacks. *This* on top of Elizabeth's bomb."

"Which bomb is that?" Katherine wasn't quite sure she wanted to know. Her older sister Elizabeth was always dropping "bombs."

"You haven't *heard?*"

"How could I have heard?" Katherine asked patiently. "It's been weeks since we've spoken."

"She's pregnant."

Katherine nearly dropped the telephone. *"Elizabeth?"*

"Undeniably."

"I didn't even realize she was seeing anybody."

"She's not," Serena intoned. "She won't tell who the father is. She wouldn't even tell *me.*"

Oh, *dear.*

"Gabe Morgan keeps looking at me as if he's sizing me

up for a chastity belt," Serena complained. "I swear, I'll never have any fun with him following me around."

"I've got a bodyguard tagging along after me, too," Katherine told her sister, her head still spinning from the news about Elizabeth. Her older sister *pregnant!* "But he just sits in a car outside the house. He doesn't follow me inside, thank goodness. It would be hard to keep my cover as a nanny if he did that."

"You better take advantage of the privacy and have a torrid affair with your gorgeous billionaire while you still can. After you get back here, you're going to be put on a very short leash. And, believe me, that's no fun."

"Yes," Katherine said. "Well, I'm afraid torrid affairs aren't high on my priority list these days." Of course, that wasn't through her own choice.

"He really thinks you're the nanny?" Serena asked. "That's so romantic. Trey Sutherland." She sighed. "Even his *name* is romantic."

"Right," Katherine said. "Look, when you talk to Elizabeth tell her…tell her I'm here if she needs me."

"I will."

"I'll call you in a few days," Katherine said. "Be careful."

She hung up the phone, feeling completely unhinged. Elizabeth, pregnant. And here Katherine had been completely aquiver over one little meaningless kiss.

It was stupid—she knew it was stupid—but she was actually jealous of her older sister. Jealous of an unplanned pregnancy, if only for the nights of passion that had preceded it. Elizabeth had acted foolishly, impetuously, sure. But the emotion and the passion she had surely felt…

Katherine took a deep breath, determined to feel relief rather than envy. She was lucky. After all, one didn't find oneself pregnant when nearly every man one interacted with preferred to stay friends.

Of course, one also could find oneself in the unfortunate position of being in love with a friend, which undeniably *stank*.

Chapter 14

Trey sat in his office. He wasn't getting a damned thing done. Over the past week, he'd cleared his desk of all the work that had been plaguing him. He'd procrastinated today to the point of polishing the rich wood of his desktop. It gleamed now, completely clear, like the desk of a man who played golf every day, instead of the desk of a man who had twelve clients screaming for delivery.

And yet he sat there, staring sightlessly at his computer screen.

Thinking about Kathy.

He closed his eyes as he rubbed his forehead, trying to banish the headache that had also plagued him for the past week.

Marry her.

He was insane.

There was no other way to explain why he couldn't stop thinking about the crazy conversation he'd had with Stacy this afternoon.

Marry her.

Kathy made him happy. A fact he couldn't deny.

So why was he working so damned hard to stay away from her?

She'd told him point-blank that she went into a relationship to explore possibilities. She had to know there were no guarantees. She'd either find true love, or she wouldn't.

Trey thought she wouldn't. But maybe she'd find something else—something more realistic. Something that he could be a part of. And maybe that would be enough for her for a while.

And maybe, instead of his crushing her hope with his cynicism, she might give him an infusion of her light and life. Why couldn't it go that way?

So what the hell was he doing, sitting alone up here, when she was downstairs?

Trey was out of his chair and halfway down the tower stairs before he realized what he was doing. He slowed his pace.

This was just great. This was perfect. He had no clue what he was going to say to her. He had no plan, no strategy, no speech prepared. How about, "Hey, Kath, you know what? I was really wrong about everything. I've had this raging attraction for you since we first met. Let's definitely try that kissing thing again, and see where it goes."

As if he didn't know damn well that it and they would go straight to her bed or his bed, or hell, maybe they'd get it on right on the floor inside his locked bedroom door.

He took a deep breath. Yeah, only in his dreams.

He stopped at the overlook onto the entryway, gripping the railing with both hands, staring down at the gleaming Mexican tile below, wishing he'd figured this all out *before* he'd pushed Kathy away.

If he had, he'd be with her right now. In her arms, in his bed, surrounded by her warmth. He'd probably be laughing instead of feeling as if he couldn't breathe.

But he knew that Kathy wasn't going to sleep with him tonight. After his farce of a let's-be-friends speech the other day—God, he felt like such a liar—and after the way he'd been avoiding her like the plague this last week, she was bound to be wary.

He was going to have to be honest when he saw her. Honest and humble and apologetic. And then, maybe then, she'd agree to spend some time with him.

Because all he *really* wanted right now was to be in the same room with her, to talk to her, to see her smile. Sex would only be a bonus.

He closed his eyes and leaned over to rest his forehead on top of his hands. God, he would sell his soul for just one of her smiles.

"Are you all right?"

He nearly fell over as he straightened and spun around. "You scared me to death."

Wide-eyed, Kathy took a step backward. "I'm terribly sorry."

He reached for her, in a vague attempt to keep her from running away, but managed to stop himself before he actually touched her. "No," he said. "I'm…I just wasn't expecting anyone to be out here at this time of night."

God, did that sound as lame to her? And did he look as wild-eyed as he felt? What did she see when she looked at him standing there? What did she see in his eyes?

Whatever it was, it made her take another step back. She hugged herself, her arms folded across her chest, as if she were cold. "I was just…" She gestured down the hall, toward the tower. "I saw your light on and I was coming to see if you were…there."

She pushed a strand of hair behind her ear and nervously moistened her lips, waiting for him to respond. But what could he say to that? She was coming to see him. Please God, don't let her tell him she was coming to tender her resignation.

Honesty. If this was going to work at all, he'd have to use honesty and he'd have to start now.

"That's what I was doing, too," he said. "Coming to see you."

The gray of her eyes was nearly swallowed by the black

of her pupils in the dim hallway light. As she gazed at him, he felt as if he were being pulled into the endlessness of outer space.

Honesty. He had to tell her he'd tried really hard, but he couldn't stay away. He just had to open his mouth and say it.

But she spoke first.

"We need to talk about Stacy," Kathy said. "And…" She looked down at the floor as if bolstering her courage. "We have to talk about the fact that although I'm the one you've been avoiding, it's been impacting the time you spend with your children, and—" she lifted her chin almost imperiously "—I won't allow that to continue."

Trey nodded. "I wanted to talk to you about this, too. I wanted to apologize—"

She cut him off. "It's not necessary. I've come up with a plan. I'll make arrangements to go out at dinnertime, so you can spend your evening meal with Doug and Stacy without having to worry about me. I'll sign up for an evening class at the college or come up with some other kind of excuse so the children won't have to know that we've been having these…personal problems."

"Kathy, I don't—"

"I'm not finished," she told him. "Please, this is difficult enough. I know the reason you've been avoiding me is because you've realized that I've become…attached to you in a manner that is not appropriate considering my…my position."

Trey opened his mouth, but she held up her hand, a picture of quiet dignity.

"I won't deny that I've been foolish," she continued, her voice shaking slightly. "But I *will* assure you that my feelings and my…*attraction* for you, if you will, are not your concern. The problem is obviously all mine, and I *will* deal with it. You don't have to be afraid that I'll accost you in any way, or say or do anything inappropriate, even when the children aren't around. I promise you that."

Trey tried to swallow, but his heart was in the way. She had just confessed that her feelings for him weren't based purely on physical attraction. Dear God, now he was really scared. Scared and oddly elated.

Make her fall in love with you.

He could do it. It would be almost laughably easy. From what she'd just told him, he knew she was already halfway there.

Just as he'd suspected, with very little effort he could have her.

And then what?

What if he couldn't give her all that she deserved? He was ninety-nine percent certain that he couldn't, that he'd be trouble and *only* trouble for Kathy.

But that one percent was what kept him from running away. That one percent chance that maybe this could work kept him standing there, gazing into her eyes.

As a businessman, the situation would be a no-brainer. He'd go with the obvious odds. After all, in the business world, ninety-nine percent was virtual certainty. A one percent chance of *any*thing happening was too high-risk, even for a hardened risk taker like himself.

But as a man, as he stood here staring at the one woman he wanted more than *any*thing in the world right now, that one percent was looking pretty damn good. Particularly since trying for it would get her back into his arms.

"So," Kathy said, trying to be brisk. "That said, that leaves Stacy for us to talk about. Did you get a chance to—"

"Can we continue this conversation in my office? I could really use a drink." And a door with a lock. God, even with privacy, this was going to be hard as hell. He'd never been good at expressing his feelings—now there was an understatement and a half.

She only hesitated briefly, then nodded and followed him silently toward the tower. Although he tried to plan exactly what he'd say once he shut the door behind them, his mind was completely blank.

He opened his office door, stepping back to let her go in first. God, she smelled so good. *Stay with me tonight.* That was what he wanted to say. Point-blank.

She made a beeline for the chairs in front of his desk, no doubt in an attempt to keep this conversation as businesslike as possible. Well, that was going to change—fast—the moment he opened his mouth.

He poured her a glass of wine without asking, setting it down on the edge of his gleaming desk. He sat in the leather chair across from her and took a long sip of his gin and tonic, hoping for that sense of relief he felt when he was done with work for the night and he let himself relax with a drink.

He took another sip, but it still didn't come.

Kathy didn't touch her wine. She sat on the edge of her seat with her arms folded, still holding on to herself.

Trey took a deep breath and got down to it. "Avoiding you isn't working out," he told her. "None of this is working out."

"I'll leave," she said without hesitation. "Of course. I'll go first thing tomorrow if that's what you want."

"God, no! No, you don't understand." Honesty. He could be even more honest. He *had* to be. He gripped his glass and brought this all down to the very bottom line. "The problem is that…I want you, Kathy."

She blinked at him, clearly still unable to make sense of his words.

"I haven't been able to stop thinking about that kiss," he explained. Just say it. Just tell her. These were facts he was reporting. It shouldn't be that hard. "I've tried. I told you that nonsense about wanting to be friends because I was trying to talk myself into believing it. And in a way, yeah, I *do* want us to be friends. But I really want to be friends who are also lovers. I want to make love to you just about more than I've ever wanted anything in my life. And I've spent most of this past week completely unable to think about anything else. All I've done, all week long, is dream about kissing you again."

There, he'd said it. He took another sip of his drink as he

watched her. He wouldn't blame her one bit if she simply stood up and left the room.

But she didn't move. She looked down at her hands. "Why did you stay away?" She laughed, looking up at him, and he saw that she had tears in her eyes. "You don't have to answer that. I already know. This is probably extremely confusing for you. I'm not exactly…your type."

"No, you're different from the other women I've known," Trey agreed. "You're nicer. Sweeter. I didn't stay away because I was confused. I did it because I'm scared to death of hurting you. See…" He cleared his throat. God, this was hard. He had to tell her the truth, but this particular truth could well make her walk away. And that was something he both did and didn't want to happen. He was completely torn in half. The good and the evil Trey in endless battle within him. The good Trey won this round, and he told her, "I can't make you any promises. If we *do* get together, it's probably not going to be anything more than great sex. And honestly, I can't even pretend I *want* it to be anything more than that."

He set down his drink and stood up, moving away from her to pace. "God, I hear myself say that, and I feel like such a bastard. I should stay away from you. If someone else said that about you, about not wanting more than sex, I'd break their nose, and kick them out of the house. But here I am, calculating the last split second you'll have to leave my bedroom in the morning so that the kids won't know you spent the night with me." He turned to look at her. "Do yourself a favor, Kathy, and say no."

Katherine stood up. "What is it that I'm supposed to say no to? You haven't exactly asked me anything."

Trey stopped moving. His pacing would bring him toward her, and he clearly couldn't handle that. But she moved closer to him, empowered by all he'd said. He wanted her. He needed her. Desperately.

It wasn't the same as if he'd told her he loved her, but it would do. Yes, after this past week, thinking he didn't want her at all, it would do very well indeed.

His eyes were impossibly blue as he looked at her. "Say no to everything," he said so intensely, so clearly tortured about all of this. "Anything. If it has something to do with me, for your own sake, say no."

She stopped in front of him, close enough to reach out and touch him. But she kept her hands at her sides as she met his gaze. "What if I'd rather say yes? And what if *I* can't make any promises, either? You know, there's so much you don't know about me."

Trey touched her cheek with just one finger. His hands were warm, his knuckle slightly rough against her face. It felt so good, she felt herself sway.

"Run away," he breathed. "Please?"

The heat in his eyes contradicted his words. It promised a connection magically profound, a pleasure unlike anything she'd ever known. And Katherine knew the intensity of her attraction truly was mutual. He wanted her as much as she wanted him.

And yet he'd tried to push her away, worried that she'd be hurt. It was heart-stoppingly sweet. "I've never met a man so determined to talk a woman *out* of making love to him as you are tonight," she whispered.

She found the courage to touch him then, lightly brushing his arm with her hand, just above the soft cotton sleeve of his T-shirt.

"It doesn't have to be tonight," he told her, his fingers now in her hair, barely touching her as well.

She slid her hand down and the sensation of his bare arm beneath her palm was incredible. He was so warm, so solid.

He laughed, but it was more a burst of emotion than real laughter. "I'm thinking, please God, let this happen tonight. But I'm also thinking that this is where I should tell you I honestly expected you'd want to take some time. Step back and think this through and—"

Katherine laughed, too, as she touched his other arm with her other hand, glad he was wearing a T-shirt, glad she was touching his skin, glad she was holding on to him with both hands. "Are you serious? No, thank you very much. I'm not letting go of you. The last time I did, you changed your mind."

"No." With a groan, he gave up and put his arms around her waist, pulling her close. "I never changed my mind. I never stopped wanting you. I was just trying to do the right thing."

He was so solid, so strong, so…aroused. Katherine looked up at him and he smiled at her crookedly, obviously aware that there was absolutely no way she could have missed the unavoidable physical evidence of his desire—not the way he was holding her. Oh, yes, he really *did* want her desperately and now she knew it, too. And that knowledge took her breath away. He wanted her. Trey Sutherland wanted *her*.

"This *is* the right thing," she whispered. "I believe that absolutely."

Time hung suspended for a moment as Trey's gaze dropped to her mouth, then lifted back to her eyes.

Need and want lingered in his own eyes, and for one brief moment, Katherine felt a flash of regret. This was going to be amazing, but she couldn't help but wonder how much better it might be if only he loved her, too.

But then he kissed her, and need and want were quite enough.

He didn't try to be gentle, and she in turn didn't try to pretend she was anything but starving for the taste of his mouth, for the sweet sensation of his lips against hers.

He made a sound deep in his throat—a sound of complete surrender, of intense need.

And she was just as lost.

She could feel his hands in her hair, on her back, slipped between the edge of her shirt and the waistband of her pants, hot against her skin. She could feel his heart beating, pounding, hear his ragged breathing as he kissed her again and again, harder, deeper, longer kisses that melted the absolute last of her doubts.

This *was* right.

The man was living, blazing passion. He lit a flame in her that burned hotter than anything she'd ever felt in her life. She opened herself to him, wrapping her leg around his, and he picked her up, pressing her against him, neither of them pretending they didn't know exactly where this was going.

And they *were* going there. To someplace a whole lot like heaven. Tonight. At long last.

Katherine kissed him, burning to feel him inside her, dying to be rid of the jeans and clothing that kept him from her. He kissed her back, moving against her, driving her nearly mad with the sensation.

She reached for his hand, aching for him, pulling him so that his palm covered her breast. *Yes.*

He laughed aloud as he broke free from their kisses, gazing down into her eyes as he touched her, first gently, then harder as she pressed herself more completely into his hand.

"I want to kiss you here," he murmured. "I want to take off your clothes and taste you."

Katherine could see her blurred reflection in the glass of one of the framed watercolors behind him, her hair messed, her face almost unrecognizable from the heat of her desire, her eyes half-closed. "I would love that," she whispered.

He lowered his head, kissing her mouth, her chin, her throat, her breasts. He kissed her through the cotton of her shirt, drawing her into his mouth. The sensation made her cry out, but it wasn't enough. She pulled up her shirt, he pushed back her bra and then he was really kissing her, his mouth hot and wet against her, his tongue rough against her taut nipple.

She reached between them for the waistband of his jeans, desperate to touch him. She fumbled with the button, searched for the zipper, her fingers grazing him, and this time he took *her* hand, and pressed it completely against his hardness.

Oh, *my.*

He lifted his head from her breast. "Come upstairs with me," he whispered and then kissed her again.

She wanted that zipper down, wanted to hold him in her

hands. ''No,'' she gasped. ''I don't want to wait that long. Does this door have a lock? Please say yes.''

''Yes.'' His laughter turned to a deep inhale as she finally got that zipper down, as her fingers closed around him. ''I locked it when we came in.''

It was all she needed to hear. The blinds were down, the door was locked. She released him only long enough to pull her shirt up and over her head.

He reached for her jeans and she helped him push them off her legs, helped him rid himself of his own T-shirt and jeans.

His skin was beautiful—tanned satin over the hard steel of his muscles. His shoulders were wide, his chest broad and sprinkled with just enough dark hair to be impossibly sexy. His stomach was a six-pack, tapering down to narrow hips, a perfect rear end, and long, gorgeous, powerful legs.

Katherine touched him everywhere, kissed him, skimmed her palms across him, even as he did the same to her.

He wore dark-green briefs, and she realized with a jolt that she was standing there in front of him in her underwear as well, very plain, very white, very boring.

But she might as well have been wearing the fanciest, sexiest lace, the way he was looking at her. The heat in his eyes couldn't have blazed any hotter.

''You're so beautiful,'' he murmured, and she was. In his eyes, for this moment in time, she was the most beautiful woman in the world, underwear be damned.

She unfastened the front clasp of her bra, and the way his breath caught made her feel as if she'd unveiled a priceless work of art. She felt impossibly sexy and completely powerful, and it didn't matter at all that she was truly neither of those things. And it didn't matter, either, that their affair wasn't going to last, that he didn't love her. The magnitude of his desire was more than enough for this moment.

She pushed his briefs down his legs, freeing him, letting herself look and touch and kiss him, laughing up at him as he cried out his pleasure.

He hauled her to her feet and she kissed him again, on the

mouth this time, as he lifted her up, against him. And this time, the only thing keeping him from her was the thin cotton of her panties.

The anticipation was wonderful as he kissed her and touched her everywhere, as she locked her legs around him and moved against him. And then it wasn't quite anticipation anymore as he slipped his fingers beneath the elastic edge of her panties and touched her. Lightly. Then harder, deeper.

She was ready for him. She'd been ready for this incredible man for *years.*

She moved against him, pushing him more deeply inside of her. "Oh," she breathed. "Please tell me you have a condom."

"In my wallet." He kissed her throat, her breasts as he kept touching her.

"Please," she gasped.

"I don't want to stop—this feels too good."

It did. It felt very, *very* good. But she wanted more. She wanted *all* of him. And she wanted him now.

Now.

Katherine pulled aside her panties, pushed aside his hand, and shifted herself up on top of him. With one smooth, deep thrust, she surrounded him, filling herself with him. *All* of him.

"Kathy!"

It *was* as good as she'd imagined and the sensation made her cry out. It was fire and giddy free fall and exploding colors. It was an explosion of music and laughter and wild song. It echoed with promises and unlimitless possibilities, rapture and ecstasy and hope.

Maybe this *would* last. Maybe...

She kissed him, moving in his embrace, filling herself with him again and again, impossibly close to her release.

"Oh, man," he breathed, moving with her. "We need to stop. I need to get that condom."

With herculean effort, he pulled away from her, setting her

down on the edge of his desk while he scrambled for his wallet.

Katherine could barely breathe, could barely hold herself upright. She leaned back against his desk, supporting herself with her elbows, just waiting for him, watching him cover himself. He was gorgeous. And tonight he was all hers.

"Let's go to the sofa." His voice was husky, his eyes hot.

"Are you kidding?" she said. "And miss this opportunity to make passionate love atop your desk?"

He laughed. He was even more gorgeous when he was laughing. "That probably won't be very comfortable."

"Come here," she said. "I'll make it comfortable."

She was serious. Quiet, polite Kathy Wind was completely uninhibited when it came to sex. She was leaning back on the cleared-off surface of his desk, looking like something out of one of Trey's wildest fantasies. She wore only the smallest white panties, nearly virginal in style. It was a delicious contradiction to the way she seemed almost unaware that her breasts were bare. She looked almost heathen, leaning back the way she was, her full breasts tightly peaked with desire.

As Trey watched, she leaned forward, slipping her panties down her long, gorgeous legs. Completely naked now, she leaned back again and, with a smile that was molten, she opened her legs to him in an invitation that was unmistakable.

Two short steps and he was making love to the sexiest woman in the world, on top of his desk.

And she was dead right. It was *not* uncomfortable.

She was fire beneath him, lightning in his arms as she moved with him, urging him on—faster, harder, deeper.

Trey felt his entire world, his entire universe spiraling down to this one small spot, this one brief moment in time. Nothing else mattered, nothing else even existed. There was only Kathy, her arms around him, her cries of pleasure, her body rising to meet him, her beautiful, beautiful eyes.

She clung to him fiercely, her hands hot and urgent against his back, her touch possessive, demanding.

It was beyond exciting, the way she moved beneath him, her hunger for him as desperate as his need for her.

And Trey completely lost control. And it didn't matter. He didn't need control, didn't need to hold back—not when she so desperately wanted more of him. He lost himself completely in the wildness of her pleasure, and when he felt the powerful storm of her release, his body followed instantly, as if he'd been waiting all his life for this one mind-blowing moment of sheer perfection.

Pleasure ripped through him, roaring in his ears, rocketing through him, blasting him higher, farther, than he'd ever been. And she was with him all the way.

Trey closed his eyes, afraid of the barrage of emotions that had struck him, focusing on the aftershocks of his physical release.

He became aware of the outside world slowly.

Kathy's breath warm against his ear. Her arms still around him. His desktop hard against his knees—a whole hell of a lot less comfortable now than it had been just a few minutes ago.

He was crushing her. He started to lift himself up, but she clung to him. "No," she whispered. "Stay. Please? Just a little bit longer."

Trey kissed her, his chest tight. A little bit longer didn't work for him. A little wouldn't be long enough. He wanted far more than a little bit of time to do this again and again and *again*.

But he couldn't quantify what he wanted, couldn't estimate just how much time would be enough.

There was only one thing he was absolutely sure of right now.

And that was that he would never, ever, for the entire rest of his life, be able to sit behind this desk and get *any*thing done.

Chapter 15

"When I was Dougie's age...?" Trey mused. "I think I wanted to be a teacher, but only because I had a raging crush on my first-grade teacher and I wanted to be able to get into the staff room to hang out with her at lunch time." He sat up. "See, even back then I had a thing for the Mary Poppins type."

Katherine laughed as she turned from the dawn that was breaking outside his bedroom windows. "Mary Poppins type?"

He was stretched out among the rumpled sheets of his enormous four-poster bed looking like the official spokesperson for hedonism. He was unshaven, his hair tousled, and he was completely, beautifully, splendidly naked. It was a shame that he ever had to wear clothes at all. His muscles were far more suited to the wardrobe of a lifeguard. Or an exotic dancer. Yes, she could definitely picture him smoldering away, wearing the smallest of G-strings as he danced on a dimly lit stage.

He patted the mattress enticingly. "Come here."

She hid her smile, trying to sound stern. "If you think

calling me a 'Mary Poppins type,' is going to make me rush into your arms—I don't look anything like Mary Poppins, anyway."

"It's an attitude thing." He had that look in his eyes that promised ecstasy. He'd promised—and delivered—more times than she could count. Yet still, all he had to do was look at her that way, and she was filled with breathless anticipation. "It really works for me. Polite as hell and a little bit bossy on the outside—sex goddess when the door's locked."

Katherine couldn't hold back her smile. "Sex goddess. I like *that*."

"Yeah," Trey said, "I like it, too."

The shirt she'd stolen from his closet was mostly unbuttoned and as he looked at her that way, it felt transparent as well.

"Come here," he said again, dead serious now.

She loved the way he couldn't seem to get enough of her. But she couldn't resist teasing him. "The sunrise is going to be lovely. Don't you want to watch?"

"If the sun's rising, you've got to go back to your own room soon. If you don't come over here now, we're going to have to wait to make love again until tomorrow night."

Tomorrow night. They'd been talking and making love all night long, but this was the first time Trey had mentioned the future. Of course, tomorrow night wasn't tremendously far into that future, considering tomorrow's sun was pushing its way over the hills to the east. But it was certainly a start.

Something must have shown on her face. She must have let a little of her uncertainty slip, because Trey instantly back-pedaled.

"Tomorrow night," he said. "There I go, Mr. Assumption, just assuming we're both automatically on the same page. I'm sorry, I need to rephrase that as a question." He moistened his lips as if they were suddenly dry, took a deep breath and gave her one of those crooked smiles that could melt her completely. "Kathy, will you—"

"What time shall I come to your room?" They *were* on

the same page. Absolutely. Already, before she'd even left him, Katherine couldn't wait for the coming night.

Fire sparked in his eyes. "What are the chances of Dougie going to sleep a half hour after dinner?"

"Eleven-thirty," Katherine decided. "I'll be here at eleven-thirty, after Stacy goes to bed. And at 11:31…"

Several long strides brought Trey to her side. He swept her up into his arms and carried her back to his bed.

The sunrise *was* lovely—even though neither of them watched.

Doug and Stacy looked up as Trey came into the kitchen.

"I thought you were at work," Doug said.

"Yeah," Stacy agreed. "I thought you left, like, *hours* ago."

"No," Trey said. Every cell in his body was aware of Kathy, standing with her back to him as she made sandwiches at the counter. "I, uh, slept in a little bit this morning."

"That's funny," Doug said. "Kathy did, too."

Kathy turned to face him, and something shifted inside him at the sight of her smile. It was odd. She looked exactly the same as she had all those other mornings he'd run into her in the kitchen. Her hair back in a ponytail. Jeans and a sweatshirt. Except now he didn't have to work to imagine her naked. Now he just had to remember back a few hours and…

Oh, dear, as Kathy always said.

"Good afternoon. Would you like me to make you a sandwich?" she asked, her cheeks heating with a delicate blush as if she could read his wandering mind. It was so contradictory. She hadn't blushed once last night, at least not after they'd started taking off their clothes.

But those were *not* the right thoughts for him to be having—not with Doug and Stacy staring at him. Doug was completely clueless to the undercurrents in the room, but Stacy was looking from him to Kathy and back a little too perceptively.

"Where's Anita?" he asked, trying to regain his equilibrium. The housekeeper usually made his lunch when he was home during the day.

Doug laughed and fell out of his chair. Mr. Slapstick.

"Earth to Trey," Stacy said. "It's *Saturday*. Why else would we be home from school?"

"Home from school," he repeated, realization dawning. School. Started again on Monday. And on Monday, Doug and Stacy would be out of the house from early in the morning until midafternoon. He could give Anita Monday off and… He looked over at Kathy.

She knew exactly what he was thinking. Her blush deepened and she turned back to her sandwiches, carrying two of the plates to the table where Doug and Stacy were sitting.

Trey cleared his throat. "So. What do you guys have planned for today?"

"Just a little Christmas shopping at the mall," Kathy told him briskly. "We'll be back by around four."

"Mind if I come with you?" The words had left his lips before he even realized he was saying them. Trey couldn't remember the last time he'd wanted to go to the mall. But he couldn't think of anything he'd rather do today, considering that the mall was where Kathy was going to be.

This was crazy.

He'd woken up feeling nearly dizzy, and that giddiness had only gotten worse when he'd seen Kathy again. He didn't want to think about what it meant, didn't want to dissect it. He just wanted to enjoy it while it lasted.

Stacy and Doug were looking at him as if he'd lost his mind, but Kathy was giving him the most beautiful, most brilliant smile he thought he'd ever seen in his entire life.

"We'd love for you to join us," she said.

Trey held Katherine's hand while he drove home from the mall.

The children were in the back seat of the sedan, belted in. They couldn't possibly see either of their hands from where they were sitting. They couldn't know that Trey was drawing maddening circles on the palm of her hand with his thumb.

Doug and Stacy also had been unaware that Trey had pulled her away from them and kissed her nearly senseless three different times while they were in the mall. He'd taken her to the back of a store on the pretense of showing her something he wanted to buy one of the kids for Christmas, and had pulled her behind a rack of clothing or a display rack of toys and kissed her. Briefly, but very, *very* powerfully. Each short kiss had been loaded with meaning. Each embrace was jam-packed with passion.

And whenever possible over the past few hours, he'd touched her. He'd touched her arm to get her attention, to point something out. He'd brushed against her. He'd draped his arm over the back of her chair in the food court. And now he held her hand.

Katherine was positively giddy. She'd never in her life been so completely in love like this.

She squeezed his fingers slightly as he pulled into their driveway. And, as she'd hoped, he was properly distracted and didn't notice her bodyguard's blue car as it continued down the street.

She knew she should tell him why she was being followed, what she really was, and why she was there in Albuquerque.

But Katherine liked knowing without a doubt that Trey wanted her for who she was, not *what* she was. She loved being just a woman in his eyes, being Kathy Wind. She had the entire rest of her life to be Princess Katherine. She could wait a little bit longer to tell him the truth.

Kathy Wind had no self-doubts. She was bold and brave and outspoken. She was interesting, colorful, passionate. She could learn new things, like how to skateboard. She wouldn't balk at windsurfing or skydiving—

Well, maybe skydiving wasn't in her future. But still.

Kathy Wind looked good in blue jeans. And she looked good naked, too. She didn't mind being naked. In fact, when

Trey looked at her the way he had last night, she'd *loved* being naked.

No, Katherine didn't want to stop being Kathy Wind. Not yet. Not until she absolutely had to.

Trey released her hand as he pulled into the garage. He glanced at her in the dim light, his eyes sparking. "I have to kiss you again," he mouthed silently. "Or I'm gonna die."

Katherine nodded at him. She knew. She felt exactly the same way. Dear Lord, this was powerful, the love she felt for this man. And it *was* love, God help her.

She was hopelessly, head over heels in love with Trey Sutherland.

She got out of the car. "The door's locked and it won't open without your father's key, Douglas, no matter how hard you try to turn the knob. Let's get jackets hung up in the mudroom, and then bring your shopping bags right upstairs. Oh, and Stacy and Doug, I have some business to discuss with your father. I think now might be a good time to do that." She turned briskly to Trey. "How about I meet you in your office in about fifteen minutes?"

The smile he gave her was pure sin.

Kathy made it up to his office in less than ten minutes. But polite as always, she knocked instead of just letting herself in.

Trey opened his office door. "We've got to tell Stacy and Doug."

"Tell them what?"

Dear God. Trey nearly jumped back in surprise. It wasn't Kathy, it was his *mother* standing there.

Penelope Sutherland breezed past him, into his office, followed closely by Diana St. Vincent.

Diana touched his face as she went past. "Darling," she murmured, chastisingly. "Why haven't you called me?"

Um.

"Mother. To...what do I owe this surprise attack?"

"Aren't you amusing today?" She didn't sound the least little bit amused as she sat down across from his desk.

His desk.

It gleamed enticingly as his mother moved her chair closer to it, as she opened her briefcase and took out some papers and placed them on its top.

And Trey began to sweat.

That desk had been the location of the best sexual experience of his life. He couldn't look at it without thinking of Kathy, without thinking about what they'd done, right there. It didn't take much to remember her leaning back, naked, inviting him to bury himself inside her with both her smile and her position.

"Maybe we should sit over here on the sofa," he suggested. "It's a little more comfortable."

Comfortable. Oh, God. He started to laugh.

His mother glanced up at him as if he'd gone stark raving Looney Tunes. Maybe he had.

"This is fine," she said. "I can spread out over here."

Diana perched on the edge of the desk and he wanted to tell her to get off. The only woman who could ever sit on his desk from this moment on was Kathy Wind. But he kept his mouth tightly shut.

"We're here to talk you into hosting the Children's Camp charity Valentine's Day Ball," Diana told him.

Kathy knocked on the door. It had to be Kathy. Well, actually, it didn't. It could be someone else he absolutely wasn't expecting. Bill Lewis, for instance. Why not?

He started for the door, but then stopped. What if it *was* Kathy, and he opened it and she grabbed him and kissed him, the way he was dying to grab her and kiss her? If they were going to go public with their affair, he wanted Stacy and Doug to hear about it first. Not his mother. Not Diana St. Vincent.

"Come on in," he called out. "Join the party."

The door opened, and Kathy peeked in, clearly aware that his words had been a warning. She looked at him, looked at his mother and Diana and stopped short. "Oh," she said. "I'm sorry. I didn't realize you were...busy."

Oh, God, if his mother hadn't come by, he could be kissing Kathy. Right now. She would have been in his arms, and he could have taken his time and—

She was looking at him as hungrily as he was eyeing her, and he turned away, afraid his mother would notice. She was very perceptive, particularly since she already suspected his relationship with Doug and Stacy's nanny was more than boss and employee. It wouldn't take much more than a few longing looks for them to completely give themselves away.

"Mom and Diana came over to coerce me into spending a lot of money," Trey told Kathy briskly, trying to sound like a man who wasn't having a torrid affair with his kids' caregiver. He turned to his mother. "Yes," he said. "I'll do it. You know I'll do it. So let's skip the part where you spend the next forty-five minutes convincing me it's worth my while. You can go home and I'll—" he looked at Kathy, trying his damnedest not to eat her alive with his eyes "—I'll do something far more valuable with my time."

"I'll come back later," Kathy told him. "Perhaps in an hour...?"

In an hour he'd be dead from wanting to kiss her. "Twenty minutes."

"Don't you let her leave," Penelope commanded. "Trey, it's been weeks and you haven't yet introduced me to your new nanny. Come over here, young lady. I assume you *are* the new nanny?"

Kathy came a little bit farther into the room. "Yes, ma'am."

Trey made the introductions. "Kathy Wind, my mother, Penelope Sutherland, and her friend, Diana St. Vincent." Her friend, not his.

Kathy smiled at him. She'd understood what he was telling her.

"Come over here, girl," Penelope said. "Don't be shy."

"I'm not," Kathy said. "But I'm making dinner tonight and I'd only intended to stop in briefly to—"

"Oh, yes." Penelope inspected Kathy. "You were at the awards ceremony for Bill Lewis." She looked at Trey. "You haven't heard from Bill yet, have you?"

"Yeah," he said. "Actually, I have."

"You *have?*" Kathy coughed. "I mean, really, have you?"

"He called to check in," Trey reported, "to let me know he's alive."

"Where is he? Where has he been?" Kathy cleared her throat. "I mean, did he tell you…?"

"He wasn't specific," Trey said. "He *did* say he wasn't planning to be back in New Mexico until after the New Year."

"Completely irresponsible," his mother sniffed.

"I think he's in love," Trey said. Bill had sounded almost giddy, almost dizzy, almost… Wait. Almost the way Trey was feeling. Was it possible…? No way. Trey wasn't in *love.* He pushed the thought away. This was definitely *not* the time to be psychoanalyzing himself, with his mother looking on.

"If Bill were in love, he wouldn't plan to come home in mid-January," his mother pointed out. "Love's just not that tidy."

Love could, too, be tidy. What Trey had had with Helena had been remarkably tidy—for want of a better word.

His mother turned to Kathy. "I was at the awards ceremony, too, you know, but Trey whisked you away before we had the chance to meet."

"I'm sorry," Kathy said so politely. She was remarkably good at sounding respectful. "My fault entirely. The children had school the next day, and I didn't want to stay out very late. Now, if you'll excuse me? It was a pleasure meeting you, but—"

"You look so familiar to me." Penelope wouldn't let her go. "Have we met somewhere before? In New York perhaps?"

Kathy shook her head. "No, I don't think so."

"It's possible she's worked for someone you know," Diana suggested, careful to stress the word *worked*.

As Trey watched, Kathy looked at Diana sitting there on the edge of his desk, looked at the papers spread out there, looked at his desk. And as he watched, Kathy became completely aware of how difficult this meeting had to be for him.

She looked up at him, her eyes dancing with amusement, her smile holding a beautiful echo of last night's steam heat.

He smiled back at her, wanting her with every fiber of his being. The night could not come quickly enough.

"I'm having a small get-together tomorrow afternoon," Penelope interrupted them. "Just a casual, impromptu thing. A buffet dinner. I was hoping you'd bring Anastacia and Douglas, Trey. And Kathy, too, of course, to keep an eye on them."

Trey shook his head. "I'm not sure if we can—"

"I haven't seen the children in *such* a long time." His mother looked at Kathy. "If Trey's too busy, won't you bring them over?"

"Of course." Kathy was a complete pushover. "It sounds lovely."

"Five o'clock."

Trey sighed. "We'll be there." No way was he letting Kathy venture unescorted into the dragon's lair.

Kathy turned to him. "May I speak to you briefly in the hall?" she asked, her eyes dropping to his mouth for just a fraction of a second, just long enough to let him know the topic of their "conversation."

He couldn't look at her without giving himself away. Somehow he managed to nod. "Sure." Somehow he managed to turn to his mother and Diana. "Excuse me for a minute." Excuse me for four hours....

Trey followed Kathy into the hall, closed the door behind him and then, God, she was in his arms, and he was kissing her, touching her, filling his hands with the softness of her breasts, pressing her hips tightly to his. He nearly wept, it felt so deliriously good.

She pulled away from him much too soon.

"Eleven thirty-one." She smiled. "You might want to fill that Jacuzzi I spotted in your bathroom."

Oh, *yeah*.

She started hurrying away, but he stopped her. "Kathy."

She turned back.

"What *is* this?" he had to ask. "Have you ever in your life...?"

She shook her head. "No. Nothing like this. Not ever."

"It's crazy. It's..."

"Wonderful?" she finished for him.

"Yes," he said. "It's beyond wonderful. It's..." *Scaring me to death.*

"See you at dinner," she said softly. "Don't forget the Jacuzzi."

Yeah, like he was going to forget *that*.

And with that she was gone.

Trey took a deep breath and went back into his office, mentally preparing himself to spend the next hour talking to his mother...across the gleaming surface of his desk.

Chapter 16

"How's Elizabeth?" Katherine asked her sister.

"Still not talking," Serena said. "She and Laura have left for Arizona, to take a look at The Sunshine Home's files. I'm not sure what they're hoping to find."

"Bill Lewis called and spoke to Trey," Katherine reported, "but he's still out of touch and unlikely to return here until January. Trey said he suspects his partner is in love."

"Which brings us back to the elusive Betty Jo, who, according to my sleuthing skills—which consisted of my cleverly calling the operator and requesting her address—resides in Las Vegas. I've called her about seven thousand times, but she's never home."

"You've got to go there," Katherine decided. "To Las Vegas. If she's off somewhere with Bill Lewis, someone—a neighbor, maybe—might know where she's gone."

"And the reason *you* can't go to Las Vegas is…?"

"I can't leave Albuquerque now," Katherine admitted. "Serena, I'm…" She was what? In completely over her head?

Undoubtedly. "I promised I'd stay until January. Trey thinks I'm a nanny and..."

"You know, I read that his wife died of extremely mysterious circumstances," Serena said.

"As a matter of fact, she didn't," Katherine all but snapped.

"My, my," Serena said, laughing. "Such certainty. What has he been doing to convince you so thoroughly?"

"Go to Las Vegas, Serena," she told her sister. "Please?"

At 11:25, Katherine went to check on Doug.

He was so soundly asleep, he didn't even stir as she pulled his blankets farther up and tucked him in. Poindexter lifted his head and wagged his tail from the spot he'd claimed next to the boy's bed. She patted him then went on to Stacy's room.

A quick listen at the girl's tightly closed door, and she'd be on her way to the tower and Trey. It was funny, really. She now knew that Bill Lewis wasn't going to show up here in Albuquerque any time soon, and although, for her parents' sake, she wished she and her sisters would find him soon, she had to admit she was torn. Finding Bill Lewis seemed so secondary to what she'd already found with Trey. In just a short time, she'd be in his arms again and...

She held her breath, leaning closer to Stacy's door, listening harder.

Stacy was crying.

Again.

Oh, dear.

Katherine knocked on the door, but this time the crying didn't stop. She knocked again, louder.

"Kathy?" Stacy's voice was quavery—and she didn't even bother to hide it.

Katherine opened the door and peeked in. "It's me," she said. "Are you all right?"

"I had a *terrible* nightmare," Stacy said in a very shaky

voice. "I purposely went to bed a little early, and I think I must've fallen right asleep, but then I had this *awful* dream."

Katherine went into the room. The light from the hallway was bright enough to illuminate Stacy, who looked very small and very young—like a real thirteen-year-old—in the middle of her big bed.

"I hate that." Katherine crossed to sit on the edge, next to the girl. "It's as if your subconscious sabotages your plan to get a good night's sleep. It happens to me sometimes, too."

She held out her hand, and to her surprise, Stacy clung to it almost desperately.

"My nightmare was about you," Stacy told her, tears welling in her eyes. "I dreamed I got an A plus on my math test, and I went into your room to tell you, but you were…"

She started to cry in earnest and Katherine drew the girl into her arms. Stacy didn't try to pull away. In fact, she clung tightly.

"You were dead," Stacy sobbed.

Oh, dear. "Shhh." Katherine stroked her hair. "I'm not dead. I'm fine and I'm here."

January was coming more quickly than Katherine herself would have imagined possible. And although Stacy might not have been consciously aware of the countdown to the day Katherine was due to leave, subconsciously she knew it was coming.

Stacy lifted her head. "I found you lying on the bathroom floor. At first I thought it was just that same old nightmare I always have, but when I looked, it was *you* lying there, not Mommy. And I tried and tried to make you start breathing again, but I couldn't do it right and no one would come and help me!"

Same old nightmare…*Mommy*…

"And I realized that I was ten again, and I hadn't taken any first-aid classes, and your head was bleeding and there was nothing I could do, *nothing!* It was happening all over again!"

Same old nightmare, happening all over again…

"Shhh." Katherine rocked the sobbing girl gently. "It's all right, it was only a dream," she said soothingly, even as her mind was racing. Maybe it wasn't Stacy's subconscious sending her a message about Katherine's impending departure. Maybe it was more than that. Had Stacy seen something awful the night her mother had died, back when she was ten?

Helena, perhaps—lying on the bathroom floor with her head bleeding, having stopped breathing.

Dear God.

Cancer, Trey had told her. And yet there had been something in his eyes, some flicker that had made her think he was leaving some of the details out. She'd thought that change in his eyes had been because the truth was too hard to deal with. She hadn't imagined that truth might include Helena dying while bleeding on her bathroom floor.

No, that was absurd.

She'd had a feeling there was more to Helena's death than Trey had told her, but this was a little extreme.

Still, Stacy's words had been chilling. Happening all over again...

Impossible. Trey Sutherland had *not* killed his wife. The man who was her lover was completely incapable of killing anyone. Or was he? He was so fiercely passionate, so wildly intense. Katherine knew that firsthand, after making love to him all night long. He'd liked it when she'd urged him to be a little wild with her. Theirs had been no slow, reverent joining, that was for certain. Each time they'd made love had been an explosion of desire, a violent, raging storm of passion.

If he'd been as passionate with Helena, mightn't it be possible some kind of awful accident had happened?

No. Katherine refused to believe it. Trey wasn't the type of man who wouldn't have faced up to killing another human being, accidentally or otherwise. And it wouldn't have happened any way but accidentally. She believed that much about him, absolutely.

Still, Stacy's nightmare warranted a certain amount of discussion with Trey. Katherine would have to tell him about his daughter's dream. Ask him about it outright, inquire as to what it could mean. He would tell her the truth, and that would be that. There was no need to turn this into some lurking gothic mystery.

Likely as not, it would turn out she was making somewhat wild assumptions based purely on a thirteen-year-old's vivid imagination.

Except, how did one go about posing that sort of question? *I know you didn't kill your wife, but…is it possible Stacy saw her lying, bleeding on the floor?* No matter how she said it, it would come out as, *I know you didn't kill your wife, but did you kill your wife?*

Stacy's breathing was still ragged, but her eyes were closed. She roused slightly as Katherine tucked her back into her bed. "Sit with me for a while, Kathy?" she murmured sleepily. "Don't leave me yet. Please?"

Katherine brushed back the girl's hair. "I'll be right here." Her meeting with Trey would have to wait.

Eleven-fifty.

Kathy was late.

Trey checked the candles in the bathroom, checked his reflection in the mirror, bumped the thermostat up another few degrees, checked the temperature of the water in the Jacuzzi and then tried not to pace.

Eleven-fifty-two.

Watching the clock wasn't going to help, but he'd been watching the clock all day. Why stop now?

Eleven-fifty-three took forever to come. Where *was* she?

Of all his skills, patience was low on his personal list.

Trey opened the door to his bedroom and looked down the tower stairs. The hallway below was dim and silent. He went back inside and tried not to pace again. Still 11:53. He'd give her another five minutes, and then he'd go looking for her.

But what if she'd changed her mind?

Trey rejected that thought immediately. There was no way Kathy was going to change her mind. Not after the way she'd kissed him in the kitchen while they were cleaning up after dinner. Not after the way she'd smiled at him and touched his foot under the table as they'd both played a game of Monopoly with Dougie in the playroom earlier this evening.

Of course, there was always the possibility that sanity had set in. It was possible Kathy had come to her senses and realized that this craziness she and Trey shared wasn't bringing her any closer to her goal of marriage and family. It was possible—

Eleven-fifty-five.

To hell with the five minutes. He'd had enough of waiting.

He blew out the candles in the bathroom and started down the tower stairs.

And found Kathy. On the sofa at the foot of the stairs, outside his office door. Just sitting.

She stood when she saw him.

"How long have you been sitting there?" *Why* was she sitting there?

She looked tired. Her face was pale and there were shadows beneath her eyes. He'd kept her from sleeping last night, and now he was going to keep her from sleeping all over again.

She made a vague gesture. "Just a few seconds, really. Stacy had a nightmare, and I had to stay with her for a while and…"

Trey had to force the words out of his throat. "If you want, we don't have to…" God, he wanted her so much, he couldn't believe he was saying this. "If you're too tired, we can—"

"Would you mind putting your arms around me?" she asked in a very small voice.

She must have known he'd never deny her a request like that, because she moved toward him as he reached for her. He tried to hold her gently, tried not to let it be about sex. If she needed to go back to her room to get some real sleep tonight, then so be it. He'd just have to deal with it. He certainly didn't want her feeling pressured by him in any way.

She was so soft in his arms. And so small. She'd made love

as if they were physical equals, but in truth, she was tiny and so very fragile compared to him.

"I was sitting there," she whispered, her cheek resting directly over his heart, "trying to figure out a way to ask you a difficult question without making it sound as if I were accusing you in any way."

"Accusing me? Of what?" But as soon as Trey said the words, he knew. This was about Helena. God, he'd forgotten about the rumors and innuendo. He'd assumed Kathy had dismissed them, that she put no weight in them. Apparently he'd been wrong. He felt himself go very, very still.

And Kathy felt it, too. She pulled away from him. "Please, may we go upstairs to talk?"

His arms felt cold without her enfolded within them. And the stillness was replaced by a surge of anger and frustration. "Are you sure you want to come up there with me? You never know, I just might kill you, too."

She drew herself to her full height, and her gray eyes were almost stern—Mary Poppins at her toughest. "Don't be foolish," she reprimanded him. "I don't believe for one second that you killed Helena. It's obvious that you loved her very much." Her voice broke slightly and she sat back down on the sofa, rubbing her forehead as if she had an awful headache. "I'm actually jealous of her, can you believe it?" She looked up at him, and the whirl of emotion in her eyes took his breath away. "I'm jealous of a woman who's dead. How pathetic is that?"

She loved him. Kathy loved him. She didn't have to say the words aloud. He knew.

And his anger was replaced by sheer, screaming terror and crazy exhilaration. She *loved* him. Somehow his heart wedged tightly in his throat as he gazed down at her and even though her question was rhetorical, he couldn't have answered it if he'd had to.

But he could kiss her. Could and did.

He knew he shouldn't. He knew that doing so gave her false hope, made her think he might someday love her, too.

But he sat down beside her anyway, pulled her into his arms and kissed her softly, sweetly. The way a woman deserved to be kissed when she'd revealed the fragile contents of her heart. He kissed her tenderly, hoping that she'd know from his kiss how much her honesty meant to him. How honored he was that she'd entrusted him with her deepest secret.

And he knew she deserved to know his secrets as well. And maybe then she'd understand why he couldn't risk giving her his heart.

"Come upstairs," he whispered, kissing her chin, her throat, her ear. "We can talk."

She sighed as he kissed her again, moving his hand so it covered her breast. "Would you mind very much if we waited to talk for about an hour?"

Oh, God. Four minutes ago, he'd wanted nothing more than to make love to her again. As soon as possible. But now he knew that she loved him, and that to her, *making love* was not just a euphemism for sex.

But what was he supposed to do? Now that he knew that she loved him, was he just supposed to never touch her again, for fear of hurting her?

She opened her eyes and looked up at him, her hand on the inside of his thigh. She had such beautiful eyes. "Perhaps if I said *please?*"

Her hand moved higher, and he laughed at himself. Yeah, like hell he'd ever be strong enough to resist this woman. It probably wasn't the right thing to make love to her knowing it would mean so much more to her, but there was no way he'd be able to keep away from her. No way. Especially not when she was touching him like that.

His voice was raspy and he had to clear his throat. "Please will get you just about anything you want."

She pulled free from him, taking him by the hand and tugging him toward the stairs. "Please…?"

She didn't have to drag him. And she didn't have to ask him twice. He followed her up and into his bedroom, locking the door behind them before he kissed her again. Slowly. Sweetly.

She trembled as he unbuttoned her shirt and slipped it off her shoulders. She sighed as he deepened his kiss, still keeping it slow. Deliberate. Languorous.

How could something so wrong be so completely right? Trey gave up trying to analyze it. He refused to feel bad about it. There would be plenty of time to feel bad later. Now was only about feeling good.

And everything about this felt good. Very, very, *very* good.

Last night he didn't believe it was possible he could make love to Kathy without losing control. Every time they so much as touched, he'd exploded with near frantic passion. But tonight, he knew he'd been wrong. Tonight, he was going to love her slowly. Tonight, he was going to savour every shiver, every sigh.

He picked her up and carried her to his bed.

When she tried to help him take off her jeans, he gently pushed her hands away. This was his show. He only moved quickly to rid himself of his own clothes and then he lay down beside her, taking his sweet time as he touched the perfect smoothness of her skin. He touched her everywhere, and he knew that making love to her slowly this way was as much for him as it was for her. She was so deliciously beautiful, and she belonged to him.

Completely.

The thought didn't scare him quite so much with her legs looped around him, with her breast filling his hand, her fingers in his hair. He followed his hands with his mouth, kissing his way down her body, tasting her, breathing in her sweetness.

He covered himself and entered her tantalizingly slowly, and she opened her eyes and smiled.

Trey felt electrified as he held her gaze, as if a circuit had been completed. She pulled him down to kiss him, moving with him, still so exquisitely slowly. And when she finally shattered around him, he followed in slow motion. Fireworks ignited behind his eyelids, colors exploding, spinning him completely and totally into outer space, well beyond all previously charted territory.

And he knew he'd been wrong. When he was with Kathy, he was never quite in control.

Katherine listened to the steady rhythm of Trey's heart.

It would be so easy just to drift off to sleep. To ignore the rest of the world, the realities of the past. To simply sink into the intense pleasure of here and now.

The here and now in which she had just made the most beautiful love to Helena Sutherland's husband.

Reality forced her eyes open and she sighed.

It shouldn't really matter how Helena had died, but it did. Until they talked about it, the uncertainty would be here, lying between them, almost as if Helena herself were in this bed.

Trey shifted beneath her, loosening his grip around her, as if anticipating her need to pull free. He sighed, too, as if he knew what she was thinking, knew this quiet moment had come to an end. And then he spoke, his voice soft in the dim light.

"Helena was diagnosed much too late for treatment," he said, almost as if he were starting in the middle of the story. "I can remember sitting in the doctor's office and listening to him say *terminal*. I heard the word, but it seemed impossible. She looked a little tired and she'd recently lost some weight, but... He initially gave her two months, if that."

Katherine closed her eyes, imagining how hard that must have been for Trey to sit there and be told that the person he loved was going to be taken from him. His heart was still beating beneath her ear, steady and strong. But she knew it was a heart that had surely been damaged, perhaps to the point of no repair.

"She wasn't very strong," he told her tightly. "She'd never been very strong. She was one of those people who quit smoking about twelve different times in a single five-year period. She was in a lot of pain toward the end, and it was very hard for her."

Katherine wanted to touch his face, but his eyes were so distant—he was back three years in the past. He *was* Helena's husband again, and it didn't seem right to touch him any more than she already was. "It must have been hard for you and the children, as well," she murmured.

His arms tightened around her. "She asked me to help her die."

Katherine pulled back to look at him head-on, searching his eyes. "Oh God, Trey!"

"Damn it, it still makes me so *angry*. And guilty, and…" His eyes were anguished. "I think, how could she have asked that of me? And then I think how could she *not* have asked? I was her husband. She knew that I loved her. God, if she knew anything at all, it was that."

"Did you…?"

He shook his head. "I didn't. I couldn't. The one time she actually asked something of me, and I couldn't deliver. So she ended up asking Mae—our nanny—to tell the pharmacist that she'd dropped her bottle of pain medication in the toilet. Mae got the prescription refilled, and Helena did it herself. She took all the pills she had at once. And she ended up dying alone. On the bathroom floor."

"Oh, Trey, I'm so sorry."

He held her gaze as if it were a lifeline. "I just couldn't do it for her, Kathy. I knew she was dying, but all I could think was that she'd already lived nearly a month longer than the doctor had thought. Maybe the cancer would stop growing, and she'd live another month or two or— God, if it were me, I would've never stopped fighting. I just…I couldn't help her quit."

There were tears in his eyes, but he blinked them back.

"But it was her choice," he continued softly. "And I feel so guilty, and so angry at myself, too, for not being there when she needed me—for not being strong enough."

"But if you'd helped her," Katherine pointed out gently, "you'd feel guilty about that, as well. Trey, there was no wrong or right in that situation."

He laughed, but it had nothing to do with humor. "Yeah, it was a real lose-lose scenario, wasn't it? And I'm the biggest loser of all."

"You had to go with your own beliefs." Katherine sat up, determined to make him listen. "Helena believed it was time to die. You believe it's never time to die. In order to help her, you would have had to compromise something you believe in absolutely. And if you *had* helped her, you would have had to live the rest of your life wondering *what if*. What if you helped her and two days later someone found a miracle cure?"

"They didn't." Trey put his arm up, over his eyes. "It's been three years and—"

"But you didn't know that at the time. And those months and years would have been hell because even if you had helped her, you wouldn't have stopped believing she was giving up too soon."

He was silent, and she knew he was listening to her.

"But you've got to try to see it from Helena's side, too," Katherine continued. "She was in pain. You have no idea, really, what that had to have been like for her. And she wasn't strong, you say. She wasn't a fighter. So her choice was to give up, to die. Even without your help. Trey, you've got to forgive her for that. You've got to forgive her for asking you to do the impossible, and you've got to forgive yourself for being stronger than she was."

He managed a crooked smile. "Easier said than done."

"Why do you let those rumors continue?" she asked him gently. "There are people in town who honestly believe Helena was murdered—and that you're the murderer."

"She killed herself, Kath," he said. "Suicide. It's such an ugly word. I didn't care—she was gone, and I didn't care about much else at the time. But her parents didn't want the news getting out. They didn't want her name connected to that word—suicide. So we just never released any kind of statement about cause of death."

He sighed, rubbing his eyes with his hands. "But it got

complicated. She must've hit her head on the vanity in the bathroom when she collapsed. There was a lot of blood, and the ambulance and the police came. I had blood all over me because I…I tried to revive her. God, I did everything but walk into hell to get her back. But she was gone, and on the surface it looked as if it might've been foul play.

"I was a suspect for all of three hours, until the police chief was contacted at his vacation house. He was close friends with Helena's father, and he knew exactly what had happened, knew how sick she was, knew I didn't kill her." He looked up at her. "The autopsy report backed us both up—I can show it to you, if you want—and he was able to keep the results private. My mother had connections and she kept the story from running in the newspapers, but the local TV news had already reported that I'd been brought in for questioning. They did an interview with the ambulance driver who used words like *murder* and *suspect.* I think the rumors first started because of the way the story just disappeared. Helena was dead, I was a suspect, and then suddenly—nothing. People who remembered thought I'd somehow bought my way free."

"So now murder is associated with Helena's name—and your name—instead of suicide."

"I don't give a damn what people think—only what you think."

That was the kind of thing handsome men with neon-blue eyes only said to Katherine in her wildest dreams.

Dreams.

Oh, dear. "Trey, Stacy had a nightmare tonight, and… She was *there.* When Helena died. Stacy found her in the bathroom, probably before you even got there."

"What?"

As Katherine quickly reported all that his daughter had told her, Trey was clearly shaken. "Oh, *God.* I had no idea."

"She described it to me exactly. The bathroom floor, the blood. I think she even must have watched as you tried to revive her."

"I was…upset." He corrected himself. "I was beyond upset, but still I can't believe I missed seeing Stacy there.'' His eyes were a very sober shade of blue. "She doesn't think…" He tried again. "Does she think *I* was somehow responsible for…?"

"I don't know what she thinks. But I *do* know you've got to talk to her first thing in the morning," she said absolutely. "You've got to tell her the entire truth. She's old enough now to know."

Trey nodded. "I will. Absolutely." He smiled at her crookedly. "You know, I really love it when you talk to me in your nanny voice when you're naked."

Katherine laughed to cover her confusion. *I really love…* Her heart had leapt foolishly at those three words, thinking that the fourth would be *you. I really love you.*

"I don't know how I managed without you," he told her. "What can I do to convince you to stay?"

Katherine just shook her head. As much as she wanted to stay, she couldn't. Not without a really, really good excuse. And embracing a career as a full-time nanny would *not* be considered a good excuse.

The Royal Court in Wynborough awaited her. As Princess Katherine, she had duties and appearances and all manner of business to attend. She was already, no doubt, sorely missed.

As Katherine sat there, she almost told him who she was, why she was there, why she couldn't stay. But Trey pulled her toward him and kissed her, and she let herself be selfish. She would let herself be daring, sexy Kathy Wind who had captured the attention of Trey Sutherland just a little bit longer.

After all, come January, she had an entire lifetime ahead of her as the very lonely, very staid Princess Katherine.

Chapter 17

"Trey, have you seen Stacy?"

Kathy's voice made Trey look up from the English muffin he was cutting open for Dougie's breakfast. He slipped the two halves into the toaster and pushed the button down.

"You got it from here?" he asked his son, who nodded as he clicked together the ends of large wooden toaster tongs. "Great." He turned to Kathy, who was standing just inside the kitchen door. "Good morning."

He knew his smile was bordering on foolish grin territory, but he couldn't help himself. Just seeing her again made him want to break into song. And it had only been about two hours since she'd crept from his room.

God, he had it bad for her. He was even looking forward to the party at his mother's house later this afternoon—simply because Kathy was going to be there.

And she...

She was frowning slightly, her gray eyes filled with concern.

He stopped grinning at her. "What's up? No, I haven't seen Stacy yet this morning."

"Doug, have you?" Kathy asked.

"Nope."

"Trey, may I please talk to you out in the hallway?"

"You in control of that toaster?" Trey asked Doug again.

"I *said* yes. Jeez."

It still felt so good to hear Doug talk, he didn't even mind indignation from the kid—as long as it was expressed in English rather than barks and woofs.

Trey followed Kathy into the hall. "Problem?"

"I think maybe yes," she said. "I was on the phone and the call waiting beeped. It was the dispatcher from Western Limousine. She was calling about a piece of personal luggage that was found in one of their cars after a seven a.m. pickup of a passenger from this address."

"*What?*"

"Trey, I think Stacy's run away. The dispatcher told me the young woman who was picked up from the Sutherland estate was taken to the *airport*."

Katherine couldn't figure it out. Los Angeles. *Why* would Stacy just leave the house without telling anyone and try to hop a flight to L.A.?

Trey had leapt into action immediately, calling the airport, calling the police, calling Anita to rush over and stay with Doug.

Within seconds, Anita was on her way.

Within minutes, Trey and Katherine were hurrying to the airport.

And before they'd even reached the airport turnoff, Trey's cell phone had rung. Sure enough, Airport security had found Stacy. Waiting to board a nine o'clock American Airlines flight to Los Angeles.

Katherine had never seen Trey so upset. He was furious and frighteningly grim.

And as they approached the airline office where Stacy was

being held, she stopped him. "If you go in there like this, she's just going to get defensive, and it'll be days before we get an explanation from her."

"What am I supposed to do? Think of something nice to say to her when I first see her? 'Good choice of airlines, kid. Way to get those frequent flyer miles?'"

Katherine laughed. She couldn't help herself. And to her relief, Trey managed a crooked smile.

He pulled her into his arms, holding her tightly. "Thank you for being here with me. I'm so not cut out to be a father."

"You can't mean that." Katherine looked up at him. "You're one of the best fathers I've ever known."

"My thirteen-year-old just tried to split for California. Don't hand me the Father of the Year Award yet." He let all the air out of his lungs in a loud exhale. "I thought we were doing all right. I thought we'd gotten past the worst of it, and…" His voice broke. "Why would she do this? I just don't get it."

"*That's* what you've got to walk in there and say."

"I don't understand."

Trey sat across a cheap plastic table from Stacy. His daughter hadn't done a whole hell of a lot more than stare at the floor since he and Kathy had come in.

She still didn't look up. "Can we just go home?"

"No. Not until you tell me why you were going to L.A."

"What does it matter?"

Trey worked to keep his voice even. "If you don't tell me, then how can I decide whether or not I'm going to let you go?"

Stacy nearly fell out of her chair as she finally looked up at him. "What?"

"I assume you've got a reason for wanting to go there, and unless I know that reason, I can't possibly let you go. But if it's a really good reason…" He shrugged.

"There's no way you'd ever let me go!"

"Yeah, you're right," Trey said. "But I got your attention, didn't I? Do you know why I'd never let you go?"

"Because I'm too young?"

"And…?"

She stared at him.

"Because you're too young *and*…" he repeated. "There's a second part to that. It's the most important part. Because you're too young and because I love you."

Tears sprang into her eyes and she quickly looked away. "I know that," she said in a very, very small voice.

God, could this be any harder? Trey felt Kathy standing behind him, felt her hand as she touched him lightly, briefly on the shoulder. Please Lord, infuse him with some of her gentle patience. Lord knows he needed it right now, badly.

He took a deep breath. "If you know that," he said, managing to sound remarkably calm, "how could you even think of packing your things and…" his voice broke "—leaving me and Dougie this way?" He no longer sounded calm. He sounded exactly like what he was—a frightened, frustrated man who was working his butt off to keep from bursting into tears.

But it was Stacy who started to cry—tough, angry Stacy who dissolved into a puddle of emotions.

"I'm sorry," she sobbed. "Daddy, Kathy, I'm so sorry. I didn't know what else to do!"

Trey moved around the table and she actually reached for him. He held her from one side, and Kathy held her from the other as she cried.

"I thought this would be a good time to leave," Stacy said, gasping for breath, crying just the way she'd cried when she had been only four years old, "because Doggie loves Kathy so much. I thought if I were gone, then Kathy would *have* to stay, because she wouldn't want to leave Doggie alone. She wouldn't want to leave you alone, either." She looked up at Trey, tears spilling from her eyes and down her cheeks. "I know you love her, too, even though you won't admit it. You're so happy when she's around."

Trey looked up and directly into Kathy's gray eyes. She quickly looked away. "But, Stace, I still don't understand. Were you leaving to try to make Kathy stay?"

"No." She wiped at her eyes and her running nose. As if by magic, Kathy produced a tissue from her purse. "Thanks." She blew her nose. "I was leaving because—" her face crumpled again with fresh tears "—because I have what Mommy had."

Trey was floored. Did she honestly think she had... "Cancer?"

The look Stacy gave him was pure exasperation. Combined with her tears, it was almost funny. Almost. "I know that she didn't *really* have cancer. I know that was just the story you told us after she died."

"Stacy, what—"

"Daddy, I know what happened," Stacy said fiercely. "I read about depression in a book, and the description about staying in bed all the time and being so tired and crying— It was *exactly* what Mommy had. I used to hear her crying. I never told you, but I used to sit outside her room and just listen to her cry. And I heard you after you found her in the bathroom. I was hiding under her bed, and I heard you shouting at her. You were so angry at her for killing herself. I *know* she killed herself."

Trey was stunned. "Oh, God, Stace—"

"The books I've read said that depression can be hereditary. I've got it, too. I know I do. I'm *so* unhappy all the time, and I'm afraid I'm going to do the same thing."

Fear made him numb and he gripped Stacy's face, searching her eyes. "Oh, Stace, do you really think about killing yourself?"

"No!" She was vehement. "No, I don't. *Never.* I don't want to do that. But the book said..." She started to cry again. "The book said people who have depression can just suddenly turn suicidal. That's why I was leaving. So you and Dougie wouldn't wake up some morning and find *me* on the bathroom floor."

Trey pulled his daughter close.

"Oh, sweetie," Kathy murmured. "Your mother really did die of cancer. She was in a lot of pain, *and* she had a tumor in her brain. We'll never know if that affected her judgment, or if it was just the pain that drove her to take those pills. Nobody made up a story about her having cancer. And if she was depressed, it was because she knew she was dying. I can't pretend to know all that she was thinking or feeling, but I do know without a doubt that she didn't truly want to leave you and Doug." She looked up into his eyes. "Or Trey." She smiled, a sweet, quavering smile. "How could she ever willingly leave you?"

Stacy had been wrong about so much, but she'd been completely right about one thing. He *was* happy when he was with Kathy. Here he was, emotionally eviscerated from all he'd just learned, skewered once again by Helena's untimely, unfair death, and yet he felt a sense of contentment, a sense of peace he doubted he'd ever felt before in his life.

Simply from looking into Kathy's eyes.

And the truth had hit him full in the face.

He was in love with her.

He had been so careful not to give away his heart, but he hadn't counted on her stealing it from him. But she had.

"Let's go home," he told the two women who made his life complete. He lifted his daughter's chin so he could look into her eyes. "I'll tell you all about your mother's illness. And we can find someone to talk to. A counselor. I don't think you're going to turn suicidal, kid, but that's not something ever to ignore. We'll find somebody who maybe knows a little bit more than those books you've read, and we'll deal with this, okay? I'm ready to do whatever it takes."

Stacy nodded, and Kathy gave him another perfect smile.

He'd deal with Stacy, and then he'd deal with Kathy, too.

He smiled into Kathy's eyes, definitely ready to do whatever it took.

"Hey," Trey said. "There you are."

Katherine looked up from the playroom floor, and the game

she was putting away. "Back so soon?" she asked. He'd spent the morning in his office, talking to Stacy. Around lunchtime, they'd both emerged, and Trey had left shortly afterward, saying he had several errands to run in town.

"I found what I was looking for right away," he told her. He glanced around the room almost nervously. "Where are the kids?"

It was funny, really. She'd seen him businesslike, seen him angry, seen him filled with passion, seen him smile that half sheepish, half embarrassed smile that made her heart swell, but she'd never really seen him nervous. Not like this. What was going on?

"Doug's in the shower, getting ready for the party at your mother's. Stacy's in her room, getting dressed, too. I told her I'd stay home with her, but she seems to want to go," she reported. She glanced up at him. "If you don't mind, I thought I'd beg off and stay home tonight."

"Oh, no," he said, crouching down on the floor next to her. "Knowing that you were going, too, was the only thing making this bearable. Please, I was counting on you being there."

She smiled at him. "Stacy and Doug will protect you from Diana St. Vincent just as well as I would have. Actually, I thought it would be good for you and the children to go out together as a family."

"But you're part of our family."

"No, Trey," she said gently, "I'm not."

"Maybe I should rephrase that. I want—*we* want—you to be part of our family." He was so serious, his eyes a very serious shade of blue. "Permanently."

Katherine turned back to the game, adjusting the pieces so that they all fit into the box. "Trey, please don't start with your outrageous salary offers again. I assure you, there's no amount high enough—"

"How about half of everything I own?"

What? She blinked. "I'm sorry…?"

That was when she realized he was holding something in his hands. Something small and black and...

A jeweler's ring box.

Trey opened it and held it out to her.

It was the most beautiful diamond she'd ever seen in her entire life. It sparkled and glimmered in a setting that was regal in its simplicity. She knew quite a bit about precious gems, and that stone had to be worth—

But it wasn't what the diamond was worth that made her breath catch in her throat. It was what it meant. And its simple message was there in Trey's eyes, as well.

And, just in case she hadn't yet caught on, he said the words, too. "Marry me."

Katherine laughed, clutching one hand to her throat, completely surprised. Never, ever, *ever* in her wildest, *craziest* dreams had she *ever* imagined Trey asking her to stay in quite this way.

"I won't even ask you to sign a prenup—because I know you don't want the money."

"Trey, I..." She didn't know what to say.

He took her hand, took the ring from the box and slid it onto her finger. It fit perfectly.

"We can get married right away," he said, as if it were already settled, already agreed upon. "Head someplace warm for a honeymoon." He kissed her. "Someplace where I can keep you naked most of the time."

His kiss was so delicious, his touch wonderful, and the ring... It looked as if it had been made specifically for her hand.

"Trey, I don't know."

It was his turn to be absolutely surprised. As if he hadn't doubted for one second that she would immediately and enthusiastically say yes.

But how could she say yes? He'd asked Kathy Wind to marry him, and she *wasn't* Kathy Wind.

But what if—*what if*—she were to tell him who she really was? And *what if* he didn't see the fact that she was Princess

Katherine of Wynborough as any kind of insurmountable obstacle?

What if?

Hope took flight as she stared at the man who ruled her heart. He wanted to *marry* her.

What would her father say? He himself had married non-royalty—a commoner and an American. But would he allow such a thing for one of his daughters? And if he *didn't* allow it, would she have the nerve to defy him?

For a lifetime with Trey? No question about it. She loved this man enough to give up everything, *every*thing.

She kissed him, unable to say in words all that she was feeling.

"How could you not know?" he whispered. He kissed her again, harder, longer this time. "I need you—so much that I sometimes feel as if I'm going to rip in half. But this isn't just about sex. When we're together, I'm so much better than I am when we're apart."

He didn't say he loved her. She tried not to care about that, but couldn't. She *did* care.

"Trey, I have to think about this," she told him. "I can't just say yes without really figuring this out. I never expected you to ask me to *marry* you."

"Yeah," he said. "I never really expected it, either, and then today it was just suddenly so obvious." He kissed her again. "Kathy, you make me so happy. Just seeing your smile…"

It wasn't "Kathy, I love you," but it was close enough.

She had to tell him who she was. And she had to do it now.

"Do you remember when you asked me how I had met Princess Alexandra?"

He nodded, clearly bemused. "I know she's a friend of yours, but I was thinking we should probably get married quietly. And any wedding that has a princess as a guest isn't going to be exactly quiet."

Oh, dear. "Well—" she began.

And the screaming started.

It came from Doug's room and got louder and louder and—

Dougie burst into the playroom, wearing only his underwear. "There's a killer bee in my room!"

Trey stood up and caught Doug around the waist, covering his mouth and cutting off the siren effect. "How could there be a bee in your room in the middle of winter?"

"I don't know," Doug continued at full decibel level. "He was in my closet! He tried to kill me when I opened the door!"

Katherine stood up.

"I'll take care of this," Trey said. "Go get ready for my mother's party. Please? We'll finish talking later." He gave her a long look. "You might as well say yes now. I'm one hell of a negotiator, and this is one negotiation I don't intend to lose."

"But, Trey, I really have to..."

He was already out the door.

Chapter 18

It had only been a moth.

Doug had pulled Trey away from what was quite possibly the most important conversation of Katherine's life, and his terrible man-eating bee had turned out to be only a very large moth.

Katherine stood at the edges of Penelope Sutherland's vast living room, feeling sadly out of place in a blue-patterned dress that she'd bought while shopping with Stacy at the mall. It was a little too casual, a little too feminine in an earthy kind of way. The softly flowing skirt went all the way to her ankles, and it had long sleeves, but the neckline was low, making her look even more generously proportioned on top than she in fact was.

It was the kind of dress one might see on a beautiful, solitary woman walking on a windswept beach.

"I love this dress," Trey whispered in her ear as he came up behind her. "I can't wait until later, when I can take it off you."

She laughed.

"You have a beautiful neck. Think anyone will notice if I kiss it?"

She turned to face him, afraid he just might do it. "Yes!"

His gaze was nearly scalding as he handed her a glass of champagne. "All you have to do is say yes one more time, and I'll make the announcement right here. And then it doesn't matter who notices if I kiss you. We can spend the rest of the evening necking in the corner and everyone will say, 'Oh, how romantic.'"

Katherine looked around. This was hardly the place to be telling him secrets, but this was the closest to alone they'd been since being interrupted in the playroom. "Trey, there's a reason I haven't just gone ahead and accepted your proposal."

"Please don't tell me you're already married."

"No!"

"Thank God." He edged closer so that she could feel his body heat, so that he brushed against her. "Look, dinner's not going to start for another hour. What do you say we pretend to mingle and then break away from this crowd. We can meet upstairs, lock ourselves into one of the bathrooms and—"

"I'd love to." There, in privacy, she'd be able to tell him the truth about who she truly was.

But it clearly wasn't the response Trey was expecting. "Really?" he said, then, "*Really?* I was kind of half teasing, but, if you really want to…" As he laughed, the look in his eyes nearly lit her dress on fire.

"Ten minutes," she said. "Upstairs."

Nine and a half minutes.

Trey tried not to stare at his watch, tried not to map out his route to the stairs as he went to the bar and freshened his drink.

It *was* amazing. He couldn't remember the last time he'd actually enjoyed one of his mother's parties. And he had a feeling that in…nine minutes and ten, nine, eight seconds this party was going to be off the charts as far as enjoyment went.

Trey didn't look at his watch, didn't look toward the stairs, but it was impossible not to stand there and watch Kathy. She stood across the room, her smile shining as she spoke to Wallace Tippins, the pastor of his mother's church. Pastor Tippins would probably be pleased to marry them and—

Kathy looked up and directly into his eyes, as if she could feel him watching her. She smiled. It was a very different smile than the one she'd been giving the pastor. It was a smile just for him. A smile loaded with shared secrets and deeply flowing love.

He smiled back at her, his heart in his throat.

He'd loved Helena. He loved Helena still and always would, but it wasn't like this. Because even though Helena had grown to care for him, she'd never truly loved him. Not the way Kathy loved him.

It had been so damned ironic. He knew his parents and Helena's parents had set them up, knew they wanted them to wed, had even bribed them outrageously. But it wasn't the money that had made Trey fall in love with Helena. He'd taken one look at her, spent one evening having dinner with her, and he'd fallen for her, hard. He'd thought she'd done the same, but she hadn't.

The money and the power she'd gain from their union had motivated her. It was true she never would have married him if he'd been boring or cruel, but who he was had been secondary in her decision. And after he knew that, he hadn't stopped loving her, but what he'd thought of as a storybook life had become imperfect and dissatisfying.

He'd honestly thought he would never find anyone that he would love as much as Helena. And he'd also been convinced that even if he *did,* he would never marry again for fear she, too, only saw him as some kind of high-society prize.

And then he'd met Kathy—who didn't care about money to the point of turning down the highest salary offer to any nanny anywhere on the planet. Kathy—who loved him with every cell in her body, who loved his children just as fiercely.

"If you keep looking at her like that, the entire world will know."

Trey's mother was standing beside him. He dragged his gaze away from Kathy, glanced as surreptitiously as possible at his watch. Seven minutes, four seconds, three, two…

"So." Penelope Sutherland took a sip of her wine as she gazed across the room at Kathy. "Are you going to do right by the girl and marry her?"

Trey couldn't believe his mother would approach the idea of his marrying the nanny quite so calmly. Still, maybe she could tell how happy he was just from looking. "I asked her this afternoon."

His mother nodded. "Good."

"Good?" He couldn't believe it. "What's wrong with this picture? I just tell you I want to marry the nanny, and you say good. Have I suddenly been transported into an alternative reality?"

Penelope started to laugh. "You are *too* funny. I know who she is. I *knew* she looked familiar. And if you think I'd object to your marrying Princess Katherine of Wynborough, then *you're* the one who's in an alternative reality."

"Princess *what?*" Trey was stunned. He looked up at Kathy, who had heard his outburst. His words had apparently cut across the crowd noise—or maybe guilty ears were capable of superhuman hearing. Because she *was* guilty. He saw it in her eyes as she looked at him. It was written all over her face.

"Katherine Wyndham, Royal Princess of Wynborough," his mother repeated. "Look at the way she stands, at the way she carries herself. I can't believe I actually thought she was a nanny."

Trey couldn't breathe.

Kathy—no, Princess Katherine's—face was pale as she wove her way through the crowd toward him. His mother was right. She moved regally. As if the crowd should part to let her pass. Why hadn't he noticed before?

"I like her," Penelope said, still chuckling. "She's clearly got initiative, posing as a nanny to catch a husband as eligible and wealthy—and as reclusive—as you."

The reality of his mother's words were like a sucker punch to his gut. Now not only couldn't he breathe, but he was in pain as well.

He'd been played.

Kathy had hinted to him that she was a player, but he'd had no idea the scope of the game she was playing. And she'd almost won. He'd almost married her.

But the pain ran deeper than mere embarrassment at nearly being conned. He was devastated. Straightforward, upfront, *honest* Kathy had told him nothing but lies.

He turned to his mother, keeping his voice cool and controlled. "I'm sorry to have to leave before dinner."

He turned to Kathy. "Get your coat. Get in the car. I'll get the kids."

"Trey—"

She was doing a remarkably good job of acting distraught.

But he didn't expect anything less than excellence from a princess.

Katherine had waited too long to tell the truth.

This was entirely her fault. She'd been dishonest, and she couldn't blame Trey one bit for wanting her out of his house.

She'd said goodbye to the children, telling them the truth about who she was and why, because of her deceitfulness, Trey wanted her to leave.

Doug had been inconsolable, and Stacy had been outraged. Her father frequently concealed his identity when they went on vacation. She didn't see the difference between that and what Katherine had done.

Katherine had tried to talk to Trey, tried to explain. About Bill Lewis, about her suspicion that he might be her missing brother. He'd listened, but he'd barely reacted. He'd just sat there, cold as stone, and after she'd done her best to apologize, he'd quietly told her to pack her things.

Now there was only one thing left to do before she got into the car that was waiting to take her to the airport.

She knocked timidly on Trey's office door. Yes, there was no doubt about it. Bold, daring Kathy Wind had vanished. She was timid, mousy, dull-as-dirt Katherine once again.

"Yes?" Trey's voice was sharp.

She pushed the door open just a little bit, peeking in.

"Ah," he said. "Your Highness. Come to collect your severance pay?"

She felt herself flush with indignation. "Trey," she said. "Please. Let's not end it this way."

"How would you like it to end, Princess? With a business merger between the country of Wynborough and Sutherland-Lewis? You in a veil? Me in tails? And a room full of well-dressed lawyers drafting up a plan to move Sutherland-Lewis—and its three thousand jobs—to Wynborough?"

His rudeness awakened the spirit of Kathy Wind. "You think you've got it all figured out, do you?" she retorted sharply. "Well, guess what, Mr. Know-It-All? You're wrong. I came here to find Bill Lewis in the hope that he was my brother. Believe what you want, but I didn't come here looking for a marriage proposal. It was the *last* thing I expected from you. I'm not even certain my father would *allow* me to marry you. From his point of view, if we *were* to wed, *you'd* be the one getting away with something—an American commoner marrying a Princess!"

"Well." Trey's voice was quiet, his eyes subdued. "Looks like we just uncovered another nasty truth."

"My *father's* truth," she told him, tears making her voice shake. "Not mine. I would have married you without a single thought to anything but how much I love you."

He crossed to the bar and began fixing himself another drink, his movements jerky. "You know, that's the problem with liars. You can just never be sure what's the truth and what's not. Close the door on your way out, will you?"

The last of Katherine's hope died.

He was right. She *was* a liar. And even if Trey could forgive her, she *wasn't* Kathy Wind.

She quietly set the ring box down on Trey's desk and closed his office door behind her.

Chapter 19

Katherine kept the shades down in her hotel room at the Albuquerque airport.

She was pathetic.

She'd been here for three days.

Hiding.

It had started when she'd arrived at the airport to find that the next available flight to Aspen didn't leave until the morning. So instead of going to Denver and taking commuter flights from there to Aspen, she'd checked into the hotel.

She didn't have the energy for anything but a direct flight. She didn't have the energy to do much besides curl up in the middle of that king-size bed and be pathetic.

She'd slept for nearly twenty hours, pathetically missing her flight.

She now sat up in bed, watching TV, unenthusiastically channel surfing. A home shopping network was trying to sell a diamond bracelet. A sports channel was showing car racing. The weather-loon was talking passionately about a storm approaching the Northeast United States on the Weather Channel, but even he couldn't hold her attention today. A movie channel was showing *Gone with the Wind.*

Frankly, Trey didn't give a damn. Katherine sniffled her way through a few scenes with Scarlett, then flipped to the local cable news. They were showing downtown Albuquerque, and she strained to see Trey's office building, only half listening to the report on local restaurants being given bad grades by the Board of Health.

The Board of Health would no doubt condemn her, as well. Her hair was a wreck, she hadn't showered in days. No doubt she looked as miserable as she felt.

And, sister, she felt *miserable.*

But everything she was feeling, every ounce of remorse and regret and spine-deep pain, was entirely her own damned fault.

Trey had called her a liar, and he was right.

She, Katherine Wyndham, one of the staunchest believers in truth and honesty, had made what she'd considered to be one little white lie, and it had cost her very, very dearly.

She had loved him.

She loved him still.

But if he'd felt anything for her at all, it had been for a woman she was only pretending to be.

She flipped to the next channel, but then sat up, quickly flipping back.

Stacy's picture was on the screen. She raised the volume. "...missing since yesterday," the news anchor reported. "The daughter of Trey Sutherland of Sutherland-Lewis was last seen on the grounds of the Wellford School, getting into a blue Toyota hatchback. Foul play is not suspected at this time, but the police are asking anyone who may have knowledge of the girl's whereabouts to call their runaway hotline."

Katherine nearly fell off the bed as she dove for the telephone. She muted the TV as she dialed. Her hands were shaking so much, she had to start over.

No way would Stacy run away from home. Not now. Not after the truth had finally come out about her mother's death.

"Come on, come on," she said as she listened to the telephone ring. "Pick up!"

"Laura Bishop." The Wyndham social secretary answered the phone.

"Laura, thank God!"

"Katherine, where have you been? I called you at the Sutherland estate and the woman there, Anita, said you'd left *days* ago!"

"I did," she said. "But I'm still here in Albuquerque. I can't explain right now. Laura, I need you to tell me something. Did Gabriel Morgan send one of his men out here to act as a bodyguard?"

"Bodyguard? No," Laura said. "You told me you didn't need anyone, that having someone assigned to you would interfere, so I made certain you were on your own."

"Nobody in a blue subcompact—a blue Toyota?"

"No one at all."

Katherine swore pungently in a most unprincessly manner. "What's going on?"

"Laura, I can't explain right now. Please forgive me for hanging up on you." Katherine cut the connection and quickly dialed the front desk. "I need a taxi and I need it now," she ordered.

She opened her suitcase and pulled out her jeans and a clean turtleneck sweater. She dressed quickly, yanked her hair back into a ponytail, and stuffed her feet into her sneakers.

Kathy Wind looked back at her from the mirror, strong and capable.

She grabbed her purse and ran for the elevators.

"This is about you, Your Highness," Trey said tightly to Kathy. "Stacy ran away because she was angry that you left."

He was mad as hell.

He was mad at Stacy for running off again, mad at Kathy for showing up at his home like this, mad at himself for having felt that hot surge of hope and pleasure at seeing her again. What, was he nuts? He shouldn't want to see this woman again, ever. He shouldn't want to pull her into his arms and kiss her until the room spun.

But he did.

And that made him mad as hell.

She hurried alongside of him as he strode toward his office.

He had a roomful of detectives waiting for him with a pile of ransom notes, no doubt sent by crazy, greedy dirtwads *after* they'd seen the news reports about Stacy having gone missing. So far they'd received seventeen different letters, all claiming to have his daughter.

He was virtually certain she was hiding out at a friend's house. This was just her way of getting back at him. "She was upset with me for letting you go," he told Kathy. "As if I had a choice."

"You *did* have a choice," she said quietly.

"Oh, what, so now it's *my* fault?"

"You've got another choice right now. You can either choose to listen to me, or you can continue to ignore me."

He stopped and faced her. "Go home, Princess," he said. "Go back to Wynborough. Your being here is only going to make it harder when I *do* find her."

"What if she really was kidnapped?" Kathy apparently hadn't heard a single word he'd said.

"She wasn't." He started walking again, faster now.

She caught his arm. "Trey, damn it, listen to me!"

No, he didn't want to listen to her. He didn't want to have to look into her gray eyes. He didn't want to face the fact that he still wanted her, still loved her.

He wanted to cry, but he pumped his anger instead, making a point to look at his watch, to look impatient. "Okay, I'm listening. You've got sixty seconds. Make it quick."

"I think I can help identify the driver of the blue subcompact."

That caught his attention. "You know which one of Stacy's friends drives a blue Toyota?"

"He's not one of Stacy's friends," Kathy told him. "I thought he was my bodyguard and—"

"Bodyguard. Right. Princesses naturally have body-guards." Trey couldn't stand it, couldn't stand here and listen to this. He started walking again, started up the stairs. "Kathy, just go home."

She ran after him. "That's not fair! You said I could have sixty seconds."

"Yeah." He pushed open his office door. "Well, I lied."

"Mr. Sutherland, I think you better look at this, sir." Joe Verrone, the police detective in charge of the search for Stacy, stepped out of the crowd of policemen that had gathered around the computer at Trey's desk.

"What is it?"

Verrone's dark brown eyes were sober. "One of the ransom letters we've received, sir. It wasn't a letter. It was a CD-ROM. You better sit down."

"Joe, you're scaring me." Trey sat and one of the other detectives activated the computer message.

The picture on the monitor jumped and crackled and then—

It was Stacy. She was sitting on the floor in the corner of a nondescript room, tied to a chair, her chin held deceptively high.

She spoke. "Daddy. I'm here, I'm safe. For now." Her voice shook slightly. "I'm supposed to tell you to get a suit-case and put one million dollars inside." She looked off camera. "Right. I'm sorry." Her voice shook again. "One million dollars in small, unmarked bills. Further instructions will fol-low."

The screen went black.

"Oh, my God." Trey felt sick to his stomach. "Oh, my *God.*" Stacy had been kidnapped and he'd been sitting around for nearly an entire day, feeling mad as hell, feeling *inconvenienced,* so certain that she'd run away just to get back at him, certain she would turn up any minute.

Kathy was beside him. She took his hand, squeezing it, calm and capable enough to start finding answers to the mul-titude of questions he had.

"What do we do?" she asked Joe. "Do we go ahead and get the money? Do we follow the instructions and try to catch whoever's done this only *after* we get Stacy safely back?"

The look on Joe's face was not a good one. "Kidnapping's a capital offense. If the perpetrator thinks the victim can identify him or her in any way…"

"We might not get Stacy back," Trey said. He held on to Kathy's hand desperately, praying that some of her ability to think clearly and calmly would penetrate this sickening fear that had completely gripped him.

"In my experience, we should try to find your daughter by all means possible," Joe told him.

Kathy put her arms around Trey. "We'll get her back," she murmured. "We'll do whatever it takes. We'll find her."

He held her tightly and let himself be glad that she was there. God, he'd been such a bastard when she'd first shown up. He'd been so convinced Stacy had run away to make a point, and Kathy… He lifted his head and looked into Kathy's eyes.

"You said you could identify the driver of that blue car."

She nodded, looking from him to the detectives. "A man in a small blue car had been following us around for weeks. I thought he was one of the Wynborough Royal Bodyguards, but I was wrong. No one was dispatched to watch me here in Albuquerque. I had a very clear look at his face a number of times. He's a grown man, about Trey's age, a little shorter than Trey, but quite a bit heavier. He's got short hair, like a soldier, and a very distinctive face. Dark eyebrows, inset eyes, rather large nose and chin, flat cheekbones."

Trey looked up at Joe Verrone who had picked up the telephone. "Can we get a sketch artist down here?"

"Already doing it, sir. With luck, she'll be here in five minutes."

Five minutes. Trey could die five hundred times over in five minutes. He stood up and moved to look out his window, pretending to stare at the mountains, when in fact his eyes were too blurred from tears to see much of anything at all.

Please God, keep Stacy safe....

He felt Kathy's familiar touch, and he reached for her, holding her tightly, welcoming her warmth.

"We'll find her," she said again.

With Kathy in his arms, infusing him with her warmth and hope, he could almost believe it himself.

Trey stared at the police sketch. "I know this man." He looked up at Joe Verrone. "He works for me. Or rather, he did. I fired him about a month ago. Bruce Baxter."

"You got a home address for him?" Joe asked.

"You're kidding," Trey said. "You honestly think he would kidnap Stacy and take her to his *house?*"

"That's always the first place we look," Joe told him. "And I'm hoping we'll find your daughter there. I know it sounds less than intelligent, but believe me, the state jails aren't filled with geniuses."

Trey broke free from Kathy's arms and sat in his desk chair, sliding quickly toward his computer. "His home address is probably still in the company's personnel files." He pulled the information up onto his screen.

Joe was on the phone again. "Okay," he said. "That matches what we've got. Now we just need to get a warrant and..."

Trey put on his jacket. "I'm going with you."

"The warrant'll meet us over there." Joe hung up the phone. "Mr. Sutherland, with all due respect, sir, you should wait here."

"I'm going with you."

Joe looked to Kathy for support.

But she shook her head and took Trey's hand. "I'm going, too."

Trey wouldn't wait in the car.

Katherine couldn't blame him one bit. The sight of the SWAT team preparing to pay a surprise visit on Bruce Baxter was frightening. The police officers' guns were enormous. And if Stacy *were* inside that house, she would likely be in the line of fire.

But it was over almost before it started.

One second the police officers were outside the house, and the next they were inside. Not a single shot was fired.

Joe Verrone waved from the open doorway, and Katherine followed Trey as he ran across the lawn. As he hit the steps up to the front door, Stacy was there.

She leapt into his arms and he held her tightly. "Are you all right? Please tell me he didn't hurt you!"

"I'm okay. He didn't touch me," Stacy told him through her tears. "I *knew* you would come for me, Daddy. I *knew* it."

Katherine couldn't stop her own tears. Thank *God*.

"He didn't really have a gun," Stacy told them. "It was just a fake gun, but I thought it was real, so I got into his car. I would never have gotten in if I hadn't thought he had a gun!"

"I know, baby," Trey murmured, kissing her hair, rocking her in his arms. "It's all right now."

"I was so afraid you would think I was being terrible, that I'd run away again," Stacy sobbed. "I was so afraid he was going to take me away and you'd never know that I had been kidnapped."

Trey looked up, directly into Katherine's eyes.

She stepped forward and put her arms around Stacy, too. "Are you kidding? Your dad was *so* upset. I've never seen him that scared. And when we got that ransom message..." She shook her head. "I had to hold him back to keep from leading the SWAT team into this house."

Stacy laughed through her tears. "Really?"

Katherine nodded. "Really."

Stacy looked at her father. "Can we please go home?"

Chapter 20

Katherine crept toward the door.

Stacy and Trey were still talking to the police. They hadn't noticed as she'd slipped from the room and headed down the stairs.

It was definitely time to go.

Nothing had really changed between Trey and herself. And she, for one, couldn't handle the emotional turmoil of another rejection.

Trey didn't want her. She didn't need to stick around and hear that again.

"Are you leaving?"

Katherine nearly jumped a mile into the air. "Doug! Please. Make some noise—don't just creep up on people that way!"

"*Are* you leaving?"

She nodded. "Yes, I am."

He was trying not to cry, but his lower lip trembled. "You promised to stay until January."

"I know, I did. And I'm sorry I have to break my promise." Her lower lip trembled, too. "I'm really, *really* sorry."

"I heard Daddy on the phone," Doug told her. "He was trying to get someone to come in and drive me and Stace to school and home again, but the only people who were available weren't people he wanted. He told me it was hard to find anyone before Christmas." He sighed. "Are you really a princess?"

"Yes."

"You look like a princess," he decided. "Poindexter thinks so, too."

Katherine had to smile at that. "Thank you."

"Are you leaving because princesses aren't allowed to be nannies?" he asked.

"Princesses are allowed to be whatever they want," she told him.

"Then why don't you stay and be our nanny," Doug suggested. "Or our mother. Stacy says that's like being a nanny who never goes away. All you have to do is marry Daddy."

Katherine laughed. "That really only works if your daddy wants to marry me."

Doug shrugged. To him that was no problem. "Why wouldn't he want to marry you? Stacy says he loves you. Don't people who love each other get married?"

Katherine didn't know what to say to that.

"You know, you make a very good princess," Doug told her, "but I think you'd make an even better mother. If mothers are like nannies… Well, you're already the best nanny in the world, so…" His lip quivered again. "Please stay. You've *got* to stay. At least until January."

"I can't do that," Katherine said softly. "I'm sorry, Dougie."

He nodded. "Yeah, I didn't think so. Thanks for saving Stacy's life. I heard Daddy telling Stacy that if you hadn't come back, they wouldn't've found her."

Outside, the taxicab she'd called tooted its horn. She had to leave. Before she started crying.

She gave Doug a swift hug. "I love you."

She peeled him out of her arms and went out the door,

closing it firmly. She climbed into the cab, gave the driver the name of the airport hotel and closed her eyes as he pulled away from the three people who'd come to be *her* family.

She didn't want to leave, but she truly had no choice.

Like hell she had no choice. What kind of thinking was that? No choice? That was the way wishy-washy Princess Katherine had thought in the past. But today she hadn't been wishy-washy. Today she'd been persistent. Today she'd been Kathy Wind—strong, bold, fascinating, daring Kathy. She'd rejected Trey's rejection and she'd gone to him because she knew he needed her, regardless of what he thought. And he *had* needed her. She'd helped him to find Stacy. She'd stood by him and supported him. She'd been strong and hopeful. *She* had been. She *was* Kathy, or rather, Kathy was *her.* They were one and the same person.

And Kathy wouldn't whine about having no real choice. Kathy would bulldoze over any obstacles. Kathy would reach out and grab Trey by the shoulders and shake him until he realized that he'd fallen in love with her, with *her.* She *knew* he had. Kathy wouldn't just let what they'd found together slip away. She would do something outrageous to win him back.

As the cab pulled up to the hotel, Kathy leaned over the seat. "Wait for me," she told the driver. "I'll be right back."

Trey sat in his office and stared out his window at the brilliant red-orange sunset.

Kathy was gone. She'd left while he was talking to the police. He hadn't even gotten a chance to properly thank her.

He closed his eyes, letting himself remember how she'd seemed to know when he'd needed a hand to hold, when he'd needed her arms around him. Her hopeful words had kept him from falling apart more times than he could count.

And then, when he'd gotten Stacy back, when his daughter was in his arms and she'd admitted she was afraid Trey had thought she'd run away...

That was exactly what he'd thought. But Kathy had known

it wasn't what Stacy needed to hear right then. It wasn't something Stacy *ever* needed to hear. And she'd known just what to say to get them both past that. She hadn't lied. Her words had all been truthful. She had simply left out the part where Trey believed Stacy had run away.

Was it lying by omission?

Trey didn't think so.

And was it lying by omission when she'd given him an aka when he'd first hired her as their nanny? Stacy had been right—he'd used a false name many times himself when they traveled.

God, he was a fool.

Kathy loved him. It didn't matter what she was—nanny or princess. She truly loved him. He believed that with all his heart.

And he loved her, too.

Yet he'd let her walk away.

He stood up and went to find his children.

Doug and Stacy were both in the playroom. Anita must have lit a fire in the fireplace before she'd left. The room was warm and cheery, and the Christmas tree in the corner of the room smelled festive and fresh. Stacy was curled up on the couch with a book, and Doug sat working a jigsaw puzzle at the table.

"Hey, guys, I need to go away for a few days," he told them. "But before I call Anita to see if she can stay with you, I thought I'd find out if maybe you want to come along."

"You don't need to call Anita, Dad," Doug said.

"Shhh," Stacy hissed at her brother. She turned back to Trey. "Where?"

"I'm not exactly sure yet," Trey admitted. "Either Aspen or Wynborough. It kind of depends where Kathy's gone."

Stacy closed her eyes. *"Yes!"*

Doug laughed so hard he fell off his chair.

And Kathy stood up from behind the sofa, where she'd been organizing a bookshelf.

"Was there something you needed?"

She was here. In his house. Mere feet away from him. Smiling at him so uncertainly.

"What..." he said, all ability to speak completely leaving him. "How...?"

"I couldn't do it," she said. "I couldn't leave you in the lurch without a nanny. Not with Christmas coming. I didn't think it would do at all if word got out that one of the Wynborough princesses had welched on a deal."

"Marry me," Trey said.

"Yes!" Stacy said. She stood up. "Come on, Doggie. Time to disappear."

"No way!"

"Yes way." Stacy picked her little brother up and carried him from the room, closing the door very tightly behind them.

"Please," Trey added, losing himself in the softness of Kathy's eyes. "God, I'm doing this all wrong. I was going to find you and plead my case and...Kathy, forgive me."

"I'm here, aren't I?"

"Out of obligation to a deal—"

She said something entirely unprincesslike. "I'm here because I love your children." Her voice shook slightly. "And because I love you. I haven't exactly kept that a secret."

"But I have," he told her. "I've been lying by omission, right from the start."

He reached for her and she came willingly into his arms. "I love you, more than you will ever know," he whispered. "Marry me."

Kathy smiled, and he knew that it could rain every day for the rest of his life, and he wouldn't lack for sunshine. "Yes."

He kissed her harder, deeper, losing himself in the sweetness of her mouth, in the fire of her touch and...

He pulled back, laughing. "My God, you're a princess. My father-in-law is going to be a king. I feel like I've been dropped into the middle of a fairy tale."

She kissed him again. "My father will like you."

"I don't know anything about royalty—about what to say

or do, or... My manners are *abysmal.* I've probably broken all kinds of rules of etiquette already and I haven't even been to court yet.''

"I'll teach you everything you need to know,'' she told him. ''Starting with the most important details.''

"Such as...?''

"Well, for one thing, this princess really loves making love to you on your desk.''

Trey laughed.

"And in other creative places,'' she added. ''As long as there's a lock on the door and shades that can be pulled down....''

Trey looked at Kathy, then at the very comfortable-looking rug in front of the blazing fire, then back into Kathy's eyes.

She was standing close enough to him to know exactly what he was thinking. And she smiled as she kissed him. ''I'll get the shades if you lock the door.''

Trey moved quickly. She did, too.

She was back in his arms in a matter of seconds. She smiled at him, and he kissed her. And together they sank down, in front of that blazing fire, and began living very, very happily ever after.

*   *   *   *   *

Turn the page for a sneak preview
of the next magnificent
ROYALLY WED *title,*
THE PRINCESS'S WHITE KNIGHT

Princess Serena's story!
by popular author Carla Cassidy,
on sale in December 1999
in Silhouette Romance...

Princess Serena Wyndham sank into the airplane with a sigh of intense satisfaction. She'd done it. She'd fooled Gabriel Morgan and very soon she'd be on her way to Las Vegas alone, without the handsome, sober bodyguard anywhere in sight.

Her self-congratulatory smile faded as she thought of the man who'd been her keeper.

While she'd been with her sisters, she hadn't paid much attention to the brooding bodyguard. It had only been since her sisters left and she and Gabe had been alone in the Aspen vacation home that she'd begun to entertain disturbing thoughts about him.

Lately her thoughts toward Gabe were more than disturbing. During the days, she found herself studying him, wondering about him. And during the nights, she had been having dreams about him, fantasizing about an intense, passionate relationship with him.

It wouldn't be so bad if she thought he reciprocated her feelings in any way, but she knew he didn't. He acted as if she were nothing more than a spoiled brat, an immature little girl who needed his presence to stay safe.

She definitely needed to get some distance from him. She needed to get some perspective. Of course she fantasized about him. Other than her father, he was the only male in her life.

A smile once again curved her lips and she slapped on a pair of sunglasses and leaned her head back against the seat.

Las Vegas. It was the perfect place to enjoy some freedom and in the process she could chase down a lead about her missing brother James…a lead that had been languishing while she fulfilled her obligations of publicizing the approaching anniversary of her father's coronation.

She eyed the empty seat next to her. Perhaps a handsome young stranger would sit beside her and they would spend the flight time indulging in playful flirting.

Or maybe she'd meet somebody wonderful in Las Vegas. He'd be tall and handsome and he'd fall in love with her not because she was Princess Serena, but just plain Serena, the princess of his heart. She closed her eyes and shivered with excitement.

Surely a couple of days in Las Vegas would put her crazy feelings for Gabe into perspective. And maybe…just maybe she'd fall desperately, helplessly in love with a man who could fulfill all the romantic fantasies that ached in her heart.

''Going somewhere?''

The deep, familiar voice washed over her with a combination of heat and dread. She opened her eyes and met Gabe's dark gaze. He grinned at her expression of utter disbelief.

He stowed a bag in the overhead compartment, then slid into the seat next to her. Instantly she could smell him. He always smelled like Aspen, like clean mountain air with a whispering breeze of pine.

She snatched off her sunglasses and eyed him in disbelief. ''How did you find me? What gave it away? Where did I mess up?'' She frowned with irritation. ''Tell the truth, you had a homing device surgically implanted in me one night while I slept."

One dark eyebrow rose wryly. "A homing device? Surgical implantation? Princess, you've been watching too much television."

Serena's irritation grew by leaps and bounds. "Of course I've been watching too much television. That's because I have no life. Eventually, I'll be the oldest living virgin in the world because my bodyguard won't give a moment of privacy."

She flushed hotly, mortified by the impetuous gallop of her tongue. "Just…just don't talk to me. Pretend you don't know me at least for the duration of this flight." She grabbed a magazine from her oversize purse and flipped it open on her lap, embarrassed and determined to ignore him for as long as possible.

"As you like it, Princess," he murmured, then leaned his head back and closed his eyes.

He'd even brought a suitcase, Serena thought as she stared down at the magazine in her lap. He'd known she was catching a flight and had been completely prepared. The man was positively amazing.

She cast him a surreptitious glance. As always, he was the epitome of a well-groomed male. He wore a navy suit with her family crest embroidered on the breast of the jacket. His dark hair was neat, his jaw without a shadow of an errant whisker. With his eyes closed, she had a full view of his sinfully long lashes.

Serena's sister, Elizabeth, had once declared that Gabe had bedroom eyes, the kind that made women think of breathless kisses and tangled sheets and heated caresses.

Bedroom eyes and a cold, unemotional heart. Heaven help the woman who falls in love with Gabriel Morgan, Serena thought.

Heaven help her.

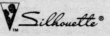

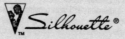

Start celebrating Silhouette's 20th anniversary
with these 4 special titles by
New York Times bestselling authors

Fire and Rain
by Elizabeth Lowell

King of the Castle
by Heather Graham Pozzessere

State Secrets
by Linda Lael Miller

Paint Me Rainbows
by Fern Michaels

On sale in December 1999

Plus, a special free book offer inside each title!

Available at your favorite retail outlet

Visit us at www.romance.net

PSNYT

Celebrate Silhouette's 20ᵗʰ Anniversary

With beloved authors, exciting new miniseries and special keepsake collections, **plus** the chance to enter our 20ᵗʰ anniversary contest, in which one lucky reader wins the trip of a lifetime!

Take a look at who's celebrating with us:

DIANA PALMER

April 2000: SOLDIERS OF FORTUNE
May 2000 in Silhouette Romance: *Mercenary's Woman*

NORA ROBERTS

May 2000: IRISH HEARTS, the 2-in-1 keepsake collection
June 2000 in Special Edition: *Irish Rebel*

LINDA HOWARD

July 2000: MACKENZIE'S MISSION
August 2000 in Intimate Moments: *A Game of Chance*

ANNETTE BROADRICK

October 2000: a special keepsake collection, plus a brand-new title in
November 2000 in Desire

Available at your favorite retail outlet.

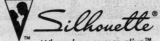

Silhouette®
Where love comes alive™

EXTRA! EXTRA!

The book all your favorite authors are raving about is finally here!

The 1999 Harlequin and Silhouette coupon book.

Each page is alive with savings that can't be beat!

Getting this incredible coupon book is as easy as 1, 2, 3.

1. During the months of November and December 1999 buy any 2 Harlequin or Silhouette books.

2. Send us your name, address and 2 proofs of purchase (cash receipt) to the address below.

3. Harlequin will send you a coupon book worth $10.00 off future purchases of Harlequin or Silhouette books in 2000.

Send us 3 cash register receipts as proofs of purchase and we will send you 2 coupon books worth a total saving of $20.00 (limit of 2 coupon books per customer).

Saving money has never been this easy.

Please allow 4-6 weeks for delivery. Offer expires December 31, 1999.

I accept your offer! Please send me (a) coupon booklet(s):

Name: _____

Address: _____ City: _____

State/Prov.: _____ Zip/Postal Code: _____

Send your name and address, along with your cash register receipts as proofs of purchase, to:

In the U.S.: Harlequin Books, P.O. Box 9057, Buffalo, N.Y. 14269

In Canada: Harlequin Books, P.O. Box 622, Fort Erie, Ontario L2A 5X3

Order your books and accept this coupon offer through our web site
http://www.romance.net
Valid in U.S. and Canada only.

PHQ4994R